The woman in black.

At the sight of the black-clad woman sitting stiffly in the cab, her hands on her umbrella, Maia faltered. This was Miss Minton, the governess, who was going to take care of her on the journey.

The tall, gaunt woman looked more like a rake or a nutcracker than a human being. Miss Minton was certainly a most extraordinary-looking person. Her eyes, behind thick, dark-rimmed spectacles, were the color of mud, her mouth was narrow, her nose thin and sharp, and her black felt hat was tethered to her sparse bun of hair with a fearsome hat pin in the shape of a Viking spear.

The cab stopped. They had reached Euston station. Miss Minton waved her umbrella at a porter, and Maia's trunk and her suitcase were lifted onto a trolley. Then came a battered tin trunk with the letters A. MINTON painted on the side.

"You'll need two men for that," said the governess.

The porter looked offended. "Not me, I'm strong." But when he came to lift the trunk, he staggered. "Crikey, ma'am, what have you got in there?"

Miss Minton looked at him haughtily and did not answer. Then she led Maia onto the platform where the train waited to take them to Liverpool and the RMS *Cardinal,* bound for Brazil.

They were steaming out of the station before Maia asked, "Was it books in the trunk?"

"It was books," admitted Miss Minton.

And Maia said, "Good."

✳   ✳   ✳

★ "The unconventional cast of characters is highly appealing, and Ibbotson does a wonderful job of turning genre themes topsy-turvy in delightfully humorous style....Recommend this to children who enjoy books by Dahl, Langton, Nesbit, and Rowling."

—*Booklist,* starred review

"Captivatingly told, funny and moving. Surely the most perfect children's book of the year."   —*The Sunday Times* (UK)

BOOKS BY EVA IBBOTSON

Dial-a-Ghost

The Great Ghost Rescue

Island of the Aunts

Journey to the River Sea

Not Just a Witch

The Secret of Platform 13

Which Witch?

Journey to the River Sea

Journey to the River Sea

BY EVA IBBOTSON

illustrated by Kevin Hawkes

PUFFIN BOOKS

For Martha

PUFFIN BOOKS
Published by Penguin Group
Penguin Young Readers Group,
345 Hudson Street, New York, New York 10014, U.S.A.
Penguin Books Ltd, 80 Strand, London WC2R ORL, England
Penguin Books Australia Ltd, 250 Camberwell Road, Camberwell, Victoria 3124, Australia
Penguin Books Canada Ltd, 10 Alcorn Avenue, Toronto, Ontario, Canada M4V 3B2
Penguin Books (N.Z.) Ltd, 182-190 Wairau Road, Auckland 10, New Zealand

Originally published in Great Britain by Macmillan Children's Books, London, 2001
Published in the United States of America by Dutton Children's Books, a division of Penguin
Putnam Books for Young Readers, 2001
Published by Puffin Books, a division of Penguin Young Readers Group, 2003

1 3 5 7 9 10 8 6 4 2

Text copyright © Eva Ibbotson, 2001
Illustrations copyright © Kevin Hawkes, 2001

All rights reserved

THE LIBRARY OF CONGRESS HAS CATALOGED THE DUTTON EDITION AS FOLLOWS:
Ibbotson, Eva.
Journey to the river sea / by Eva Ibbotson; illustrated by Kevin Hawkes.—1st American ed.
p. cm.
Summary: Sent with her governess to live with the dreadful Carter family in exotic Brazil in 1910,
Maia endures many hardships before fulfilling her dream of exploring the Amazon River.
ISBN 0-525-46739-4
[1. Amazon River Region—Fiction. 2. Brazil—History—1889–1930—Fiction.
3. Orphans—Fiction. 4. Governesses—Fiction.] I. Hawkes, Kevin, ill. II. Title.
PZ7.I11555 Jo 2001   [Fic]—dc21   2001028733

Puffin Books ISBN 0-14-250184-0

Printed in the United States of America
Typography by Richard Amari

Except in the United States of America, this book is sold subject to the condition that
it shall not, by way of trade or otherwise, be lent, re-sold, hired out, or otherwise
circulated without the publisher's prior consent in any form of binding or cover
other than that in which it is published and without a similar condition
including this condition being imposed on the subsequent purchaser.

Journey to the River Sea

1

IT WAS A good school, one of the best in London.

Miss Banks and her sister Emily believed that girls should be taught as thoroughly and as carefully as boys. They had bought three houses in a quiet square, a pleasant place with plane trees and well-behaved pigeons, and put up a brass plate saying: THE MAYFAIR ACADEMY FOR YOUNG LADIES—and they had prospered.

For while the sisters prized proper learning, they also prized good manners, thoughtfulness, and care for others, and the girls learned both algebra and needlework. Moreover, they took in children whose parents were abroad and needed somewhere to spend the holidays. Now, some thirty years later, in the autumn of 1910, the school had a waiting list, and those girls who went there knew how lucky they were.

All the same, there were times when they were very bored.

Miss Carlisle was giving a geography lesson in the big classroom which faced the street. She was a good teacher, but even the best teachers have trouble making the rivers of southern England seem unusual and exciting.

"Now, can anyone tell me the exact source of the River Thames?" she asked.

She passed her eyes along the rows of desks, missed the plump Hermione, the worried-looking Daisy—and stopped by a girl in the front row.

"Don't chew the end of your pigtail," she was about to say, but she did not say it. For it was a day when this particular girl had a right to chew the curved end of her single heavy braid of hair. Maia had seen the motor stop outside the door, had seen old Mr. Murray in his velvet-collared coat go into the house. Mr. Murray was Maia's guardian, and today, as everyone knew, he was bringing news about her future.

Maia raised her eyes to Miss Carlisle and struggled to concentrate. In the room full of fair and light brown heads, she stood out, with her pale triangular face, her widely spaced dark eyes. Her ears, laid bare by the heavy rope of black hair, gave her an unprotected look.

"The Thames rises in the Cotswold hills," she began in her low, clear voice. "In a small hamlet." Only what small hamlet? She had no idea.

The door opened. Twenty heads turned.

"Would Maia Fielding come to Miss Banks's room, please?" said the maid.

Maia rose to her feet. Fear is the cause of all evil, she told herself, but she was afraid. Afraid of the future . . . afraid of the unknown. Afraid in the way of someone who is alone in the world.

Miss Banks was sitting behind her desk; her sister, Miss Emily, stood beside her. Mr. Murray was in a leather chair by a table, rustling papers. Mr. Murray was Maia's guardian, but he was also a lawyer and never forgot it. Things had to be done carefully and slowly and written down.

Maia looked round at the assembled faces. They looked cheerful, but that could mean anything, and she bent down to pat Miss Banks's spaniel, finding comfort in the feel of his round, warm head.

"Well, Maia, we have good news," said Miss Banks, a woman now in her sixties, frightening to many and with an amazing bust which would have done splendidly on the prow of a sailing ship. She smiled at the girl standing in front of her, a clever child and a brave one, who had fought hard to overcome the devastating blow of her parents' death in a train crash in Egypt two years earlier. The staff knew how Maia had wept night after night under her pillow, trying not to wake her friends. If good fortune was to come her way, there was no one who deserved it more.

"We have found your relatives," Miss Banks went on.

"And will they . . ." Maia began but she could not finish.

Mr. Murray now took over. "They are willing to give you a home."

Maia took a deep breath. A *home*. She had spent her holidays for the past two years at the school. Everyone was friendly and kind, but a *home* . . .

"Not only that," said Miss Emily, "but it turns out that the Carters have twin daughters about your age." She smiled broadly and nodded as though she herself had arranged the birth of twins for Maia's benefit.

Mr. Murray patted a large folder on his knee. "As you know, we have been searching for a long time for anyone related to your late father. We knew that there was a second cousin, a Mr. Clifford Carter, but all efforts to trace him failed until two months ago, when we heard that he had emigrated six years earlier. He had left England with his family."

"So where is he now?" Maia asked.

There was a moment of silence. It was as though the good news had now run out, and Mr. Murray looked solemn and cleared his throat.

"He is living—the Carters are living—on the Amazon."

"In South America. In Brazil," put in Miss Banks.

Maia lifted her head. "On the *Amazon*?" she said. "In the jungle, do you mean?"

"Not exactly. Mr. Carter is a rubber planter. He has a house on the river not far from the city of Manaus. It is a perfectly civilized place. I have, of course, arranged for the consul out there to visit it. He knows the family, and they are very respectable." There was a pause. "I thought you would wish me to make a regular payment to the Carters for your keep and your schooling. As you know, your father left you well provided for."

"Yes, of course, I would like that—I would like to pay my share." But Maia was not thinking of her money. She was thinking of the Amazon. Of rivers full of leeches, of dark forests with hostile Indians and blowpipes, and nameless insects which burrowed into flesh.

How could she live there? And to give herself courage, she said, "What are they called?"

"Who?" The old man was still wondering about the arrangements he had made with Mr. Carter. Had he offered too much for Maia's keep?

"The twins? What are the names of the twins?"

"Beatrice and Gwendolyn," said Miss Emily. "They have written you a note."

And she handed Maia a single sheet of paper.

Dear Maia, the girls had written, *We hope you will come and live with us. We think it would be nice.* Maia saw them as she read: fair and curly-haired and pretty; everything she longed to be and wasn't. If they could live in the jungle, so could she!

"When do I go?" she asked.

"At the end of next month. It has all worked out very well because the Carters have engaged a new governess and she will travel out with you."

A governess . . . in the jungle . . . how strange it all sounded. But the letter from the girls had given her heart. They were looking forward to having her. They *wanted* her; surely it would be all right?

"Well, let's hope it's for the best," said Miss Banks after Maia left the room.

They were more serious now. It was a long way to send a child to an unknown family—and there was Maia's music to consider. She played the piano well, but what interested the staff was Maia's voice. Her mother had been a singer; Maia's own voice was sweet and true. Though she did not want to sing professionally, her eagerness to learn new songs, and understand them, was exceptional.

But what was that to set against the chance of a loving home? The Carters had seemed really pleased to take Maia, and she was an attractive child.

"The consul has promised to keep me informed," said Mr. Murray—and the meeting broke up.

Meanwhile, Maia's return to the classroom meant the end of the tributaries of the Thames.

"Tomorrow we will have our lesson on the Amazon and the rivers of South America," said Miss Carlisle. "I want all of you to find out at least one interesting fact about it." She smiled at Maia. "And I shall expect you to tell us how you will travel, and for how long, so that we can all share your adventure."

There was no doubt about it: Maia was a heroine, but not the kind that people envied—more the kind that got burnt at the stake. By the time her friends had clustered round her with "oohs" and "aahs" and cries of distress, Maia wanted nothing except to run away and hide.

But she didn't. She asked permission to go to the library after supper.

The library at the Academy was a good one. That night Maia sat alone on top of the mahogany library steps, and she read and she read and she read. She read about the great broad-leaved trees of the rain forest pierced by sudden rays of sun. She read about the travelers who had explored the maze of rivers and found a thousand plants and animals that had never been seen before. She read about brilliantly colored birds flashing between the laden branches—macaws and humming-birds and parakeets—and butterflies the size of saucers, and curtains of sweetly scented orchids trailing from the trees. She read about the wisdom of the Indians who would cure sickness and wounds that no one in Europe understood.

"*Those who think of the Amazon as a Green Hell,*" she read in an old book with a tattered spine, "*bring only their own fears and prejudices to this amazing land. For whether a place is a hell or*

*That night Maia sat alone on top of the mahogany library steps,
and she read and she read and she read.*

a heaven rests in yourself, and those who go with courage and an open mind may find themselves in Paradise."

Maia looked up from the book. I can do it, she vowed. I can make it a heaven and I will!

Matron found her there long after bedtime, still perched on the ladder, but she did not scold her, for there was a strange look on the girl's face, as though she was already in another country.

Everyone came well prepared to the geography lesson on the following day.

"You start, Hermione," said Miss Carlisle. "What did you find out about the Amazon?"

Hermione looked anxiously at Maia.

"There are huge crocodiles in the rivers that can snap your head off in one bite. Only they're not called crocodiles, they're called alligators because their snouts are fatter, but they're just as fierce."

"And if you just put one hand in the water there are these piranhas that strip all the flesh off your bones. Every single bit. They look just like ordinary fish, but their teeth are terrible," said Melanie.

Daisy offered a mosquito which bit you and gave you yellow fever. "You turn as yellow as a lemon and then you die," she said.

"And it's so hot the sweat absolutely runs off you in buckets."

"Not sweat, dear, perspiration," corrected Miss Carlisle.

Anna described the Indians, covered in terrifying swirls of paint, who shot you with poisoned arrows which paralyzed you and made you mad; from Rose came jaguars, silent as shadows, which pounced on anyone who dared to go into the forest.

Miss Carlisle now raised a hand and looked worriedly at Maia. The girl was pale and silent, and the teacher was very sorry now that she had told the class to find out what they could.

"And you, Maia? What did you find out?"

Maia rose to her feet. She had written notes, but she did not look at them, and when she began to speak, she held her head high, for her time in the library had changed everything.

"The Amazon is the largest river in the world. The Nile is a bit longer, but the Amazon has the most water. It used to be called the River Sea because of that, and all over Brazil there are rivers that run into it. Some of the rivers are black and some are brown and the ones that run in from the south are blue and this is because of what is under the water.

"When I go I shall travel on a boat of the Booth Line and it will take four weeks to go across the Atlantic, and then when I get to Brazil I still have to travel a thousand miles along the river between trees that lean over the water, and there will be scarlet birds and sandbanks and creatures like big guinea pigs called capa . . . capybaras which you can tame.

"And after another two weeks on the boat I shall reach the city of Manaus, which is a beautiful place with a theater with a green and golden roof, and shops and hotels just like here, because the people who grew rubber out there became very rich and so they could build such a place even in the middle of the jungle. . . . And that is where I shall be met by Mr. and Mrs. Carter and by Beatrice and Gwendolyn—"

She broke off and grinned at her classmates. "And after that I don't know, *but it's going to be all right.*"

• • •

But she needed all her courage as she stood in the hall a month later, saying good-bye. Her trunk was corded, her traveling cape lay on the small suitcase which was all she was allowed to take into her cabin on the ship, and she stood in a circle of her friends. Hermione was crying; the youngest pupil, Dora, was clutching her skirt.

"Don't go, Maia," she wailed. "I don't want you to go. Who's going to tell me stories?"

"We'll miss you," shrieked Melanie.

"Don't step on a boa constrictor!"

"Write—oh, please write lots and lots of letters."

Last-minute presents had been stuffed into her case: a slightly strange pincushion made by Anna, a set of ribbons for her hair. The teachers, too, had come to see her off, and the maids were coming upstairs.

"You'll be all right, miss," they said. "You'll have a lovely time." But they looked at her with pity. Piranhas and alligators were in the air—and the housemaid who had sat up most of the night with Maia after she heard of her parents' death was wiping her eyes with the corner of her apron.

The headmistress now came down the stairs, followed by Miss Emily, and everyone made way for her as she walked up to Maia. But the farewell speech Miss Banks had prepared was never made. Instead she came forward and put her arms round Maia, who vanished for the last time into the folds of her tremendous bosom.

"Farewell, my child," she said, "and God bless you!"—and then the porter came and said the carriage was at the door.

The girls followed Maia out into the street, but at the sight of the black-clad woman sitting stiffly in the back of the cab,

*And indeed the tall, gaunt woman looked
more like a rake than a human being.*

her hands on her umbrella, Maia faltered. This was Miss Minton, the governess, who was going to take care of her on the journey.

"Doesn't she look fierce?" whispered Melanie.

"Poor you," mumbled Hermione.

And indeed the tall, gaunt woman looked more like a rake or a nutcracker than a human being.

The door of the cab opened. A hand in a black glove, bony and cold as a skeleton, was stretched out to help her in. Maia took it, and followed by the shrieks of her schoolmates, they set off.

For the first part of the journey Maia kept her eyes on the side of the road. Now that she was really leaving her friends it was hard to hold back her tears.

She had reached the gulping stage when she heard a loud snapping noise and turned her head. Miss Minton had opened the metal clasp of her large black handbag and was handing her a clean handkerchief, embroidered with the initial *A*.

"Myself," said the governess in her deep gruff voice, "I would think how lucky I was. How fortunate."

"To go to the Amazon, you mean?"

"To have so many friends who were sad to see me go."

"Didn't you have friends who minded you leaving?"

Miss Minton's thin lips twitched for a moment.

"My sister's canary, perhaps. If he had understood what was happening. Which is extremely doubtful."

Maia turned her head. Miss Minton was certainly a most extraordinary-looking person. Her eyes, behind thick, dark-rimmed spectacles, were the color of mud, her mouth was narrow, her nose thin and sharp, and her black felt hat was tethered to her sparse bun of hair with a fearsome hat pin in the shape of a Viking spear.

"It's copied from the armor of Eric the Hammerer," said Miss Minton, following Maia's gaze. "One can kill with a hat pin like this."

Both of them fell silent again, till the cab lurched suddenly and Miss Minton's umbrella clattered to the floor. It was quite the largest and ugliest umbrella Maia had ever seen, with a steel spike and a long shaft ending in a handle shaped like the beak of a bird of prey.

Miss Minton, however, was looking carefully at a crack in the handle which had been mended with glue.

"Did you break it before?" Maia asked politely.

"Yes." She peered at the hideous umbrella through her thick glasses. "I broke it on the back of a boy called Henry Harting-ton," she said.

Maia shrank back.

"How—" she began, but her mouth had gone dry.

"I threw him on the ground and knelt on him and bela-bored him with my umbrella," said Miss Minton. "Hard. For a long time."

She leaned back in her seat, looking almost happy.

Maia swallowed. "What had he done?"

"He had tried to stuff a small spaniel puppy through the wire mesh of his father's tennis court."

"Oh! Was it hurt badly? The puppy?"

"Yes."

"What happened to it?"

"One leg was dislocated and his eye was scratched. The gardener managed to set the leg, but we couldn't do anything about his eye."

"How did Henry's mother punish him?"

"She didn't. Oh, dear me, no! I was dismissed instead. Without a reference."

Miss Minton turned away. The year that followed, when she could not get another job and had to stay with her married sister, was one that she was not willing to remember or discuss.

The cab stopped. They had reached Euston station. Miss Minton waved her umbrella at a porter, and Maia's trunk and her suitcase were lifted onto a trolley. Then came a battered tin trunk with the letters A. MINTON painted on the side.

"You'll need two men for that," said the governess.

The porter looked offended. "Not me. I'm strong."

But when he came to lift the trunk, he staggered.

"Crikey, ma'am, what have you got in there?" he asked.

Miss Minton looked at him haughtily and did not answer. Then she led Maia onto the platform where the train waited to take them to Liverpool and the RMS *Cardinal,* bound for Brazil.

They were steaming out of the station before Maia asked, "Was it books in the trunk?"

"It was books," admitted Miss Minton.

And Maia said, "Good."

2

THE CARDINAL WAS a beautiful ship, a snow-white liner with slender, light blue funnels. She had two salons, a dining room, and lots of deck space where people could lie about and drink beef tea or play games.

"Isn't it lovely?" said Maia, and she imagined herself standing by the rail with the wind in her face as she watched the porpoises play and the white birds wheel and circle overhead.

But the beginning of the voyage wasn't at all like that, because after the ship left Lisbon, the *Cardinal* ran into a storm. Great green waves loomed up like mountains, the ship rolled and shuddered and pitched. Hardly anyone got as far as the dining room, and the doors to the decks were closed so that any passengers still on their legs did not get washed overboard.

Maia and Miss Minton shared a cabin with two Portuguese ladies who spent their time in their bunks groaning, being sick, praying to the Virgin, and begging to die. Maia thought this was going too far, but it is true that being seasick is so awful that people do sometimes wish that the ship would simply sink and put them out of their misery.

Maia was not seasick and nor was Miss Minton. They did not feel exactly hungry, but they managed to get to the dining room, holding on to everything they could find, and to eat some of the soup that the waiters poured into the plates fastened onto the table with a special gadget that was brought out in storms. It is difficult not to feel superior when everyone is ill and you aren't, and Maia couldn't help being a bit pleased with herself. This lasted till Miss Minton, hanging on to the saloon rail with her long, black arms, said that this would be a good time to start learning Portuguese.

"We shall be undisturbed."

Maia thought this was a bad idea. "Maybe the twins would teach me. They must speak it if they've been there for so long."

"You don't want to arrive in a country unable to make yourself understood. Everyone speaks Portuguese in Brazil. Even the Indians mix it with their own languages."

But the lessons did not go well. Miss Minton had found a book about the family of Senhor and Senhora Olvidares and their children, Pedro and Sylvina, who did all the things that people do in phrase books, like losing their luggage and finding a fly in their soup, but fixing their eyes on a page when the boat was heaving made Miss Minton and Maia feel definitely queasy. Trying to read when you are being tossed about is not a good idea.

Then, on the second day of the storm, Maia made her way to the main salon, where the passengers were supposed to sit and enjoy their drinks and have parties. Miss Minton was helping the Portuguese ladies, and Maia wanted to get out of the way.

It was a huge room with red plush sofas screwed to the floor and long gilt-edged mirrors lining the walls, and at first she thought it was empty.

Then she saw a boy of about her own age peering into one of the mirrors on the far wall. He had fair hair, long and curly, and was dressed in old-fashioned clothes—velvet knickerbockers and a belted jacket too short in the sleeves—and when he turned round she saw that he was looking unhappy and afraid.

"Are you feeling sick?" she asked him.

"No. But I'm getting a spot," he said, pointing to a red pimple on his chin. His voice trembled, and to her amazement Maia saw that his big blue eyes had filled with tears.

"It's not chicken pox," said Maia firmly. "We just had chicken pox at school and it doesn't look like that."

"I know it isn't chicken pox. It's a spot because I'm growing up. There's another one starting on my forehead." He lifted his blond curls to show Maia, but at that moment the boat tilted violently and she had to wait till the boy was level with her again to see the small red pimple over his right eye. "And the other day my voice suddenly cracked. It went down a whole octave. If it happens onstage, I'm finished."

"Of course. You came with those actors, didn't you? The Pilgrim Players," said Maia. She remembered now seeing a whole crowd of oddly dressed people getting on at Lisbon, talking at the top of their voices and waving their arms. "But surely the spots wouldn't show under your makeup?"

"I can't wear makeup on my voice. If it cracks in *Little Lord Fauntleroy*, they'll throw me out."

"They won't do that," said Maia firmly. "You're a child. People don't throw children out like that."

"Oh, don't they?" said the boy. He looked at Maia: her neat, expensive clothes, her carefully braided hair. "You don't know what it's like—"

The boat lurched again, throwing the children against each other, and they struggled toward a sofa fastened to the floor.

The boy's name was Clovis King. "It's not my real name. My real name is Jimmy Bates, but they changed it when they adopted me."

"Who did? Who adopted you?"

"The Goodleys. Mr. and Mrs. Goodley. They own the acting company and they play most of the leads. Then there's Mrs. Goodley's daughter, Nancy—she's awful—and Mrs. Goodley's sister, and Mr. Goodley's nephew. He's the stage manager and does the box office. And old Mrs. Goodley does the costumes, but she can't see too well. They found me when they were on their way to York. I was playing cricket on the village green with my friends and they said they'd teach me to act and play juvenile leads—you know, all the children's parts and the page-boys and all that. Because I had a good voice and could sing and looked right."

"Didn't your parents mind?"

"I don't have any parents. I was living with my foster mother. She cried and cried when I went, but the Goodleys said it would be a good chance for me—I could make a lot of money and come back rich and famous. But I don't make *any* money because no one ever gets paid, and we're always in debt and we just trail about from one awful hot place to another."

"But isn't it fun—the acting and the traveling?"

"No, it isn't. We stay in beastly hotels full of bedbugs, and the food makes me feel sick. My foster mother used to be a cook in a big house; she made toad-in-the-hole and treacle pudding and custard and I had a clean vest every day," said Clovis, and once again his eyes filled with tears. "We haven't been back to England for four years, and if they throw me out I'll never get back there on my own because I haven't any money."

Maia did her best to comfort him, but later when she was alone with Miss Minton she said, "Could they do that? Could they throw him out?"

"Unlikely," said the governess. "It depends on whether they adopted him legally or not."

But when the sea became calm again and the passengers came out on deck, they weren't so sure. The Goodleys were not exactly nasty, but they behaved as if no one existed in the world except themselves.

Mr. Goodley was tall with a red face, white hair, and a loud braying voice. Mrs. Goodley's hair was dyed a fierce red and she wore layers of scarves and boas and shawls which got caught in things, and Nancy Goodley, who was nineteen, simpered and minced and ordered everyone about. As well as the Goodleys there was an Italian couple, the Santorinis, who did the music and the dancing, and a very old man whose false teeth were so white that one wanted to blink when one looked at him.

"He's got another set of teeth for when he plays villains; they're yellow with black holes in them, and they're terrifying," whispered Clovis.

The first thing Mr. Goodley did when all the actors had piled onto the deck was to move away the other passengers who were trying to read or have a game of quoits.

"We must be quite undisturbed for at least two hours," he said.

Then they started doing their acting exercises. Mr. Goodley had invented these, and he was very proud of them. He had even written a book about them, but nobody would publish it.

They threw their arms out toward the sea and cried, "Merry to the Right," while their faces became violently cheerful, and then they threw them in the other direction and cried, "Merry to the Left." Then they did "Wretched to the Right" and "Wretched to the Left," and their faces stopped being cheerful and became extremely sad.

Clovis had to join in with the others, but whenever he could, he came over to talk to Maia and Miss Minton and asked them questions about England.

"Do they still play conkers," he wanted to know, "and make a Guy on Bonfire Day? And what about snowmen? Has there been a lot of snow?"

"Yes, it was good last year," said Maia. "We always run out when the first flakes fall and try to catch them on our tongues. The first snow tastes like nothing else in the world."

Clovis agreed, but the thought of tasting things set him off on what he missed most from England: the food.

"Did you have semolina bake for pudding? The kind with squelchy raisins in it? And what about jam roly-poly . . . and plum duff with cornflour sauce?"

Maia said, yes, they had all those at school, but she couldn't help being sorry for Clovis, who was so homesick for the stodgy puddings she hoped never to eat again.

The next day the company rehearsed *Little Lord Fauntleroy*. Maia had read the book. It was soppy, but a good story all the same, and she thought Clovis acted very well. He was the hero, of course, the little American boy who finds he is the heir to a great castle in England owned by his crusty old grandfather, the earl. The boy's name was Cedric, and he called his mother "Dearest" and together they traveled to England and melted the heart of the earl and did good to the tenants and were loved by everyone.

"I thought you were very good," said Maia. "It can't be easy to call your mother 'Dearest.'"

"No, it isn't. Especially when she's Nancy Goodley, who'd pinch you as soon as look at you."

"And your voice didn't wobble in the least."

Clovis looked worried again. "It had better not! Beastly Lord Fauntleroy is supposed to be seven years old."

He told Maia that they were staying for two weeks in Belem, the first port on the Amazon, and then going on to Manaus. "It's a really good theater there—usually we wouldn't get a booking in a big place like that, but the ballet company that was going to come had to cancel. We're putting on a matinee of *Fauntleroy* every day. If it goes well, we might be able to clear our debts, but if not—"

"Of course it'll go well. And I'm so glad you're going to play in Manaus, because I'll be able to come and see you."

It seemed to her really sad that a boy should have to worry about getting spots—and that he shouldn't be at all excited about traveling to the Amazon. They were sailing into warm waters now; the sun shone day after day and the sea was a brilliant blue, but Clovis hated the heat. When he wasn't following Maia about and asking her about Yorkshire pudding and apple crumble, he lay under a fan and swatted flies and sighed. "I *must* get back to England," he said—and made her tell him about tobogganing and skating on frozen ponds, and muffins afterward for tea. "My foster mother made the best muffins in the world," he said.

For Maia it was quite different. When she was small, her parents had taken her along when they went to dig up ancient ruins in Greece and Egypt; she remembered the happiness of being warm even at night, and the freedom of the camp. And the closer she got to her destination, the more certain she became that what she had felt there on the ladder in the library was true and that this new country was for her.

"I'm going to stay with twins," she told Clovis. "Twins are special, don't you think? Like Romulus and Remus, though they were brought up by wolves, of course."

"If they're nice it'll be all right," said Clovis. "But if they're nasty you'll have a double dose."

"They won't be nasty," said Maia.

When they had been at sea for nearly four weeks, they came on deck one morning to smell not only tar and engine oil, and the salt in the wind, but a warm, rich, moldering smell. The smell not just of land but of the jungle—and within a few hours they saw a dark line of trees fringed by surf—and then they steamed into the mouth of the river and put down anchor at Belem.

It was here that the Pilgrim Players left the ship. They disembarked with as many shouts and arm-wavings as when they came on board. Maia and Clovis hugged each other; she was really sorry to see him go. She gave him her address at the Carters' so that he could come and see her as soon as he arrived in Manaus.

"The name of the house is *Tapherini*. That means 'A Place of Rest,' Miss Minton says, so it's sure to be beautiful," she said. "The twins will be excited to see a proper actor."

"And you'll come and see me in the play?"

"I promise," said Maia. "I absolutely promise."

Clovis didn't just hug Maia, he hugged Miss Minton, too. It struck Maia that though he was afraid of so many things, he didn't seem to be afraid of her fierce-looking governess.

The journey down the Amazon was one that Maia never forgot. In places the river was so wide that they sailed between distant lines of trees and Maia understood why it was called the River Sea. But sometimes they made their way between islands, and then, on the sandbanks, they saw some of the creatures that Maia had read about. Once a litter of capybaras, like outsized guinea pigs, lumbered after their mother, and they were close enough for the passengers to see their funny snouts and sandy fur. Once they passed a tree whose roots had been killed by the rise of the water, and its bare branches were full of scarlet and blue parakeets which flew up, screeching, when the boat came past. And once Maia saw a gray log lying in the shallows which suddenly came to life.

"Oh look," she said. "A croc—I mean an alligator. My first one!" and a man standing close by nodded, and said he was glad that she knew there were no crocodiles in this part of the world. "You'd be surprised how many people never learn."

They passed plantations of rubber trees and Indian villages with the houses built on stilts to stop them being flooded when the river rose. The Indian children came out onto the landing stage and waved and called out, and Maia waved back and didn't stop till they were out of sight.

Sometimes the boat went close enough to the shore for them to pass by old houses owned by the sugar planters or coffee exporters; they could see the verandas with the families taking tea, and dogs stretched out in the shade, and hanging baskets of scarlet flowers.

"Will it be like that?" Maia kept asking. "They're sure to have a veranda, aren't they—perhaps we can do lessons looking out over the river?"

She was becoming more and more excited. The color, the friendly waving Indians, the flashing birds, all delighted her, and she was not troubled by the heat. But at the center of all her thoughts were the twins. She saw them in white dresses with colored sashes like pictures in a book, laughing and welcoming and friendly. She imagined them getting ready for bed, brushing each other's hair, and lying in a hammock with a basketful of kittens on their laps, or picking flowers for the house.

"They'll have a big garden going down to the river, don't you think," she asked Miss Minton, "and a boat with a striped awning probably. I don't really like fishing because of the hooks, but if they showed me . . . I suppose you can live off the land in a place like that."

Since the letter the twins had written to her was only two sentences long, Maia was free to make up their lives, and she did this endlessly.

"I wonder if they've tamed a lot of animals? I should think they would have, wouldn't you? Raccoons get very tame—or maybe they'll have a pet monkey? A little capuchin monkey that sits on their shoulders? And a parakeet?" she asked Miss

Minton, who told her to wait and see, and set her another exercise in Portuguese grammar.

But whatever Miss Minton said made no difference. In Maia's head the twins paddled their boat between giant water lilies, trekked fearlessly through the jungle, and at night played piano duets, sending the music out into the velvet darkness.

"They'll know the names of everything, too, won't they? Those orange lilies; no one seems to know what they're called," said Maia.

"The names will be in a book," said Miss Minton quellingly, but she might have spared her breath, as Maia wandered further and further into the lives of Gwendolyn and Beatrice.

"They'll shorten their own names, do you think? Gwen perhaps? And Beattie?"

It occurred to Maia that Miss Minton knew quite a lot about the creatures they came across along the river, and when her governess pointed out freshwater dolphins swimming ahead of them, she plucked up courage to ask what had made her decide to come out to the Amazon.

Miss Minton stared out over the rails. At first she did not answer and Maia blushed, feeling she had been impertinent. Then she said, "I knew somebody once who came to live out here. He wrote to me once in a while. It made me want to see for myself."

"Oh." Maia was pleased. Perhaps Miss Minton had a friend here and would not be lonely. "Is he still here, your friend?"

The pause this time was longer.

"No," said Miss Minton. "He died."

After a week of sailing down the river they stopped at Santarem, a port where a big market had been set up. The passengers were allowed ashore, and Maia heard the familiar *snap* and saw that Miss Minton had opened her large black handbag.

"Mr. Murray gave me some money for you to spend on the journey. Is there anything you want to buy?"

Maia's eyes shone. "Presents for the twins. And perhaps for Mr. and Mrs. Carter. I should have done it in England, but it was all such a rush. Have I got enough?"

"Yes," said Miss Minton dryly, handing over a packet of notes. She would have been glad to earn in three months what Mr. Murray had given Maia.

The market was dazzling. There were watermelons bigger than babies, and green bananas, and yellow ones, and some that were almost orange. There were piles of nuts heaped on barrows, and pineapples and peppers and freshly caught fish, and fish that had been dried. There were animals tugging at their ropes, and delicate lacework and silverware and woven baskets and leather bags. And selling them, talking and laughing, were beautiful black women in brilliantly colored bandannas, and Indians in European clothes, and Indians with painted chests and feathers, and slender Brazilian girls with golden skins.

But buying presents for the twins was far from easy because Maia was sure that what they would really like were some fluffy baby chicks or a duckling or even a white mouse.

"Things that are alive are always the best presents," she said, but Miss Minton was firm.

"You can't buy them animals till you know what pets they have already. You don't want to get your present eaten on the first day."

"Things that are alive are always the best presents,"
she said, but Miss Minton was firm.

So Maia bought two lace collars for the twins and an embroidered shawl for Mrs. Carter, and for Mr. Carter a leather wallet with a picture of a jaguar on it.

Then she disappeared and Miss Minton was just getting anxious when she came back, carrying a blue-fringed parasol with a carved handle.

"Because you ruined your umbrella on Henry Hartington," she said, "and this will be better for the sun."

Miss Minton took the sunshade. It was impossible to guess from her face if she was pleased or not.

"And you, Maia? What did you get for yourself?"

But the only thing Maia wanted was a mongrel puppy, scratching its fleas in a wicker basket, and once again Miss Minton was firm.

"They'll probably have a dog already, to guard the house," she said. "Several I daresay" . . . and Maia had to be content with that.

They still had a few days to travel down the brown, leaf-stained river. Then, a few hours before they were due to dock at Manaus, the passengers were called on deck by a loudspeaker and shown a famous sight.

They had come to the Wedding of the Waters, where the brown waters of the Amazon join the black waters of the River Negro, and they could see the two rivers flowing distinct and side by side.

Then, as they steamed up the Negro, Maia saw the green-and-gold dome of the theater; she saw church spires and the yellow building of the customs house.

They had reached Manaus. They had arrived.

3

MAIA HAD BEEN certain that the twins would be at the docks to meet them, but there was no sign of them or of their parents.

The passengers had all left the ship, their luggage had gone through customs, the bustle of the quayside had died away, and still no one came up to them.

"Do you think they've forgotten us?" said Maia, trying to sound offhand. Suddenly she felt very forlorn and incredibly far away from everyone she knew.

"Don't be silly," snapped Miss Minton, but her nose looked even sharper than usual as she turned her head from side to side, searching the quayside.

They had waited for over an hour when a man in a crumpled cream suit and a Panama hat came up to them.

"I am Rafael Lima, the agent of Mr. Carter," he said. He had a sad yellow face and a drooping mustache, and his hand, as he shook theirs, was moist and limp. "Mr. Carter has sent the boat for you. He could not come himself."

They followed him and the porter to a floating dock on which were moored boats of every kind: dugout canoes, fleet sailing boats with names like *Firefly* and *Swallow*, and trim launches with gaily striped awnings and gleaming paint.

But the Carters' boat was painted a serious dark green, like spinach; the awning was dark green, too, and there was no name painted on the side, only the word CARTER to show who owned it.

As they came up to the boat, an Indian who had been perched on one of the bales of rubber waiting to be loaded, got up and threw away his cigarette.

"This is Furo, the Carters' boatman. It is he who will take you there." And with another limp handshake, Lima was gone.

Furo was not like the Indians they had passed, smiling and waving, not like the sailors on the boat with whom Maia had joked. He showed them into the cabin and shrugged when they said they wanted to sit out on the deck. Then he started the engine, lit another cigarette, and stared, unsmiling, out at the dark river.

They traveled for an hour up the Negro, leaving all signs of the town behind them. Without realizing it, Maia had edged closer to Miss Minton. It was oddly different, this stretch of the river: straight and silent with no sandbanks or islands and no animals to be seen, and the Indians working the rubber trees along the shore who looked up as the boat passed, and turned away. . . .

Then Furo pointed to the right-hand bank and they saw a low, wooden house painted the same dark green as the boat, with a veranda running its length.

And down on the jetty, waiting to greet them, were four people: a woman holding a parasol, a man in a sun hat—and two girls!

"The twins!" cried Maia, her face alight. "Oh look, there they are!"

Her spirits rose with a bound. They were there, and everything was going to be all right. Miss Minton gathered up their belongings, the boat came in quietly, and without waiting for Furo to help her, Maia jumped out onto the jetty.

Remembering her manners, she went first to Mrs. Carter and curtsied. The twins' mother was plump with a heavily powdered face, a double chin, and carefully waved hair. She looked like the sort of person who would smell of violets or lavender, but to Maia's surprise she smelled strongly of Lysol. It was a smell Maia knew well because it was what the maids had used at school to disinfect the lavatories.

"I trust you had a good journey," Mrs. Carter said, and looked taken aback when Maia said it had been lovely. Then she called, "Clifford!" and her husband, who had been giving orders about the boat, turned round to do his duty. Mr. Carter was a thin, gloomy-looking man with gold-rimmed spectacles. He was wearing long khaki shorts and mosquito boots and did not seem very interested in the arrival either of Maia or her governess.

And now, as Miss Minton, in her turn, shook hands with the Carters, Maia was free to turn to the twins.

She had imagined them well. They were fair, they were pretty, and they were dressed in white.

They wore straw hats, each with a different colored ribbon round the rim, one pink, one blue, and the sashes round their flounced dresses matched their hats. Their fair ringlets, a little limp in the heat, touched their collars, their round cheeks were flushed, their light blue eyes were framed by pale, almost colorless lashes.

"The twins!" cried Maia, her face alight.
"Oh look, there they are!"

"I'm Beatrice," said the one with the pink ribbon and the pink sash. She gave Maia her hand. Even so short a distance from her house, she was wearing gloves.

Maia turned from one to the other. Though they were so alike, down to the slight droop of their shoulders, she thought she would always be able to tell them apart. Beatrice was just a little plumper and taller; her eyes had a little more color, her scanty ringlets had more body than Gwendolyn's, and she had a tiny mole on her neck. It was as though Beatrice was the mold from which Gwendolyn had been taken, and she guessed that Beatrice was the older, if only by a few minutes.

But now Gwendolyn held out her hand. She had taken off her glove, and her hand stayed in Maia's a little longer than Beatrice's had done.

Then they turned to follow their parents into the house. But Maia lingered for a moment, looking down at the palm of her outstretched hand. Then she shook her head, ashamed of her thoughts, and ran off after the others.

An hour later Maia and Miss Minton sat on upright chairs on the veranda, having afternoon tea with the family.

The veranda was a narrow, wooden structure which faced the river but was completely sealed off from it by wire netting and glass. No breath of wind came from outside, no scent of growing things. Two flypapers hung down either side, on which dying insects buzzed frantically, trying to free their wings. On low tables were set bowls of methylated spirit in which a number of mosquitoes had drowned, or were still drowning. The wooden walls were painted the same dark clinical green as the house and the boat. It was like being in the corridor of a hospital; Maia would not have been surprised to see people lying about on stretchers waiting for their operations.

Mrs. Carter sat at a wicker table, pouring tea and adding powdered milk. There was a plate of small, dry biscuits with little holes in them, and nothing else.

"We have them sent specially from England," said Mrs. Carter, looking at the biscuits, and Maia could not help wondering why they had taken so much trouble. She had never tasted anything so dull. "You will never find Native Food served at my table," Mrs. Carter went on. "There are people here who go to markets and buy the food the Indians eat, but I would never permit it. Nothing is clean, everything is full of germs."

The word "germs" made her mouth pinch up into a disapproving O.

"Couldn't it be washed?" asked Maia, remembering the lovely fruit and vegetables she had seen in the market, but Mrs. Carter said washing was not enough. "We disinfect everything in any case, but it doesn't help. The Indians are filthy. And if one is to survive out here, *the jungle must be kept at bay.*"

The jungle certainly had been kept at bay. There were no plants on the windowsills—none of the lovely orchids and crimson flame flowers that had been on the balconies of the houses they had passed along the shore, and the garden was a square of raked gravel.

"In England I always had cut flowers in the house," Mrs. Carter went on. "Lady Parsons used to say that no one could arrange roses better than me, didn't she, girls?"

The twins nodded in exactly the same way, once down, once up. . . .

"Yes, Mama," they said.

"But not here." She sighed. "Lady Parsons is a relation," she explained. "A second cousin on my mother's side."

"Do you have any pets?" Maia shyly asked Gwendolyn, who was sitting next to her. There seemed to be no kittens, no dogs, no canary singing in a cage anywhere in the dark house. In the corner, propped up against a chair, was a large flit gun, a canister full of fly spray.

Gwendolyn turned to Beatrice. Maia had noticed already that it was usually Beatrice who spoke first.

"No, we certainly don't have any pets," she said.

"Pets bring in fleas and lice and chiggers," said Gwendolyn, smoothing down her spotless white dress.

"And horrible worms that crawl into your insides," said Beatrice, looking meaningfully at Maia.

"All right, girls, that will do," said Mrs. Carter.

A maid came to bring more hot water; she had two gold teeth and the same sulky closed look as Furo the boatman, and when Maia smiled at her she did not smile back.

"Did you bring us any presents?" Beatrice asked, and Maia said yes, and asked if she could get them from her case.

"Oh, but those are made here; they're market things," said the girls when she came back. "We want proper presents from England."

Maia tried not to feel snubbed. Then she caught Miss Minton's eye and said, "I wanted to bring some baby chicks"— and the twins shuddered.

"Now, Miss Minton, if you will come with me, I will inform you of your duties," said Mrs. Carter. "Beatrice and Gwendolyn will show Maia where she is to sleep."

The Carters had built their bungalow on land that had belonged to the Indians. The main rooms faced the river: the dining room with a large oak table and button-backed chairs; the drawing room, furnished with overstuffed sofas, a marble clock, and a large painting of Lady Parsons wearing a choker of pearls; and Mr. Carter's study. All the windows were covered in layers of mosquito netting and the shutters were kept partly closed so that the rooms were not only hot but dark.

From the front of the house two extensions ran back toward the forest. Maia's room was at the end of one of these: a small bare room with a narrow bed, a chest of drawers, a wooden table. There were no pictures, no flowers. The smell of Lysol was overpowering.

"Mama made them scrub it out three times," said Beatrice. "It used to be a storeroom."

There was only one window, very high. But there were two doors: one which led out into the corridor and one which was bolted.

"Where does that door lead?" Maia asked.

"Out to the compound where the servants live. The Indians. You must keep it locked always. We never go out there."

"So how do you go outside?" Maia asked. "To the river, I mean, and the forest."

The twins looked at each other.

"We don't go out because it's too hot and full of horrible animals. When we go anywhere we go in the boat to Manaus."

"For our dancing lesson."

"And our piano lesson."

"And you mustn't go out either. If you did, we'd have to tell Mama and you'd get into trouble."

Maia tried to take this in. It looked as though the Carters were pretending they were still in England.

"The maid'll help you to unpack," said Beatrice. "She's stupid, but it's her job."

"What's her name?" Maia asked.

"Tapi."

"Is she the one who brought hot water for tea?"

"Yes."

Remembering the heavy, sullen face of the woman, Maia said she could manage on her own.

"All right. Supper's at seven. There's a gong."

As they opened the door, Maia heard Mrs. Carter's voice raised loudly in the corridor. "Just remember this, Miss Minton: I shall always know. *Always.*"

The twins looked at each other and giggled. "She's warning her not to remove her corset," they whispered. "Some of the other governesses tried to do it, but Mama can always tell!"

"Oh, but surely in this heat—" began Maia, and bit off her words. She could imagine how uncomfortable those stiff, wired garments would be in this climate.

Supper in the dining room, under the whirr of a creaking fan, was not a cheerful meal. They ate tinned beetroot and tinned corned beef, both shipped out from England, followed by a green jelly which had not set and had to be chased over the plate with a spoon.

When the Carters first came from England, their servants had cooked all the best dishes that were eaten in Brazil: freshly caught fish served in a saffron sauce, sweet peppers stuffed with raisins and rice, roasted sweetcorn and chunky soups. They had picked fresh fruit for the Carters: mangoes and guavas and pomegranates, and had gone out at night to search for turtle eggs.

But not for long.

"Only *British* food will be served at my table," Mrs. Carter had said.

So the servants had given up. They opened the tins that came from England; they poured boiling water onto whatever pudding powder Mrs. Carter had put out for them, not caring if it was rock hard or running off the plate—and went back to their huts to make themselves decent food at night.

"Shall I call Miss Minton?" Maia had asked as they sat down. "Perhaps she didn't hear the gong?"

"Miss Minton will have supper in her room," said Mrs. Carter. "Governesses join us at breakfast and lunch, but never at dinner."

"Miss Porterhouse never had dinner with us," said Beatrice. "Nor did Miss Chisholm."

Maia was silent. She had had a governess before she went to the Academy. She'd been part of the family, sharing all meals except formal dinner parties, when she and Maia ate together in the schoolroom, and to her dismay Maia felt a lump come to her throat as she remembered the warmth and laughter of her old home.

After supper the girls worked on their embroidery and Mr. Carter went to his study. He had said almost nothing during the meal, only complaining once because the servants had moved some papers on his desk. "You can't trust anyone out here," he grumbled, and told Maia to beware because all the Indians were out to cheat you.

"I expect you must be tired after your journey," said Mrs. Carter, and Maia said yes, she was, and went back to her room.

Presently there was a knock at the door, and Miss Minton came in. She looked at Maia's room in silence. "I'm next door," she said. And then, "Do you need any help with your hair?"

Maia shook her head, but Miss Minton took the silver-backed hairbrush and started to brush the long thick hair. She said nothing for a while, letting Maia gather herself together.

"It's not quite like I thought it would be, is it?" said Maia ruefully. "I don't think the twins like me."

"They will do when they get to know you. Remember, twins are used to living in their own world." She put down the brush and began to rebraid Maia's hair. "Give them time."

"Yes. It's just . . . I don't really understand why the Carters offered to have me."

Miss Minton opened her mouth and closed it again. She knew exactly why they had offered to have Maia. Her interview with Mrs. Carter had made that absolutely clear, but she would not tell Maia. The child had been hurt enough by her parents' death.

"You'll see, it will all look different in the morning. Have courage. Courage is the most important thing."

"Yes."

Left alone, Maia climbed into bed. There was no fan; it was incredibly hot and stuffy. But she would have courage. She stretched out her hand and looked at the tiny bruise in the skin. It was silly to think that Gwendolyn had dug her finger-nail into her palm. Why should she want to hurt someone she had never met? She must have had something caught in her glove and not realized it; a little piece of wire or a thorn.

But not a thorn from a rose, in this house without flowers. And had she been wearing her glove?

Maia turned out the lamp, but still she could not sleep. After a while she got up and pulled a chair up to the window.

Out there in the forest were the huts of the Indians who worked for the Carters—not cool, native huts with thatched roofs, but wooden shacks built to house servants. She lifted a corner of the mosquito net and saw fireflies—a hundred points of dancing light—and heard the croaking of frogs. How alive it was out there, and how dead inside the house!

As she watched she saw a girl in a bright frock, carrying a baby on her hip, go into the middle hut. As she opened the door there was the jabber of a tame parrot, the brief yapping of a little dog. Then came the sound of singing—a slow crooning song. A lullaby for the baby perhaps.

Then silence again. . . . But just before she left the window, she heard somebody whistling. The sound came from behind the end hut, set a little way back in the forest. The strange thing was that she knew the tune. It was a North Country air— "Blow the Wind Southerly." Her mother had sung it often.

She listened till it died away and went back to bed. Hearing the familiar tune so far away from home had comforted her, and almost at once she slept.

Mr. and Mrs. Carter had come to the Amazon from Littleford-on-Sea, a small town in the south of England.

Mr. Carter had worked in a bank, but he had lost his job and decided to take his family to the Amazon to make his fortune. Many Europeans went out at the beginning of the century, some to plant coffee or cocoa, some to try to find gold—

but most to harvest rubber, the "black gold" of the Amazon. It sounded like an easy way to get rich. Rubber trees grew all over the Amazon basin; all one had to do was hire some Indians to collect the sap from the trees, take it to the sheds to be smoked, and send the balls of crude rubber down the river to be exported.

And certainly a lot of people had made their fortunes. There were people in Manaus who lived like princes. But not the Carters. Because to get the juice from the rubber trees you need Indians who know the forest and understand the trees. And Indians are proud people who have their own lives. If you treat them like slaves they don't revolt or go on strike; they simply melt back into the forest, join their tribes, and disappear.

This is what had happened to the Indians whom the Carters had employed. Every month Mr. Carter lost some of his workforce, and far from making his fortune, he was getting poorer and poorer.

So when Mr. Murray had written to ask if they would have Maia to live with them, the Carters had been overjoyed. They did not want Maia, they were far too selfish to want anybody, but they needed her.

Or rather they needed the money she brought with her. Mr. Murray had never told Maia how much money her father had left her; she knew she did not have to worry about having enough and she seldom thought about it. But the fact was that she was rich now, and would be richer when she was twenty-one. The Carters had explained that life was very expensive on the Amazon; everything had to be shipped from England— every digestive biscuit, every jar of marmalade. So they had asked for a very large sum of money for having Maia to live with them. They had also insisted that a large part of Miss Minton's salary be paid by Mr. Murray.

We'd love to have Maia for nothing, Mrs. Carter had written, *but times are hard.*

Mr. Murray had agreed, but he was a careful man, as lawyers are. He had sent the first month's keep with Miss Minton, for he knew she could be trusted. Later Maia's allowance and the money for Miss Minton would go straight into a bank in Manaus.

And Miss Minton had only needed a few minutes to realize why the Carters wanted Maia. Mrs. Carter had not been able to hide her relief and her greed as Miss Minton counted out the notes the lawyer had trusted her with. As for Beatrice and Gwendolyn, they had been told nothing—only that a distant cousin was coming to stay with them and must be welcomed. But the twins had never welcomed anybody in their lives.

Maia woke next morning not to the sound of birdsong, but to a noise she could not place at first. A sort of swishing, squelching noise followed by thumps and bumps and cries of "Out!"

She put her head round the door. In the corridor, wearing a dressing gown and a turban to protect her hair, was Mrs. Carter. She had the flit gun in her hand and was carefully squirting every nook and cranny with insect killer. Then she disappeared into the cloakroom, fetched a broom, and began to thump and bang on the ceiling to get rid of possible spiders. Next came a bucketful of disinfectant and a mop which she squelched across the tiled floor—and all the time she muttered, "Out!" or "That will settle you!" to the insects that she thought might be there. Mrs. Carter did nothing else in the house, but this early-morning hunt was one she did not trust to the servants.

Then, after breakfast, Maia started lessons with the twins.

They did them in the dining room, sitting at the big oak table. The room was already hot at eight in the morning. They could not use the fan because it blew the pages of the books about, and to the smell of insect killer were added the other morning scents of the house: carbolic soap, Lysol, and Jeyes disinfectant fluid.

Mrs. Carter had given clear orders to Miss Minton. "The girls work from a set of books by Dr. Bullman. As you see, the books cover all the subjects they will need."

She pointed to *Dr. Bullman's English Grammar, Dr. Bullman's English Compositions, Dr. Bullman's French Primer, Dr. Bullman's History of England,* and *Dr. Bullman's Geography.* All the books had the same brown covers and on each one was a picture of Dr. Bullman himself. He had a pointed beard, staring eyes, and a bulging forehead, and as Maia looked at him she felt a slight lurching of the stomach.

"I want you to stick absolutely to the exercises in the books," Mrs. Carter went on. "No making things up. No straying. I have always made this the rule—then, when a governess leaves, the next one knows exactly where to take over."

"Yes, Mrs. Carter."

"Every three months a progress report is sent out to Dr. Bullman in England. You will, of course, show me yours before you send it." She gave a couple of squirts with the flit gun in the direction of the window, where a small fly had appeared. "You will find the books very clear and easy to use," she said, and left.

The twins were dressed in white again. Today Beatrice had a green ribbon in her hair and Gwendolyn's was yellow. Seeing them so fresh and pretty made Maia ashamed of her thoughts the night before, and she smiled at them. They would be friends in the end, she was sure of it.

Miss Minton looked at the timetable. English grammar was first. She opened Dr. Bullman at the page with a marker.

"That's where we were when Miss Porterhouse left," said Beatrice with a sly look at her governess.

"She left suddenly," said Gwendolyn.

"Mama sent her away."

Miss Minton gave her a steely glance. "Beatrice, read out the paragraph on 'The Use of the Comma,' please."

"'The comma is used . . . to divide . . . a sentence into . . . phrases,'" read Beatrice. She read slowly and with difficulty, and Maia looked up, surprised, for Beatrice was older than her, and they had done "The Use of the Comma" two years earlier at the Academy.

"Now, Gwendolyn. Look at the first exercise. Where does the comma go in that sentence?"

Gwendolyn's round blue eyes looked puzzled. "After . . . after 'station' . . ."

"No. Have another look."

The morning dragged on. Dr. Bullman's exercises were the most boring Maia had ever seen, and the girls worked so slowly that she had to look away so as to hide her expression. But when Miss Minton asked Maia to read a paragraph, she stopped her almost at once. "All right, Maia, that will do," she said crossly, and Maia looked up, puzzled. It was a ridiculously easy passage; surely she had not read it wrong? But Miss Minton did not ask her to read again.

After English grammar came English composition. Dr. Bullman did not believe that children should write stories using their imaginations. He gave set subjects, examples of how to begin, how to end, and the number of words they were to use. Then came French—and Maia had to sit in silence while the twins stumbled over phrases she had learned in her first year.

But the boredom was not as bad as knowing she had upset Miss Minton. The governess gave her no chance to read or take part—she did not even look at her. Maia had begun to think of Miss Minton as her friend, but clearly she was wrong.

At eleven Mrs. Carter came back with the flit gun, followed by the sullen maid with a jug of tinned orange juice and four of the dry biscuits they had had the day before.

"Would you like to take your elevenses in the garden?" suggested Miss Minton.

The twins looked at her in amazement.

"We never go out into the garden," said Beatrice, looking at the raked square of gravel which an Indian was spraying with something.

"You get stung," offered Gwendolyn.

So they stayed in the hot room with the loudly ticking clock. After break came arithmetic. The twins were better at that, and as it was Maia's weakest subject, she was able to work at the sums without too much boredom. But history, which for Dr. Bullman was the history of England and nowhere else, was deadly: the repeal of the Corn Laws and a list of pointless dates. There was not one lesson which touched the lives of the twins in Brazil; geography was about coach building in Birmingham, and religious instruction was about a girl

47

who would not read her Bible and was struck down by a terrible disease.

After lunch the twins did needlework in the drawing room, watched by their mother, who kept the flit gun by her chair as other women might keep a pet dog—a dachshund or Pekingese.

Another hour of lessons followed. Then Miss Minton suggested they might like to read some poetry, and Maia's face lit up.

"Must we?" asked Beatrice. "Can't we just go on with the exercises?"

"Very well," said Miss Minton, ignoring Maia's disappointed face.

The afternoon ended with the twins' piano practice. They did exactly half an hour each, with the metronome set. Scales, arpeggios, "The Dance of the Butterflies," "The Merry Peasant" . . . And after half an hour exactly they stopped, even if they were in the middle of a bar.

"And you, Maia?" asked Mrs. Carter. "Did you have piano lessons in England?"

"Yes, I did."

"Well then, you had better practice, too," said Mrs. Carter. "Of course, Beatrice and Gwendolyn are exceptionally musical, but you mustn't be jealous."

So Maia went to the piano. With anything else she might have pretended to have less skill, but music was too important. She, too, practiced her scales and her arpeggios. Then she began to play the Beethoven sonata she had been studying at the Academy.

Mrs. Carter allowed the first movement to soar out over the room. But when Maia began on the heartbreakingly lovely adagio, she put down her sewing.

"All right, that will do," she said pettishly. "I have a head-ache coming."

As she sat at supper, to which Miss Minton was not allowed to come, it occurred to Maia that the twins had not once been out of doors, not for five minutes to look at the river or take a stroll.

How am I going to stand it, thought Maia, shut up like a prisoner?

Back in her room she turned out the lamp and pushed the chair under the window as she had done the night before. She was beginning to make out the people who lived there. In the middle hut lived Furo the boatman, and Tapi, the sullen maid to whom he was married—but it was from there that the singing had come, so there had to be other people living there: so sulky a woman could not have sung such a lullaby.

The girl with the baby lived in the hut on the left: she was the wife of the gardener who sprayed Mrs. Carter's gravel and was half Portuguese, which was why her baby sometimes wore nappies instead of running naked as the Indian babies did. The little dog belonged to her. There was a chicken run behind the huts—an old woman with long gray hair came out sometimes to feed them—and Maia had heard the grunt-ing of a pig, but all the animal noises were quickly hushed—for fear of the Carters, she guessed.

The next three days were exactly the same. The sound of squirting and stamping at dawn, Dr. Bullman's boring lessons, unspeakable meals—tinned fish in bluish sauce, endless beet-root, and a cornstarch "shape" that seemed to quiver with fear as Tapi brought it to the table. The twins, who always looked so clean and fresh in the morning, were flushed and grumpy by the end of the day. Mr. Carter scarcely spoke and disappeared into his study, and whenever it was Maia's turn at the piano, Mrs. Carter had a headache.

But Maia could have coped with it all. What really upset her was Miss Minton. Her governess went on ignoring her in lessons, and never let her read or answer questions, while Beatrice and Gwendolyn became more and more smug as they saw Maia being shown up as a fool. I must have made her angry, thought Maia, but try as she would, she could not think what she had done.

Then, on the fourth night, there was a knock at the door and Miss Minton entered.

"Right," she said. "Come down off that chair. I think we are ready for the next step."

"What do you mean?"

"I am going to see Mrs. Carter tomorrow. I shall tell her that you are not able to keep up with the twins in lessons."

"But—"

Miss Minton held up her hand. "Don't interrupt, please. I shall tell her that I will set you to work separately because you are holding the twins back. That means I am trusting you to work on your own. I shall, of course, help you whenever I can, but you must keep up the deception." She gave one of her tight smiles. "I don't see why we shouldn't have an interesting time. I have a book about the history of Brazil, and one by Bates, the explorer who first described this part of the Amazon. And another by Humboldt—a very great scientist. The twins may live as though they are still in Littleford-on-Sea, but there is no need for us to do so."

Maia jumped from the chair. "Oh, Minty," she said, and threw her arms around her governess. "Thank you. I'm sorry . . . I thought—"

"Well, don't," said Miss Minton briskly. And then: "Come along, it's time we opened my trunk."

Miss Minton had been poor all her life. She had no trinkets, no personal possessions; her employers underpaid her when they paid her at all—but her trunk was an Aladdin's cave. There were travel books and fairy tales, novels and dictionaries and collections of poetry. . . .

"How did you get them all?" Maia asked wonderingly. "How did you manage?"

Miss Minton shrugged.

"If you want something enough you usually get it. But you have to take what goes with it"—and she pointed to her shabby blouse and mended skirt. "Now, let's see—what shall we start with? Ah yes, here is Bates. He must have sailed down this very river not sixty years ago. Look at that drawing of a sloth. . . ."

4

MRS. CARTER WAS delighted to hear that Maia could not keep up with the twins. The first real smile they had seen lit up her flabby face, and she gave permission readily enough for Maia to work on her own.

"Of course, Beatrice and Gwendolyn are very intelligent, I've always known that." She gave Maia a smug look. "I daresay you'll catch up soon enough if you apply yourself."

So each morning Maia was set to work on the veranda at a small wicker table. Miss Minton gave her exercises and projects and occasionally she left Dr. Bullman and the twins to see if she needed help, but mostly Maia worked on her own and she loved it.

She learned about the explorers who had braved incredible hardship to map the rivers and mountains of Brazil, she copied the drawings made by the early naturalists: drawings of marmosets and tapirs and anacondas . . . and of the great trees which supplied the world with precious woods and rare medicines. It was as though Miss Minton's books gave her back the mysterious country she had longed to see, and which the Carters had shut out. She was told to write stories about whatever interested her; she learned poetry by heart, and she wrote it.

From time to time she would knock on the door of the dining room, where the twins were doing their lessons, and ask how to spell a word, choosing an easy one so that the girls could despise her. . . .

"How do you spell 'table'?" Maia would say, trying to sound worried, and Beatrice would tell her how to spell it, and say, "Goodness, can't you even spell that?"

But mostly no one took any notice of what Maia was doing. The teaching had been good at the Academy, but Miss Minton was a born teacher. Not that Maia enjoyed all her lessons. Minty insisted on an hour of math each day. She also made her go on learning Portuguese, and Maia was about to complain when she tried out a few words on the sullen maid, Tapi, and found that Tapi understood her, and almost smiled!

It was because Miss Minton was determined that she should learn about the country that she lived in that Maia had her first meeting with Mr. Carter in his study.

The girls were drawing a teapot according to the instructions of Dr. Bullman, narrowing their round blue eyes as they measured the exact distance from the handle to the spout, when Miss Minton came to Maia and said, "It's time you learned to draw proper maps. Go and ask Mr. Carter if there's a chart or a map of the country surrounding his house."

Maia looked up, alarmed. She had scarcely spoken to Mr. Carter, who mostly sat silent and gloomy at meals and vanished as soon as he could.

"Must I?" asked Maia.

"Yes," said Miss Minton, and returned to the twins.

Mr. Carter's room was the end one in the main part of the house. As Maia knocked on the door she heard a shuffling and a rustling, as though papers were being quickly put away. Then he called, "Come in."

The room was dismal and dark like all the rooms in the house and the air was full of smoke from the cigarettes which hung from Mr. Carter's lower lip whenever he was alone. It was also dusty because he did not allow the maids to come in and clean. The charts and sales figures tacked to the wall had curling edges and looked as though they had been there for years; piles of paper lay in untidy heaps on the drawers and filing cabinets.

But in the center of Mr. Carter's desk was a cleared space covered in a white cloth, and on it were small, round objects which he was examining carefully through a lens. At first Maia thought they might be samples of rubber or specimens of soil, or seeds. But when she came closer she gave a little gasp.

They were eyes.

Glass eyes, but still definitely eyes. And not the eyes of dolls or teddy bears. No, these were human eyes—and so carefully made that it was hard to believe they were not real.

The back of the eyes were hollowed like seashells to fit over the muscles of the person who had worn them, but the front was a perfectly copied ball. There were blue eyes and brown eyes and hazel eyes, and in the center of the colored part, a black pupil which looked as though it really must let in light.

"As you see, I am sorting my collection," said Mr. Carter. He picked up one of the largest of the balls, crisscrossed with tiny scarlet veins, and held it to the light. "This is the left eye of the Duke of Wainford. He lost the real one in the Battle of Water-loo. It's worth a pretty penny, I can tell you."

"*As you can see, I am sorting my collection,*" said Mr. Carter.

Maia swallowed. "How do you get hold of them?"

"Oh, I have a man who sends them out from England. There's quite a few dealers in the business. They get them from the undertakers as often as not—most people don't mind too much what happens . . . afterward." He put down the duke's eye and picked up another one. "Now this one's really special. It's the right eye of a famous actress who was burnt in a fire in the theater. Tilly Tyndall, she was called. Look at the color—it's as blue as the sky, isn't it? You wouldn't believe what that would fetch. Of course the really valuable ones are the doubles, but they're rare."

"You mean two eyes from the same person? From someone who's lost both eyes?"

Mr. Carter nodded. "I've got three pairs and they're worth more than the rest put together." He put out a hand toward a blue velvet box, then changed his mind. The doubles were too valuable to show a child. "I tell you," said Mr. Carter, "if this house went up in flames, it's my collection I'd save."

"After you'd saved your wife and the twins," said Maia.

He looked up sharply. "Eh? Yes. Yes, of course—that goes without saying. Now, what was it you wanted?"

"Miss Minton wondered whether you might have a map or a chart of the country round the house. It's just to borrow for a little while."

Mr. Carter sighed, but he got up and began to rummage in a number of drawers. "Here you are," he said, returning with a rolled-up chart. "It covers ten square miles behind the house. Bring it back."

Maia thanked him and left. She had never seen such a sad room or such a sad hobby.

But the map was interesting. She took it to her room and waited till evening when Miss Minton came to do what she called "hearing Maia read." Since Maia had read fluently since she was six years old, this mostly meant asking Maia what she thought of *David Copperfield* or arguing with her about sentimental poems which Maia liked, and Miss Minton didn't.

"Look—I've been trying to copy this, but it's difficult. Would you believe there are so many little rivers and streams and channels behind the house?"

Miss Minton bent to look. "They're called *igapes*," she said, "and the Indians go up and down them in their canoes. Even the ones that seem to be choked with reeds are often navigable."

"It looks as though one could go to Manaus the back way—not down the main river—if one had a canoe."

"And if one knew the way," said Miss Minton, looking at the maze of little waterways

After she left, Maia again climbed onto the chair and looked out to the huts at the back. She had found out how to loosen the netting nailed over the window, and so could undo the catch. She knew the lullaby now that came from the middle hut where Tapi and Furo lived; sometimes she hummed it to herself in bed. And she was beginning to make out more and more people. The girl, the gardener's wife, who had walked across the first night in her bright dress was called Conchita. Her baby was a demon, always trying to wriggle out of her grasp, and the old lady in the middle hut who tended the chickens was Furo's aunt. . . .

But "Blow the Wind Southerly," the tune she had heard someone whistle on the first night, never came again.

. . .

That Maia's lessons were so interesting was a good thing because the twins went on being unfriendly and rude. Each day when she saw them in the fresh white dresses which Tapi's young sister, Unini, washed and ironed in a small steamy hut beside the boathouse, she felt hopeful. The fair girls, their pretty dresses, their pink and blue ribbons, seemed to belong to the twins she had imagined before she came.

But the girls lived strange lives inside the dark and stuffy house.

Like those pale insect grubs that exist only to be fed and groomed by others, the twins ordered the servants to comb their hair, pick up their handkerchiefs, iron their hair ribbons. . . . They never went anywhere alone, following each other even to the bathroom, and when they shook their heads or nodded they moved absolutely together, as though they were puppets pulled by the same string. Yet one did not get the feeling that they were fond of each other—or indeed of anyone or anything else.

As for Maia, the girls never lost a chance of snubbing her or making her feel unwanted. Mostly it was just words, but sometimes, when no one was there, they pushed her against the roughcast wall of the corridor, or dug their elbows into her. She had caught them coming out of her room and knew that they picked over her things, and whenever they could they tried to get her into trouble. It was a long time since Maia had thought that Gwendolyn's pinch that first day had been an accident.

. . .

Then, at the beginning of the following week, they went into Manaus.

"Perhaps Maia may prefer to stay behind and rest," suggested Mrs. Carter hopefully.

"Oh no. Please!"

"Mr. Murray has made it clear that Maia is to have dancing and music lessons also," said Miss Minton firmly.

Since the twins' lessons were being paid for by the money Maia had brought, there was nothing Mrs. Carter could do.

They traveled down the Negro in the same dark green launch that had brought them from the ship. Mrs. Carter and the twins sat in the cabin with the doors and windows shut, Maia and Miss Minton sat on deck.

"Your hair'll get all messy," said Beatrice.

But Maia needed to feel the wind on her face. She felt as if she had been in prison for a week.

Though they had docked there, Maia had not really seen the city. Now, as they drove from the harbor in a cab drawn by an old horse in a sun hat, she was amazed by the beauty and elegance of Manaus.

They drove past mansions painted in every color: pink and ocher and blue, with flowers tumbling from window boxes. In the gardens surrounding them were blossoming orange and lemon trees, and mangoes, and wonderful creepers climbing over the railings. They passed two churches, a museum, a little park with a bandstand and a children's playground. Everywhere were busy people: black women carrying baskets on their heads, Indian women with babies on their hips, messenger boys, smartly dressed Europeans, and nuns ferrying lines of little children.

And on the far side of a huge square, paved in swirling mosaics, stood a magnificent building roofed in tiles of green and gold, with the eagle of Brazil in precious stones soaring over the top.

"Oh look!" said Maia. "The theater! Isn't it beautiful! That's where Clovis is going to act. The boy we met on the boat."

"We're going there later to pick up our tickets," said Beatrice.

"We're going to see *Little Lord Fauntleroy*," said Gwendolyn.

"Oh good!" said Maia innocently. "That's the play he's got the lead in."

The twins looked at each other, but they said nothing then.

They drove down a street of elegant shops: dress shops and shoe shops, saddlers and hatmakers. It was incredible, this luxury a thousand miles from the mouth of the river. There seemed to be everything here that one could find in Europe.

The dress shops excited the twins; they leaned out of the cab, peering and arguing.

"Fleurette's still got that polka-dot muslin in the window. Can we go in, Mummy? You said we could shop properly this month. Can we have new dresses?"

Mrs. Carter nodded. She would be able to pay off the money she owed Fleurette. Well, not all of it; she owed money everywhere and Maia's allowance would have to be doled out carefully. Fortunately, Maia herself wouldn't need new clothes for a long time. The child was dressed very plainly, she thought, looking at Maia's blue poplin skirt and white blouse, but the materials were good.

But first they stopped at Madame Duchamp's Academy of Dance.

Madame Duchamp was a Frenchwoman who had the wit to understand that the wealthy rubber growers and merchants who had come to Manaus wanted to make sure that their children missed nothing they could have had in Europe. So she ran classes in ballroom dancing, folk dancing, ballet . . .

The class the twins went to was a mixed one of boys and girls. There were children of all nationalities: Russian, English, French, and of course, Brazilian—some pure Portuguese, some of mixed race, Indian with Portuguese, black with Indian, for the people of Brazil had intermarried for centuries and were proud of their mixed blood.

Maia changed quickly into her dancing shoes and turned round to see the twins sitting side by side on a locker, their plump legs sticking out in front, waiting for Miss Minton to come and help them.

"Miss Porterhouse always put on our shoes and tied up our hair," said Beatrice.

"So did Miss Chisholm," said Gwendolyn.

Maia went ahead into the big room with its tall windows and *barre*. It was full of chattering, swirling children, waiting for Madame Duchamp. An old lady with mottled hands sat at the piano, absently touching the keys.

A tall Russian boy with red hair came over and introduced himself. "I'm Sergei," he said with a friendly smile. "And this is my sister Olga."

Maia put out her hand. "I'm Maia. I'm staying with the Carters."

"Yes, we heard."

A sunny-looking Austrian girl with braids around her head came to join them. This was Netta Haltmann, the daughter of the twins' piano teacher. Maia was usually shy with new people, but the relief of seeing all these ordinary, welcoming children was overwhelming, and she was soon chattering in the same mixture of languages that the other children used. She had not realized that every word she spoke to the twins had to be thought about and weighed.

Madame Duchamp now entered, an elegant Frenchwoman of about fifty with a black bun skewered high on her head.

"So, now we are ready. Find a space and point the toe, please."

Maia's toe was already pointed. She loved to dance. The old woman at the piano began to play a Chopin waltz.

While the children danced, the governesses and the nursemaids sat on chairs round the wall.

"Is that the little cousin who comes to live with the Carters?" said a friendly-looking, plump lady on Miss Minton's left, and introduced herself. "I am Mademoiselle Lille, the governess of the Keminskys'—Sergei and Olga."

"Yes, that's Maia," said Miss Minton.

"She is charming. So graceful."

"Yes, she is a good child," said Miss Minton.

Mademoiselle Lille looked at her from under arched eyebrows. "And of course the twins," she added politely. "They are always so tidy . . . so clean. . . ."

Both women watched the two stolid girls, revolving as relentlessly as metronomes to the music.

"Yes . . . it is difficult for them," said Miss Minton. "They have not been used to having other children."

"But now your Maia is happy," said Mademoiselle Lille, who seemed to know a little too much about life at the Carters

"How musical she is! She and little Netta and my Sergei also. You must bring her to visit us. The countess is always wanting that her children meet new friends."

The music stopped.

"Now you will take partners," said Madame Duchamp.

Maia looked down at the floor. There were more girls than boys; she would wait and dance with whoever was left over. A Portuguese boy with a rose in his buttonhole claimed Netta. Then she found that Sergei was at her side.

"Will you?" he said. And she nodded happily, then saw the twins watching her balefully before they turned to each other.

"They always dance together," explained Sergei. "I don't think they like other children."

Maia was not so sure. "Perhaps next time you can ask one of them."

"No! They make me frightened," he said, and laughed.

It was a wonderful hour. The shabby old lady had played for the Imperial Russian Ballet School; she coaxed real music out of the battered piano. Maia forgot the twins, forgot the dark and gloomy house—and danced.

But five minutes before the end of the lesson, something happened that changed her mood completely.

Two men came into the room. They were dressed in black— black trousers, black jacket, black shoes—and as they walked over to Madame Duchamp, it was as though a pair of gloomy crows had stalked into the room.

The larger of the crows put up his hand; the piano fell silent. Then both men approached Madame Duchamp and spoke to her in a low voice.

Maia could not hear what they were saying, but she felt a shiver of unease, and when she looked at Miss Minton, she saw that her governess was frowning.

"I know nothing of such a boy," said Madame Duchamp firmly. "Nothing."

The men spoke again, and when she nodded they turned to the class.

"Now, please listen very carefully," said the taller of the crows, as though he were speaking to a group of two-year-olds. He had a square forehead and a bulbous nose covered in broken veins. "My name is Trapwood and my partner here is Mr. Low, and we've come to Manaus on an important mission. A very important mission. We have come to find a boy who is living somewhere near here and who must be brought back to England."

Mr. Low, the thinner, smaller crow, blinked his watery eyes and nodded. "Must be brought back," he repeated in a high voice. "Quickly. Must be taken back without delay."

"The boy is the son of an Englishman called Bernard Taverner, who settled out here and who is now dead." Mr. Trapwood went on. "He was drowned when his canoe overturned in the rapids. Now, does anyone here know such a boy?"

The children looked at each other. Those who spoke English translated what the crows had said into other languages, and everybody shook their heads.

"What does he look like?" asked a tall girl.

"We don't know. Nor do we know his first name. But he must be found."

Mr. Low was getting agitated; his voice had risen to an even higher squeak.

Still the children shook their heads.

"Well, if you see anything unusual, anything at all—or if anything occurs to you later that makes you think you know where he might be found, you must go at once to the police station. Do you understand me?" said Mr. Trapwood, who seemed to think that the children had lost their wits. "Or you can come to the Pension Maria and ask for Mr. Trapwood and Mr. Low."

"What has he done?" asked a brave child, the son of the customs officer.

"That is neither here nor there," said the taller crow. "But he must be found and he must be taken back to England," he said. "We will be offering a reward," he added in an oily voice. "And remember, anyone hiding such a boy would be guilty of interfering with the law."

"Which means he could be locked up. Or she. They could be put in prison," squeaked Mr. Low.

They left then, and Madame Duchamp called for a final polka, but the lightness had gone out of the day.

Sergei knew about the crows. "They arrived yesterday on the mail boat and they've been prowling round ever since, asking questions," he said.

"I 'ope they do not catch 'im," said Netta.

Maia hoped so, too, she hoped so very much indeed. To be found by Mr. Low and Mr. Trapwood and be dragged back to England seemed to her a most horrible fate.

After the dancing class, the twins and Mrs. Carter went off to shop and have lunch before their piano lessons in the afternoon. Since the time for Maia's lesson had not yet been fixed,

Mrs. Carter gave permission for Miss Minton and Maia to wander around Manaus on their own.

"You will of course not go into any place where they serve Native Food," she told Miss Minton, and Miss Minton said, "No, Mrs. Carter," and did not bother to point out that since the Carters had not paid her yet and she had used Mr. Murray's first check on the voyage, she could hardly afford to buy Maia a banana, let alone give her lunch in a restaurant.

But they had a lovely time. It had rained earlier, but now a fresh breeze blew from the river, and wherever they looked there was something to interest them: a howler monkey sitting on a telegraph pole outside the post office; a cluster of brilliant yellow butterflies drinking from the water troughs put out for the horses, a pint-sized child lugging a mule on a rope. Maia bought some postcards to send to her friends and asked Miss Minton if she would like one to send to her sister, but Miss Minton said her sister thought postcards were vulgar, so she could do without.

"I think we might have a look in the museum," she said. "It's probably free. Perhaps I could offer them my necklace."

"What necklace is that?" asked Maia, surprised. She had never seen her governess wearing jewelry.

"It is made up of all the milk teeth of my sister's children. She gave it to me as a farewell present. She has six children, so there are a lot of teeth," said Miss Minton in an expressionless voice.

The museum was behind the customs house, not far from the river and the docks. It was a yellow building with a domed roof and the words MUSEUM OF NATURAL HISTORY painted on the door. Inside, it was a marvelous jumble of stuffed animals in glass cases, skeletons hanging from wires; drawers full of rocks and insects and feathers. There were three rooms downstairs and two more upstairs, which housed tools and carvings made by Indians from all over Amazonia.

Maia and Miss Minton wandered about happily. Some of the stuffed animals were unusual: a manatee, which was a kind of sea cow that looked like a great gray potato with little bumps and knobs on its skin, and a golden tamarin, a small orange-gold monkey with a mane of fur around its face like a lion's. But some were just ordinary animals that people had brought in from the jungle. And in one glass case there was a stuffed Pekingese labeled: *Billy: the faithful friend of Mrs. Arthur Winterbotham.*

Museums do not usually show stuffed lapdogs, but the curator was an Englishman with a kind heart, and Mrs. Winterbotham, who raised a lot of money for the museum, had really loved her dog.

Maia was admiring a shrunken head when she heard a small exclamation and turned to find that Miss Minton was standing in front of a display case showing specimens of dried plants. The plants did not seem to be particularly exciting, but Miss Minton was so absorbed that Maia came over to stand beside her.

The Bernard Taverner Collection of Medicinal Plants from the Tajupi Valley, she read.

The plants were carefully labeled with their names and what they were used for. A few Maia had heard of—quinine bark to treat malaria, morning glory seeds to bring on sleep— but most were strange to her.

"This is one of the most important collections in the museum," said a voice behind them, and they found that

Professor Glastonberry, the curator, had come out of his office. "He was a fine naturalist, Taverner."

The professor was a big, portly man with a fringe of white hair framing a pink skull, very blue eyes, and an old linen jacket from which a handkerchief protruded. The handkerchief did not have much to do with the professor's nose; it was used to mop up dye or formalin, wrap up a delicate specimen, or wedge a rickety stand. He had been putting together the skeleton of a giant sloth and was still carrying one of its claws in his hand.

"When did Mr. Taverner present the collection?" asked Miss Minton.

"Five years ago, when he came back from the Tajupi. But he often brought things in—that banded armadillo came from Taverner. He never killed more than he needed, though; once he had a specimen, he left the rest alone."

He sighed, remembering the man who had been his friend. Then the door was flung open, loud footsteps sounded on the wooden floor, and they found Mr. Trapwood and Mr. Low making their way toward them.

"Oh no, not the crows again," whispered Maia, and was frowned into silence by Miss Minton, who pulled her away from the display case and led her out of sight behind the manatee.

"Professor Glastonberry?" asked Mr. Trapwood, wiping his face. Black suits are not the best things to wear in the tropics and he was sweating heavily.

The professor nodded.

"We understand that you knew Bernard Taverner? That he gave a collection to the museum?"

The professor nodded again. "Medicinal herbs, very interesting; over there."

"We would like to ask you some questions about Mr. Taverner," said Mr. Trapwood. "Trapwood and Low, private investigators." He took a card out of his pocket and handed it to the professor.

The professor looked at it and gave it back. "I'm afraid I'm very busy."

"It won't take long. We know that Bernard Taverner died about four months ago. What we want to know is the whereabouts of Taverner's son."

"What we *must* know," squeaked Mr. Low. "He is to be brought back to Westwood without delay."

The professor blinked at him.

"I'm afraid that won't be possible," he said.

"Why is that?"

"Because Bernard Taverner didn't have a son," said the professor. "And now if you'll excuse me . . ."

"I'm glad," said Maia as they left the museum. "I'm glad he hasn't got a son. I don't know what Westwood is, but it sounds horrid. I suppose it's a prison, like Wormwood Scrubs or Pentonville?"

And Miss Minton said, "Yes."

They were to meet the Carters at the theater box office at four o'clock. As they crossed the square with its tall brass lamps and flowering trees, Maia was more and more awed.

"Imagine Clovis acting there . . . " she said. "It's a really famous place, isn't it?"

Miss Minton nodded. "Pavlova danced there," she said. "And Sarah Bernhardt came to act; she was seventy years old, but she played Napoleon's young son and she was a sensation!"

"Goodness!" Maia was impressed. If a woman of seventy could act Napoleon's son, then surely Clovis could manage *Little Lord Fauntleroy*. "I'm really looking forward to seeing him again," she said. "It's only a week now before they come."

The twins and their mother were waiting.

"We've got our tickets," said Beatrice. "We're going to *Little Lord Fauntleroy* on Monday afternoon, and on Saturday we're going to see *Twelfth Night*. That will be boring because it's Shakespeare. But *Little Lord Fauntleroy* will be good."

"Yes, it is. We saw Clovis rehearsing. He was splendid."

The twins stared at Maia. "Oh, you aren't going! We got the tickets weeks ago, before we knew you were coming. They're all sold out, aren't they, Mummy?"

Mrs. Carter nodded absently. She was sending the doorman out for a cab.

"I promised Clovis I would be there," said Maia, fighting off tears. "I promised."

"He'll have forgotten," said Gwendolyn. "Actors don't remember people. He'll have forgotten that he ever met you."

And they followed their mother to the waiting cab.

The twins were wrong about Clovis. He wasn't clever, but he was faithful, and as soon as the Pilgrim Players arrived in Manaus, he asked where he could find a place called Tapherini or House of Rest, and a family called Carter.

No one seemed to know about the House of Rest, but h

was told that the Carters lived in a bungalow an hour's journey from Manaus and could only be reached by boat.

"You can't go gallivanting off now," said Mrs. Goodley. "We've got the dress rehearsal this afternoon. And when you see the theater you won't want to. It's twice the size of anything you've played in before."

This did nothing to cheer up Clovis, who said he felt sick.

"Everyone feels sick in this dump," said Nancy Goodley.

The company had taken the top floor of the Hotel Paradiso, which was the cheapest hotel in Manaus. It was also the worst. Gray slugs crawled over the wooden floors of the showers, the lavatories were filthy, and the smell of bean stew being tortured to death in rancid cooking oil stole through the rooms and corridors all day.

"It's no good having the vapors now," said Mrs. Goodley sharply. "Remember, everything depends on you. If *Fauntleroy*'s a sellout we can pay off the sharks and get a passage to the next place, but if not, God help us all." They had left Belem at night and in a hurry, without paying the hotel bill, and they owed money everywhere.

Clovis sighed. He knew his lines, he knew his movements. The part was not difficult, and his voice seemed to be all right, most of the time. . . .

If only he could have seen Maia before the first performance. Maia and Miss Minton always made him feel safe.

But Maia was coming. She had promised.

Clovis stamped on a large cockroach making its way across the floor and decided to be brave.

5

I KNOW EXACTLY what Cinderella felt like," said Maia to Miss Minton.

It was the night before the twins and Mrs. Carter were going to Manaus to see the opening of *Little Lord Fauntleroy*. They had bought dresses at Fleurette's—white and frilled, with pink curly embroidery that made them look rather like wedding cakes. The little maid, Tapi's sister, had been sent back three times to the steamy laundry to iron the flounces to perfection. Hair ribbons were chosen and tossed to one side, bracelets slipped on and off.

"We need some proper jewelry," said Beatrice crossly. "Maia ought to lend me her mother's pearls."

"And what about me?" complained Gwendolyn. "I'm not going to sit there while you wear Maia's pearls and not me."

They weren't satisfied with the way their white shoes had been cleaned—they wriggled and complained as the hot curling tongs crimped their ringlets into shape. . . .

In the morning, as the boat waited, it was even worse.

"Where's my purse? Maia, you find it. It was on my bed."

"We must have some scent, Mama. Proper scent—not lavender water. That's for babies."

As Maia helped them she felt completely unreal; she was so certain that at the last minute Mrs. Carter would relent and let her at least go to Manaus with them.

"I know I can't come to the play, but I could wait and see Clovis afterward," she had begged.

"Now, Maia, don't be foolish; as though I would allow you to hang about the theater like a common beggar."

But at last the girls' hair was safely netted against the breeze, and the maids, looking as sullen as Maia had ever seen them, fetched the twins' shoe bags and cloaks.

As the boat drew away, Tapi standing beside Maia said clearly, *"As Pestinhas."*

Maia looked at her, startled. She must have heard wrong, but when she looked the words up in the dictionary, they meant what she had thought they meant.

"Pigs," Tapi had called the twins. "Nasty little pigs."

It was very quiet when the noise of the boat had died away, and Maia no longer tried to hide her misery.

"It's not the end of the world," Miss Minton had said the night before. "We'll have a good day exploring. They can't lock us in the house."

But when Maia went to find her, the governess was still in her room sitting in her one upright chair. She was very pale and her eyes were closed.

"I'm just coming. I've got a little headache, but it will be gone in a minute."

"No, you haven't," said Maia. "You've got a proper migraine. My mother had them and they're awful. You just have to lie down till they're over. Have you got aspirin?"

"Yes, but there's no need to make a fuss."

But when Miss Minton tried to get up there was a blind look in her eyes, and she gave up and let Maia turn down the bed.

"I'll be fine," said Maia. "I'll go and read on the veranda."

But though the book was *David Copperfield* and she'd got to the part where Betsy Trotwood was chasing the donkeys out of her garden, she couldn't concentrate. She kept seeing Clovis's face and hearing him say, "You will come, Maia, won't you? You will be there?"

After a while she went along to Minty's room and very quietly opened the door. Miss Minton was fast asleep in the darkened room, and Maia knew she would not wake for a long time.

She went into her own room. On her worktable was the map she had gotten from Mr. Carter. She picked it up and studied it. She had managed to push back the heavy bolt on the door to the compound at the back several days ago. According to the map, there was a path running from the back of the house along the water channels which eventually came out behind the docks at Manaus. The channels themselves were as tangled as boa constrictors, but if she kept the sun on her right . . . Today there really was some sun, not only the dark rain that fell so often.

It was only ten o'clock. The play didn't begin till two o'clock. Even if it took her a long time, she should still get there—and at least she would have tried.

She changed into walking shoes and buttoned her purse into the pocket of her dress.

Then slowly, carefully, she pulled back the bolt.

She had looked at the Indian huts so often from her window that it was strange to be walking past them. The little rootling pig was there, tethered, and a few chickens, but the Indians were all away, working in the forest or the house.

The beginning of the path was exactly where it should have been, with a narrow plank over the stream it followed. Maia plunged into the forest.

Away from the compound, the great trees grew more thickly; dappled creepers wound round the trunks searching for the light; a scarlet orchid, hanging from a branch, glowed like a jewel in a shaft of sun.

"Oh, but it is beautiful!" she said aloud, and drew the damp, earthy, slightly rotten smell into her lungs.

But it was a mistake to be so rapt about the beauty of nature, because the path was not quite as simple as it had appeared on the map. She knew she had to keep the sun on her right, but the sun could not be relied upon; sometimes the canopy of leaves was so dense that she seemed to be walking in twilight. And the streams kept branching. . . . She stayed beside the widest of them, but the path made by the rubber gatherers was overgrown; she stumbled over roots of trees, trod on strange fungi, orange and mauve . . . Sometimes a smaller stream cut across her path and she had to jump it or wade across. Once something ran through the trees ahead of her, a gray snuffling creature. . . .

She couldn't have told the exact moment she knew she was lost. First there was just doubt as she took one path rather than another. Then doubt became fear and fear became panic, and she had to take deep breaths to stop herself from crying out. At the same time the clouds began to cover the sun. Even those rays of light she had had to steer by had gone.

They're right, the beastly Carters—the jungle is our enemy, she thought. Why didn't I listen?

She would have done anything to be back in the gloomy bungalow eating tinned beetroot and being glared at by the twins. Trying to pull herself together, she walked faster. The stream she was following was quite big, a river really, and the current was fast: it must lead to Manaus.

Blinking away tears, she trudged on. Then her foot caught in a liana, a long branch hanging like a rope from the top of a tree, and she fell.

It was a heavy fall; her foot was trapped—and in putting out her hand to save herself, she had clutched a branch of thorns. Furious with herself, hurt, lost, she lay helpless for a few moments.

When she sat up again something strange had happened. The stream by which she had fallen disappeared behind her in a curtain of green; more than a curtain, a wall of reeds and creepers and half-submerged trees. Yet from this green barrier there had appeared a canoe, coming toward her silently like a boat in a dream.

The canoe was being poled by an Indian boy who stood in the prow and was steering it in an unhurried, easy way, so that the water seemed scarcely to be disturbed.

Maia watched for a moment, not quite believing what she saw. Then she stumbled to her feet.

"Please, can you help me?" she shouted, stupidly in English, then desperately in her few words of Portuguese.

The boy looked at her; he seemed surprised by her look of agitation. Then he brought the canoe silently alongside. Still he did not speak.

"I have to get to Manaus. I have to," Maia said, and pointed to where she thought the city was. "Manaus is there?"

The boy smiled and suddenly he seemed just a boy of about her own age, not a mysterious and possibly threatening stranger, emerged from a curtain of green.

He shook his head. "Manaus," he said, and pointed almost in the opposite direction.

She was utterly crestfallen. So much for her map, her understanding of the jungle—and her hand was bleeding.

"I have to get to Manaus. I promised a friend . . . *amigo* . . . I have to . . ." she repeated. What little Portuguese she had learned seemed to have gone from her. She could only look at him and entreat.

The boy did not answer. He was dressed in the work clothes worn by the local Indians—a blue cotton shirt faded from washing and cotton trousers—but round his head he wore a broad band which partly covered his thick, coal-black hair, and a pattern of red zigzags was painted on his cheekbones. His skin was a light bronze and his eyes the same color as Maia's own, a deep dark brown.

For a moment he stood upright in the canoe, thinking. Then he stretched out his hand and made a movement of his head which was unmistakable. She was to get into the canoe.

"Will you take me? Oh will you!"

She did not know if he understood, but her instinct was to trust him. As he pulled her into the canoe, she winced and he looked down at her hand. Then he took out a big thorn embedded in her palm, and she thanked him.

"Sit," he said in Portuguese.

He took the pole, and the boat moved with surprising speed down the river. As soon as they were under way, she thought what an idiot she was being. He would hit her on the head . . .

*The boy smiled, and suddenly he seemed
just a boy of about her own age.*

he would take her off to his tribe as a slave . . . or worse. . . .

I am thinking like the Carters, Maia told herself.

The boy had stowed the pole now and was using a paddle. She moved to take the other one, but he shook his head, pointing to her injured hand. As he pulled on the paddle, she saw on the inside of his wrist a small, red mark, like a four-leafed clover. A good-luck sign? The mark of his tribe?

But even this sign of his foreignness couldn't frighten her for long. He moved so gracefully; he was so quiet and companionable. She was an idiot to trust him, but she did.

"Thank you," she said—in English, in Portuguese. She even remembered the word for "thank you" in the Indian language that the servants spoke. "I have to go to the theater. The Teatra Amazonas."

He nodded and they glided on down the river. Sometimes they moved between lush green trees which leaned so far over the water that she felt as though they were traveling between the roots of the forest. Birds rose as they went past: scarlet ibis, white herons flapping in slow motion . . . As they took a side branch of the river, Maia cried out because the boy was steering between gigantic leaves from which spotted frogs flopped into the water.

"That's the Victoria Regia lily, isn't it?" she said. "I've read about it."

It was difficult to believe that he did not understand her; he had such a listening face.

Then in an instant the worst happened. The boy gave a wild shout, a shout of pure rage. He put down the paddle, threw himself on top of her, pressing her down against the floorboards of the boat, and kept her there pinioned. She felt his breath on her cheek.

Then he released her and pointed. They had passed underneath a wicked-looking branch with spikes the size of knives. If he hadn't forced her down, Maia would have been knocked unconscious or even blinded. As he clambered back and picked up the paddle, he was still muttering furiously in his own language and glaring at her. Without deciphering a single word, she knew he was scolding her for her carelessness, trying to explain that one had to be alert the whole time in the jungle.

"*Idiota!*" he said finally, and though Senhor and Senhora Olvidares in the phrase book had not used the word, Maia understood it well enough.

She was very careful after that, keeping a proper lookout, but nothing could quite quell her delight in the beauty she saw about her. It was as though she was taking the journey she had imagined on top of the library ladder the day she heard about her new life.

Then the stream became wider, the current stronger, and she caught a glimpse of low, color-washed houses and heard a dog bark.

"Manaus," he said. He drew up to the bank and helped her out. She took out her purse, but he wouldn't take her money, nor would he listen to her thanks. "Teatra Amazonas," he said, pointing straight ahead.

He would go no farther toward civilization.

The boy watched her as she ran off. She looked back once and waved, but he had already turned the boat.

He poled swiftly back through the maze of waterways. When he reached the place where he had found Maia, he smiled and half shook his head. Then he set the canoe hard at the curtain of green and vanished into his secret world.

6

THE POLICE CHIEF was in a bad temper. He had hoped to go to the matinee of *Little Lord Fauntleroy*. Colonel da Silva was in his fifties, a crack shot, and a man of steel with an amazing mustache, but he loved the theater. Opera, ballet, stories about little boys melting the hearts of ancient earls, it was all the same to him.

But he had had a cable from police headquarters in London asking him to give help to Mr. Low and Mr. Trapwood, who had come to the Amazon to find a missing boy and bring him back to England. The detectives were acting for an Important Person in Britain, the message had said, and he was to do everything he could to make their search easier.

It wasn't the first time that the unpleasant Englishmen had been to see him. They had asked him to put up notices in the police station, and around the city, asking for news of the son of Bernard Taverner, and they had made him put the amount of the reward on the notice. Not that he expected anyone to come forward.

"I am not prepared to go on like this any longer," said Mr. Trapwood, whose face had turned a livid puce in the heat.

"We've talked to a hundred people and no one knows about the boy. It's ridiculous! It's a conspiracy!"

"We have to get back to England," croaked Mr. Low in a hoarse voice. He had swallowed the backbone of a spiny fish in his breakfast stew and it had scratched his throat. "The boy *must be brought to Westwood.* There's no time to be lost."

Both men glared at Colonel da Silva, who looked at the clock and realized that he was going to miss the play.

"I tell you, no one knows of such a boy. Unless . . . perhaps—ah yes . . . wait . . . I think I heard something. I didn't tell you because I wasn't sure. . . . There is a boy living with the Ombuda Indians. Some say he is Mr. Taverner's son, and he left him there to be looked after."

"To be looked after by Indians!" Both men stared at him, outraged. "Let me tell you, sir, that Taverner may have been a wastrel, but he was born a British gentleman."

The colonel opened his mouth and shut it again. The less the crows knew the better. Then: "I, too, am a gentleman, *senhors,* and I have an Indian grandmother: a woman of great wisdom who brought me up. There are many mixed marriages here and we are proud of all our ancestors."

Mr. Low and Mr. Trapwood put their heads together. "You have good evidence that the boy might be Taverner's son?"

Colonel da Silva shrugged. "It is rumored. He is said to be a handsome boy, and fair. I will show you the place on the map. It is only two days on the riverboat; it will not take you long to find out. And the Ombuda people are very gentle," he said, producing a crumpled chart and wondering why he hadn't sent them to the Curacara, who had been cannibals for generations. "The boat goes at nine in the morning," he said. "

will send an interpreter with you, and I hope your journey will be a success."

When they had left, the colonel picked up a toothpick and watched them out of the window. At least that would get them out of the way for a few days. Not that he expected anyone to give Finn away. What Westwood had done to Bernard Taverner was well known to his friends. Taverner had been fearless in the jungle, but those who had camped with him on his collecting trips remembered nights when he had woken in terror after a dream, with the name "Westwood" on his lips.

After a while the colonel opened the door to his office.

"Go to the museum and tell Professor Glastonberry that I've sent the Englishmen upriver," he said to the boy who came out. "But he's to tell Finn to stay where he is—I don't know how long they'll be away."

The professor would send the little lad from the fish market, who was Tapi's nephew, up to the huts behind the Carters' house. The Indians there would do anything for Taverner's son.

In the beautiful theater in Manaus, with its crimson-and-gold decorations, its pillars and statues, the audience was waiting for the curtain to go up on *Little Lord Fauntleroy*.

Beatrice and Gwendolyn were in the front stalls with their mother. The box of chocolates they were guzzling was on the arm of the seat between them, and their plump fingers stirred the tissue paper as they dug for their favorite centers, making a loud, rustling sound.

"I wanted that one," complained Gwendolyn as Beatrice's jaws moved up and down on the hazel nougat. "Mama, why can't we have *two* boxes of chocolates? We ought to have one each."

Mrs. Carter was craning her head, peering at the people in the audience.

"Look at that ridiculous Russian woman," she said as Sergei's mother came down the aisle, "wearing her emeralds in the middle of the afternoon. And they're bringing their governess—giving her ideas!"

As he passed the twins, Sergei turned and said, "Where's Maia?"

"She couldn't come. She isn't well," said Beatrice.

"Oh, I'm sorry. Is it anything serious?"

The twins shook their heads—both together, left to right, right to left—and Sergei moved on.

"Doesn't Netta look silly in that dirndl?" said Gwendolyn. "I suppose her parents couldn't afford a proper party frock."

It wasn't true that there were no seats left; they could have bought a ticket for Maia quite easily. All the same the theater was nearly full. The Pilgrim Players might have been a small company that no one had ever heard of, but out here people went to everything. Old ladies had come to see *Little Lord Fauntleroy* even without a grandchild in tow, and army colonels with fierce mustaches . . . and of course every child whose parents could afford a ticket was there.

Mrs. Carter opened her program. There was a picture of Clovis King inside; it had been taken three years earlier and he looked very sweet.

"I bet Maia doesn't really know him. I bet she made it up," said Gwendolyn.

"Clovis King in the part he has made particularly his own," read Mrs. Carter.

Clovis was Cedric, the American boy who finds he is heir to his grandfather's title and has to leave his simple life in New York, where he is friends with the grocer and the shoeshine man, and travel to England to start a new life as an aristocrat.

"*With his beautiful mother, Dearest, he melts the heart of his stern old grandfather, the earl, and starts doing good to the peasants on the estate. But there is a dastardly plot—*"

"What's 'dastardly'?" said Beatrice, her mouth full of chocolate.

"Wicked," said Mrs. Carter. ". . . *dastardly plot to usurp Little Lord Fauntleroy's place which is foiled . . .*"

But the houselights had dimmed. The curtains parted. The play had begun.

Maia ran across the empty square toward the theater. She was out of breath, her efforts to scrub the blood off her hand and tidy herself up had not been very successful, but she thought of nothing except to keep her promise to Clovis.

But she was too late. Everyone had been sucked into the theater; there were a few beggars on the steps, an old woman selling peanuts. Nobody else.

She ran round to the side of the building and found the stage door, which she pushed open. She was in luck. The Goodleys' nephew was sitting in the cubbyhole, with his feet on the desk, smoking a cigarette.

"Oh please," said Maia trying to get her breath. "I promised Clovis I'd be here for his opening—we met on the boat. Would you let me wait for him?"

"Sure. But why don't you go out front and see the show? I'll tell him you're here."

"I can't. There aren't any tickets."

The youth raised his eyebrows. "Who told you that?" He turned to the noticeboard and took down an envelope. "Here— front row of the stalls. Saved for the police chief, but he hasn't turned up. Eaten by a croc, most likely."

"Would that be all right?" asked Maia, not wanting to waste time in explaining about crocodiles on the Amazon. "But I don't know if I've got enough money."

She felt for her purse, but the boy waved it away. "It's free for friends of the company. Better hurry up, it's started."

Slipping into her seat, Maia was glad the theater was dark. If the twins saw her they would do their best to get her into trouble.

Then in an instant she was in New York, in a grocer's shop where little Cedric was talking to his friend the grocer about the wickedness of the aristocracy.

Clovis was good. He didn't look seven, of course—or even eight or nine—but in his sailor suit with his wig of long fair curls, he certainly looked like an appealing little boy. And his voice was steady—a clear, high treble. Maia could feel the children in the audience hanging on his words.

Now a gentleman from England came onstage—a lawyer rather like her own Mr. Murray—and with him was Dearest, Cedric's mother, who explained to her son that he was really a lord. Clovis was being very good about calling his mother Dearest—even better than on the boat.

Maia forgot her worries and settled down to enjoy the play. Soppy or not, *Little Lord Fauntleroy* was a good story, and when the little boy was given a lot of money which he gave to his poor friends and did not keep for himself, a great sigh went round the audience.

Maia stayed in her seat during the first intermission and kept her head down. The twins were several rows farther back and hadn't seen her, but she could hear them giggling about something and then nagging their mother to buy them some more chocolates.

In the second act, little Lord Fauntleroy and Dearest reach the great castle that he will inherit, and Cedric melts the hard heart of the old aristocrat, his grandfather. In the book he also made friends with a large, fierce dog, but the Goodleys had left the dog out, which was a pity. It was really very touching how just by believing that his grandfather was a good man, Cedric was making him *become* good, and Maia wondered if it might work with the twins. If she really believed they were kind, would they become kind? By now Maia had forgotten all her anxieties; Clovis was really a very good actor and the audience was loving him.

The last act, as in most plays, is the exciting one. A wicked woman turns up at the earl's castle and pretends that her son is the real Lord Fauntleroy. Of course, it turns out not to be true, but everyone is very much upset, though Cedric, needless to say, behaves beautifully. When he thinks he may not be the real Lord Fauntleroy, Cedric doesn't worry at all about not being rich and grand anymore—all that worries him is the thought that his grandfather might stop loving him. And he turns to him and puts his hand on the old man's knee and says, *"Will I have to stop being your little boy?"*

And it was on this moving sentence that it happened.

Clovis turned his face to the old man and began his speech—and suddenly his voice cracked. He stopped, tried again . . . and this time he said, *"Will I have to stop being your little boy?"* in a deep bass voice.

If no one had taken any notice, it would probably have righted itself. Everyone was on Clovis's side. But the twins started it; they giggled and tittered; their titters grew louder, and then the other children who had held back joined in, and in a moment the audience was laughing and the children were falling about. Not all of them. Not Netta, not Sergei . . . certainly not Maia, who sat with her hand over her mouth.

But enough of them. Enough to go on jeering and laughing through the next two speeches—and then Clovis gave a gasp, and turned and ran away into the wings.

And the curtain came down.

Maia had been standing outside the stage door for half an hour. She had no idea how she was going to get home, but she couldn't leave Clovis in this state of misery. Many of the actors had gone past, but not him. At last she pushed open the door. There was a babble of loud voices talking about cancellation, about financial losses and disaster and disgrace. Everyone was angry, everyone was in a state.

"Can I see Clovis?" she asked bravely, and they motioned with their heads to the stairs which led to the dressing rooms.

It took her a while to find him in the huge theater, but at last she pushed open the right door and found her friend, face-down on a couch, with his shoulders heaving.

"Clovis, don't! You mustn't be like that. It's something that can happen to anyone and you were terribly good until then."

He sat up. His face was blotched; he was still crying.

"You don't understand. They're furious. They'll have to cancel all the matinees and lose lots of money and I can't stand it any longer. I'm going to stow away on the boat and go back to England."

Maia looked at him in dismay. "They'll find you. Stowaways are always found. Haven't you got an understudy?"

Clovis shook his head. "There was a boy in the last place, but he got typhoid." He got up and really seemed to see Maia for the first time. "You've got blood on your hand, did you know?"

She shook her head impatiently. "It doesn't matter. Clovis, you've got to pull yourself together. It's such a little thing."

"It is to you because you're not on the stage—and you don't know the Goodleys." He looked at her and there were still tears in his eyes. "Maia, I've got to get home. Can't you help me? I'll do anything to get away."

"I'll try, Clovis. I'll really try."

She broke off as a furious voice out in the corridor was heard calling her name. Mrs. Carter had tracked her down!

"I have to go! Look, Clovis, let me think. Just give me time. And don't be so sad. I'll help you somehow. There has to be something we can do!"

7

FOR TWO DAYS after the matinee, Maia was in disgrace.

"I couldn't believe my eyes," said Mrs. Carter, glaring at her over a dollop of macaroni cheese so solid that she was cutting it with a knife. "A girl in my care creeping out secretly, going backstage, and looking like a ragamuffin. The girls told me they thought they'd seen you on the way out, but I didn't believe it."

"We told you, Mama," said Beatrice, smirking.

"She's stuck on that actor boy with the bass voice."

Then they both started doing imitations of Clovis saying *Will I have to stop being your little boy?* in a deep, growly voice, and laughing. "Oh, it was so funny, I thought I was going to die!"

At first Maia had tried to defend Clovis and make them see what the mishap had meant to him. But soon she gave up. Making the twins imagine the feelings of anybody except themselves was a waste of time. Instead, Maia had to put up with Mrs. Carter's threats to send her back to England.

Maia had told her that she had gone to Manaus on a boat ferrying rubber downriver and Mrs. Carter did not understand why she had not been murdered and thrown overboard. "As for Miss Minton, I'm afraid she is really not fit to have charge of young girls. I shall have to replace her as soon as I can find someone suitable."

In the evening, when Miss Minton came to "hear her read," Maia said, "I'm not staying here without you. I shall write to Mr. Murray."

"I think you will find that at the salary the Carters are paying me, it might take a little while to find someone else," said Miss Minton dryly. She picked up Maia's hairbrush. "Don't tell me you're doing a hundred strokes a night because I don't believe it. I've told you again and again that you must look after your hair." She brushed fiercely for a while. And then: "Do you want to go back, Maia? Back to England?"

"I did," she said, thinking about it. "The twins are so awful and there seemed no point in being here, shut up in this house. But not now. I don't want to go now because I've seen that it is there. What I thought was there."

Miss Minton waited.

"I mean . . . the forest . . . the river . . . the Amazon . . . everything I thought of before I came. And the people who live in it and know about it."

Then she told Miss Minton about the boy who had taken her into Manaus.

"He didn't speak English, but he had such a listening face; I couldn't believe he didn't understand everything I said. Oh Minty, it was such a wonderful journey, like floating through a drowned forest. You can't believe it's the same world as the Carters live in."

"It isn't," said Miss Minton. "People make their own worlds."

"I wish I could find him again." And then: "I will find him again. If they don't send me away."

"They won't send you away," said Miss Minton. Mrs. Carter was already waiting greedily for the next month's allowance for Maia from the bank in Manaus. "However, it seems to me we must find a way of getting you out of doors." She wrinkled her formidable forehead. "I think a disease might be best. Yes. Something that makes it necessary for you to go out and breathe fresh air. Even damp air. Let me think. What about pulmonary spasms?"

Maia stared at her. "I've never heard of them."

"Well, no. I've just made them up. We'll tell Mrs. Carter that if your lungs get dry from the disinfectant indoors you have spasms. You know what they are, don't you?"

"Sort of twitchings and convulsions?"

"Yes. Convulsions will do. Mrs. Carter won't like them. But I may not always be able to go with you, so please understand that I am trusting you to stay close to the house and to be sensible. Which you do not seem to have been."

"Yes. I will, honestly." But she could try to make friends with the Indians in the huts. She could find out who sang that lullaby—and ask them about the person who had whistled "Blow the Wind Southerly" on her first night. They might even know who her rescuer had been, so that she could at least thank him properly.

But Maia had not forgotten her promise to help Clovis.

"He wants to stow away on a boat to England, but he's sure to be caught, don't you think?" she asked Miss Minton.

"Certain to," said the governess. "Fortunately, the next boat to England doesn't go for two weeks."

"Do you think Mr. Murray would be willing to pay his passage? He could take it out of my pocket money."

"I doubt if you'd see any pocket money for the rest of your life if you did that."

"But he might," persisted Maia. "Could I send him a cable? They don't take very long, do they—they sort of snake along the sea. He could arrange with the shipping company in Manaus for Clovis to pick up a ticket, couldn't he? My father was always doing things like that."

"He could," said Miss Minton, but she doubted very much whether Maia's guardian would trouble himself about a stranded actor.

But she did not stand in Maia's way. Maia copied out a message to Mr. Murray and gave it to Mr. Carter to take to the post office with enough money to send it. Then she settled down to wait for a reply.

Mrs. Carter was not pleased about the pulmonary spasms. She had never heard of them and said so, and she did not want Maia wandering about outside by herself. "I shall expect you to accompany her whenever possible," she said to Miss Minton. "And to make up the lesson time with the twins out of your free periods."

Miss Minton could have said, "What free periods?" but she did not. But she was quite right in thinking that while she could not bring herself to be nice to Maia, Mrs. Carter dreaded losing her. Since Maia came they had been able to pay the bill for the dressmaker, the piano lessons, and the dancing class. Next month they might even be able to pay some of the rubber gatherers—not their full wages, but enough to stop them running back into the forest.

So Maia was allowed to go outside for her midday break and again after tea. She was not allowed to go out in the evening, but she went anyway. Once she had pushed back the heavy bolt on her door, she left it open.

She was careful not to go too near the huts of the Indians without being asked, but when she met anyone she smiled and greeted them.

Then, on the third night, she was walking along the river beside a grove of dyewood trees, when she saw a small shape run out of the darkness toward her. In the dusk she had no idea what it was, and for a moment she was frightened. There were so many animals, still, that she knew nothing about.

Maia looked down . . . and laughed. The strange animal was a baby—the baby she had seen carried by the Portuguese girl. It had only just escaped and was enjoying its freedom, but the river was nearby.

Maia picked it up. The baby kicked and struggled, but she held it firmly and began to make her way back toward the huts.

"Oh hush," she said. "Don't make such a fuss"—and she began to hum the lullaby she had heard the Indians singing. She didn't know the words but the tune quieted the baby, and he stopped wriggling and let his head fall against her shoulder.

As she neared the middle hut she saw three people standing outside the door, staring at her: Tapi, Furo, and the old woman with long, gray hair. Then Tapi ran into the next hut and the Portuguese girl, Conchita, came out and rushed up to Maia, seizing the baby and letting off a torrent of words. She had left him asleep on his mat and he must have woken when she was out at the back getting water.

"He is a terror; he is wickedness beyond belief. . . ."

Now that she had handed over the baby, Maia turned to go—but this was not allowed. The silent sulkiness of the Carter servants had vanished. Tapi led her into the hut, the old lady brought coffee and nuts; fruit was offered, and little cakes . . . a party was brewing up.

"You sang 'im good," said the baby's mother, and nodded. "Where you learn our song?"

"From my window," said Maia, pointing back to the house. "But I don't know the words."

It was the old woman, Lila, who was the singer, and she sang it again now for Maia.

"Is it a lullaby?" she asked, pretending to go to sleep, and Lila said it was a song about love and pain like so many songs, but she always sang babies to sleep with it. She had been a nurse to many children, European ones also, she told her.

They knew and understood far more English than they admitted to the Carters—and they spoke with their hands, their eyes. Maia met the little white dog; the parrot sat on her shoulder; they had a tame gecko that lived on a potted palm in the window—and every time her cup was empty, or her plate, it was filled again. She had never met such friendliness. These Indians lived the kind of life she had imagined for the twins before she came.

After that she slipped in to see them whenever she could. The old lady, who was Furo's aunt, taught her other songs: songs that the African slaves had brought over when they came to work in the sugar plantations, songs she had learned from her Portuguese employers when she was a nursemaid in Manaus. They showed her the end hut, the one where the rubber gatherers had slept, but which was now empty, because the men had slipped back into the forest when Mr. Carter hadn't paid them for three whole months.

But nobody knew the North Country tune she had heard whistled on the first day, nor could they tell her anything about the Indian boy who had taken her to Manaus. There were many such boys on the river, they said, and Maia began to feel that she would never see her rescuer again.

Several days had passed since the disaster of the matinee, and in the Hotel Paradiso things were going badly. The Goodleys had called a meeting in their bedroom to decide what to do, but as usual they started by nagging Clovis.

"You'd think you could have waited another week before you started honking like an old grandfather," said Mrs. Goodley.

"You realize you've turned us into a laughingstock," said Nancy Goodley. "After all we've done for you, making you into a star."

Clovis hung his head. He was crouched on a dirty footstool, clutching his stomach, which was heaving after the Paradiso breakfast of bean stew and fish bones, and he was covered in bites because the hotel sheets were crawling with bedbugs.

It was all his fault, he knew that—and now even more things were going wrong. A banana boat had come in from Belem the night before and the captain had told the manager of the Paradiso that the company had left there without paying their hotel bill. Since then the manager shot out of his office when-ever any of the actors came past, asking for money and threat-ening to take their clothes and belongings if they didn't pay.

They had tried to put on a funny play that Mr. Goodley had written instead of *Fauntleroy,* but it wasn't funny and had to be pulled out, and now not only the hotel but the theater was losing money, and the management was threatening to cancel the second week of their booking.

They were due to go on to Colombia and Peru—but how?

"Perhaps we could steal out of the hotel one by one at night, and hire a van?" suggested the old actor with the flashing teeth.

"Hire a van with what?" Mr. Goodley sneered. "Pebbles? Coconut shells?"

Clovis stopped listening. He felt as wretched as he had ever felt, and frightened, too. What was going to happen to him and to everyone? He could see himself staring into the dark pit of the theater and listening to that awful tittering that had started everyone off. Two girls, high-pitched and cruel. One thing was certain: no one was going to get him onto a stage again.

Only Maia was still his friend. She'd promised to help him; she'd said there was something they could do—and he trusted Maia as he trusted no one else. The loud, angry voices crashed over his head. The room was sweltering; a centipede fell from the ceiling at his feet. Downstairs, someone opened a door and the smell of the dreaded bean stew came up and hit him. He couldn't face it again. He couldn't face any of it. . . .

Then suddenly he sat up very straight. He didn't have to face it, now that he wasn't acting anymore. He knew where Maia lived, and Miss Minton—a few miles up the river to the north. The twins would like to see him, Maia had said on the boat; and Clovis saw them now, welcoming and kind.

Yes, that's what he'd do. He'd go and find Maia. He had a few coins still; someone would take him up the river. And once he was with Maia and Miss Minton, everything would be all right. They would help him to get home. Maia and Miss Minton together could do anything.

Miss Minton's afternoon off fell two days later. She was going to Manaus and Maia hoped she would ask her to go with her, but she didn't. She was going to see if there was a reply yet from Mr. Murray, but after that she had business to attend to, she said. Since the Carters were going into the town to visit the only family in Manaus with whom they were still on speaking terms, they could hardly help offering her a place in the launch.

"Where is Furo?" asked Mrs. Carter as one of the other Indians waited by the boat.

"Sick," said the man, letting his knees go soft and miming a fever.

"Oh, really they are impossible, these people," said Mrs. Carter angrily. "The slightest thing and they stay off work."

Maia waved them off. Then she went into the sitting room and opened the piano. It was almost impossible to practice when the Carters were at home. She started on her scales, her arpeggios, but sooner than she should have done she began to play the Chopin ballade she had been learning in London. She was so absorbed that at first she did not see Furo beckoning to her outside the window.

He did not seem to be in the least sick. He looked, in fact, rather pleased and excited.

"Come," he said, making signs that she was to be quiet.

Maia followed him. She was puzzled—during the day the Indians always ignored her; it was only at night that they showed her their true selves. Tapi and old Lila were standing at the door of their hut, smiling, but they said nothing, and Maia followed Furo to the creek she had found on the day she tried to go to Manaus.

By the wooden bridge, a shabby dugout was moored. It was the one Furo used to go fishing in the evening.

"In," he said, holding out a hand.

She hesitated only for a moment, then obeyed him.

They traveled down a number of twisting rivers. Sometimes Maia thought she had been there before; sometimes everything looked different. Whenever she tried to question Furo he shook his head, but he went on looking pleased. No one could have been more different from the surly boatman who had brought them to the Carters in the first place.

They paddled down a side stream, and now Maia did feel uneasy, because Furo took out a square piece of cloth, put it over his own eyes to show her what she was to do, then over Maia's.

"Put on," he said, and when she shook her head, repeated it, leaning forward to tie the blindfold over her eyes.

She began to be frightened. The boat eased slowly forward; she heard rushes making a dry sound against the side of the canoe, felt branches brushing her arm. Then the boat surged forward, and Furo leaned forward to unbind her eyes.

They were in a still lagoon of clear, blue water, shielded from the outside by a ring of great trees. The only entrance, the passage through the rushes, seemed to have closed behind them. They might have been alone in the world.

But it was not the secrecy of the lake that held Maia spellbound, it was its beauty. The sheltering trees leaned over the water; there was a bank of golden sand on which a turtle slept, untroubled by the boat. Clumps of yellow-and-pink lotus flowers swayed in the water, their buds open to the sun. Hummingbirds clustered in an ever-changing whirl of color round a feeding bottle nailed to a branch. . . .

On the far side of the lagoon, in the shade of two big cottonwoods, was a neatly built wooden hut, and in front of it, a narrow wooden jetty built out over the lake. A small launch with a raked smokestack and the letters ARABELLA painted on the side rode at anchor nearby, and made fast alongside was a canoe which Maia recognized.

But she did not at first recognize the boy who stood outside the hut, quietly waiting. He seemed to be the Indian boy who had taken her to Manaus, but his jet-black hair had gone, and so had the headband and the red paint. With his own fine, brown hair, he looked like any European boy who has lived a long time in the sun.

Except that he didn't. He looked like no boy Maia had ever seen, standing so still, not waving or shouting instructions, just being there. And the dog who stood beside him was unlike other dogs also. A thin dog, the color of dark sand, he knew when to bark and when to be silent, and as their canoe drew up alongside the wooden platform, he permitted himself only a half wave of his tail.

The boy stretched out his hand and Maia jumped out.

"I've decided to trust you," he said in English.

She had known really before he spoke. Now she was sure.

Maia looked into his eyes. "You can do that," she said seriously. "I wouldn't betray you to the crows—not for the world."

"The crows . . . yes, that's the right name for them. So you know who I am?"

*But it was not the secrecy of the lake that
held Maia spellbound—it was its beauty.*

"You're Bernard Taverner's son. The boy who Professor Glastonberry said didn't exist. But I don't know your first name."

"It's Finn. And you're Maia, and you sing beautifully but you don't like beetroot and sums."

Maia stared at him. "How do you know all that?"

"The Indians tell me. They see everything. Old Lila used to be my nurse when I was a baby. I go and talk to them sometimes—at least I used to before the crows came—but only at night. The Carters have never seen me and they never will."

His voice, when he spoke of the Carters, was suddenly full of hatred.

"It was you, then," said Maia. "It was you who whistled 'Blow the Wind Southerly' the first night I came. It was such a comfort!"

Finn turned and said a few quick words to Furo in his own language. "He'll fetch you in a couple of hours," he said. "Come on, I'll show you everything. And then I'll tell you why I sent for you." He grinned and pulled himself up. "I mean, why I wanted you to come."

When Furo disappeared through the narrow channel of rushes the silence seemed overwhelming—yet she heard the noise of the water lapping the *Arabella*, the whirr of the hummingbirds' wings, the dog yawning. It was as though sounds had been freshly invented in this secret place.

Finn led her to the door of the hut. "My father built it and we lived here whenever we weren't away on collecting trips. I still can't believe he isn't coming back, though it's four months since he was drowned."

"Do you see him sometimes?" Maia asked—and he turned sharply because she seemed to have read his thoughts. "I see mine. My father. Not a ghost or an apparition . . . just him."

"Yes. It's exactly like that. Often he's showing me something. A new insect or a plant."

"Mine shows me things, too. Little bits of pottery . . . shards. He was an archaeologist."

"Mine was a naturalist. He collected over a hundred new species."

"I know—I saw some of the things in the museum. You must be proud of him."

"Yes. Maybe that's the point of fathers. They're people who show you things."

The hut was just as Bernard Taverner had left it when he went out with an Indian friend to look for the blue water lily whose leaves were used as a painkiller. His collecting boxes and specimen jars, his plant press and dissecting kit and microscope, were all stacked neatly on his worktable. His carpentry tools were hung carefully on the wooden wall; on the other side of the hut was the tackle for the boat. The khaki sheet still lay folded on his hammock as though he expected to return to sleep that night.

And on shelves made from palmwood planks were rows of old books—books on natural history, books on exploration, and all the well-known classics. But the book that lay open on the table with a marker was *Caesar's Gallic Wars* in Latin, and as he looked at it Finn sighed.

"He made me promise to go on with Latin whatever happened. He said there was nothing like it for sharpening the mind. But it's difficult on one's own."

"Yes." Maia nodded. "Everything's difficult on one's own."

But she thought she had never seen a place she liked more. The hut was spotlessly clean with a slight smell of woodsmoke and the watery scent of the reeds coming in through the window. There was a small oil stove and a sink, but she could see that mostly the boy cooked outside on the stone fireplace built on a spit of land that ran between the hut and the sandbank.

"You must have been very happy here—you and your father."

"Yes, we were. I used to wake up every morning and think, 'Here I am, exactly where I want to be,' and there aren't many boys who can say that. I thought of waking up in those awful English boarding schools with a bell shrilling."

He took her outside and showed her his oven, the place where the turtles laid their eggs, the bottle of sugar water that he filled each day for the hummingbirds, just as his father had done. "We've had twenty different kinds on that one tree," he said. His bow and arrow were hung on a branch, but she had seen a rifle, too, propped under the windowsill.

"Do you see that?" he said, pointing to some marks in the sand. "That's an anteater—he comes down at night to drink."

His father had planted a simple garden—manioc and maize and a few sweet potatoes, protected by a wire fence. "It's difficult, keeping the animals out—and keeping it weeded."

"It looks fine. All of it." She waved her hand over the hut, the boat, the lagoon. "It looks like a place where one would want to stay forever and ever."

He gave her a startled glance. "Yes. But I can't stay. I'm going on a journey."

"Oh!" For a moment she was devastated. She had only just met him and now he was going away.

"I'm going to find the Xanti."

She waited.

"They're my mother's tribe. She was Indian. My father brought her here and she died when I was born. I promised him that if anything happened to him, I'd go there. He said they'd keep me safe till I was of age, and then no one could make me go back to Westwood. I thought he was making a fuss, but now that the crows have come . . ."

"How will you go?"

"In the *Arabella*. As soon as the dry season starts properly. The rivers in the north are still flooded now, but it won't be long."

They clambered over the boat together and it was clear that she was the apple of his eye. She was a steam launch, rakish and sturdy, with a tall copper funnel and an awning running the length of her deck.

"My father got her cheap from a rubber baron who'd gone bankrupt. She can do five knots when she's in a good mood."

"Can you manage her on your own?"

"Just about. You have to have a lot of wood chopped at the beginning of the day and then you go on pretty steadily. It'll be difficult because there aren't any reliable maps for the last part of the journey. I'll have to go by what my father remembered."

Maia put her hand on the tiller. Five minutes ago she had wanted to stay in the lagoon forever. Now, just as much, she wanted to make this journey with Finn—to go on and on up the unknown rivers . . . not getting there, just going.

But now the dog, who had been following them silently, jumped back ashore and made his way to the door of the hut, which he pushed open with his muzzle.

"He's telling us it's time for afternoon tea."

Maia looked at him to see if he was joking, but he wasn't. Afternoon tea was exactly what Finn now produced. He put on the kettle, warmed the teapot, took down a tea caddy, and measured out three spoonfuls of Earl Grey. Then he found a plate, filled it with biscuits—proper ones with raisins—put out the sugar tongs and a milk jug; he even handed her a napkin. They might have been in any British drawing room.

The dog waited. "He only drinks China tea," said Finn, putting down a saucer and adding a spoonful of sugar. "If you give him anything else, he *looks* at you."

While they ate and drank, Finn made polite conversation, asking her how she liked Manaus, and whether her friend was still upset about the play.

"Clovis, do you mean? Yes, he is. But how do you know everything?"

He shrugged. "The Indians hear, and they tell me. The cleaner in the theater is old Lila's cousin."

When they had finished and swilled out the cups, he said, "Right. I suppose I'd better explain. I think I might need your help, you see."

Maia looked at him, flushed with pleasure.

"I'll do anything."

"Just like that?" he asked. "Even though I'm on the run?"

"Yes."

Finn grinned. "They said you weren't like the porkers."

"The porkers?"

"That's what the Indians call the twins. You know, little fat pigs that snuffle and eat."

Maia tried to look shocked and failed.

"Are they as bad as people say?" he asked.

Maia sighed and stopped trying to be good. "Yes," she said. "It would be lovely if they were pigs. One could really get fond of pigs."

"We'll go outside," said Finn. "The mosquitoes are fairly quiet at this hour."

So they sat side by side on the wooden deck outside the hut, and Finn told her the story of his father's marriage.

"When he came out here my father was just seventeen. He'd been absolutely wretched in England, but as soon as he came out here he knew it was the place for him. At first he had no money or anything, but he found he could live by collecting plants and berries people needed for medicines and selling them to traders in Manaus. He made friends with the Indians and learned their languages, and they taught him their skills.

"For nearly ten years he lived like that, exploring the rivers, building his hut. The awful memories of England only bothered him at night, when he was dreaming. He was sure he had gotten away."

Finn was silent, looking out over the lake.

"Then one day he went a very long way—not in the *Arabella,* in the canoe—and he fell ill with a fever, one of the really awful ones, and he passed out.

"When he came round he was with the Xanti. He'd heard of them—they were supposed to be special, very gentle and full of knowledge about healing, but they were very shy and mostly stayed hidden. Not many people had seen them.

"He said waking up there was like waking up in Paradise:

the kind, quiet people, the dappled trees. One girl in particular nursed him—her name was Yara—and when he was better the Xanti let her marry him, which was an honor.

"He brought her back here, but when I was due to be born, the English doctor wouldn't come out to an Indian woman in the night, and she died."

He paused. "After that he didn't have much to do with his own people. He found Lila to nurse me and we got on all right, though I think he never got over my mother's death. But we were good friends." His voice faltered for a moment. "I can stay here and live as he did, finding medicines, selling stuff to museums . . . oh, lots of things. But he said if anyone came for me from England I was to fight for my life. I was to go back to the Xanti. He never went back himself, but he said the tribe would know me." And he turned his wrist to show her the mark she had noticed in the canoe. "The trouble is, I've got to get away without being seen and the crows seem to be every-where, and no one knows how long they're going to stay and hunt around. The Indians won't give me away, but it's a big reward they're offering and there are people in Manaus who are very poor."

"You said perhaps I could help you?"

"Yes. I've got an idea, but I don't know if it will work." He pulled the dog closer and began to scratch his ear.

"You don't have to tell me if you don't want to," she said quickly. "I'll help you anyway."

"It isn't that; it's just that I haven't thought out the details yet. And anyway it doesn't depend only on me. What I'd like you to do now is tell me about your friend. About Clovis Where did you meet him? What's he like?"

So Maia told him about meeting Clovis on the boat, how homesick he was and how upset he'd been about his voice breaking. "All he wants is to get back to England. He says he's going to stow away."

"It won't work. They search the boats with a fine-tooth comb. People keep trying to smuggle out rubber seedlings so they can grow them somewhere else, which would kill the rubber trade here. He's sure to be caught."

"That's what Miss Minton says."

"Ah yes, Miss Minton. What does she think of Clovis?"

"I think she likes him. Yes, I'm sure she does. He does cry rather a lot, but he's very decent."

"Well, I suppose he would be if he's your friend."

They sat for a while in companionable silence. Then Finn said, "You don't happen to know Miss Minton's Christian name?"

Maia screwed up her face thinking. "She never uses it, but it begins with an *A*, I think, because she lent me her handkerchief once and there was an *A* embroidered in the corner."

Finn nodded. "Good," he said. "I thought it might."

Furo's canoe now appeared through the reeds, and Maia said quickly, "What I don't understand is how they can *make* you go back to Westwood. You're only a child; they don't lock up children in prisons."

Finn slapped a mosquito on his arm.

"They do at Westwood. At Westwood they lock you up as soon as you're born."

CLOVIS HAD COME up the river in an old tramp steamer which carried anything from cattle to timber.

He had paid the last of his money to the captain, who had allowed him to crouch on deck between a crate of bleating nanny goats and a leaking sack of maize. But he wouldn't put Clovis off at the Carters' landing stage.

"Bad place," he said.

And he made Clovis get out onto an old jetty higher up and walk back along the bank, so that by the time he reached the bungalow he was scratched and tired and very hot.

But now, as he made his way up the gravel path to the house, his spirits rose. It was so neat and tidy and quiet. No chickens to give you fleas, no barking dogs running the length of their chains.

Dusk had fallen and two of the windows were lit up. Clovis walked quietly toward them and looked in.

He saw a most comforting sight. The Carters were having supper, sitting around a large table spread with a clean white cloth. He could see Mrs. Carter—a kind-looking, plump woman in a blue dress with frilly sleeves, serving something onto pudding plates. A pink blancmange; Clovis could see it shaking a little on the dish and his mouth watered. *Shape* his foster mother had called it. She made it with strawberries and cornstarch and milk fresh from the cow. Opposite Mrs. Carter was her husband, a thin man in gold-rimmed spectacles—and facing him the twins.

They looked just the way Maia had described them on the boat: pretty and dressed in white, with ribbons in their hair. And beside them, Maia . . . The twins were pretty, but Maia was special; with her serious face and kind eyes; he could see her pigtail looped over her shoulder. Just looking at it made him feel safe, as if he could hold on to it and be all right.

Miss Minton didn't seem to be there. Perhaps it was her day off and she had gone to visit friends.

He stood and looked a little longer, unseen by the people in the room. It was a good name for this house: Tapherini—a Place of Rest. Then he went round to the side of the house and knocked on the door.

It took only a few moments to shatter Clovis's dream. First came the violent shrilling of an alarm bell. Then a maid with a sullen face led him to the dining room and opened the door— and the twins looked up, stared at him—and exploded. It wasn't laughter that came from them, not really. It was that awful giggling, that high-pitched, merciless titter that had spread across the footlights in the theater and set the other children off. Clovis recognized it at once. So it was the twins' laughter that had hounded him!

"Oh!" gasped Beatrice. "It's Little Lord Fauntleroy," and then both girls said, *"Will I have to stop being your little boy?"* in a deep and growly voice and repeated it, their voices getting lower and lower . . . and in between they choked and spluttered and patted each other on the back, and started taunting him again.

Clovis stood perfectly still by the door. He looked at Maia to see if she, too, was going to join in, but she looked horrified, and now she jumped up and came to stand beside him.

"Don't!" she said passionately to the twins. "Please don't; can't you see—"

Mrs. Carter now took charge. "All right, girls," she said to her daughters, "that will do," and to Maia, "Sit down, please. We have not finished our meal."

But it took some time for the twins to quiet down. They still growled and gulped, and then Beatrice said, "Look at Maia, protecting her boyfriend!"

"Enough," said Mr. Carter, dabbing his mouth with his napkin. It was the first word he had spoken at table, and was to be the last, but the twins now managed to control themselves.

"Now," said Mrs. Carter, staring at Clovis, "might I ask what brings you here?"

Clovis looked at the soft, rounded face. Close up, it did not look kind and motherly as it had looked through the window. He felt that under the puffy cheeks one would find stone.

"I wondered if I could stay with you for a few days. We have to leave the hotel, the Paradiso—all of us—and I thought . . ." His words died away.

Maia now turned to Mrs. Carter and stretched out her hands to her as if she were begging for her life. "Oh please, please, Mrs. Carter, couldn't he stay? He could have my room and I'll go and sleep with Miss Minton. I'm sure Mr. Murray will help him to—"

"*Stay?*" Mrs. Carter interrupted in a horrified voice.

"Stay with *us?*" said Beatrice. "We don't have actors to stay, do we, Gwendolyn?"

Both twins shook their heads slowly, left to right and right to left. They reminded Maia of the women knitting by the guillotine during the French Revolution, while heads rolled into baskets.

"Heaven knows what he might have picked up in the Paradiso," said Mrs. Carter. And to Clovis, "What are those bites on your leg? Fleas or bedbugs?"

Clovis flushed. There *were* bedbugs at the Paradiso; he minded it just as much as Mrs. Carter. But it was true that he no longer looked like a boy wonder of the stage. It had been impossible to get hot water at the hotel. His long hair was unwashed; his clothes were too small for him, and stained.

"We can't just turn him out," said Maia desperately.

"I hope you don't think we can take in every verminous stray that comes to the door. The boy must go back. Beatrice, go and fetch Miss Minton."

"I'll go," said Maia quickly.

"No. I asked Beatrice."

But Gwendolyn, who wouldn't even go to the bathroom by herself, had slipped out after her sister.

Maia had not sat down again; she stood beside Clovis as though she could come between him and his misery. In its bowl in the center of the table, the pink "shape," which had looked so good through the window, had sunk into a watery mush.

Miss Minton appeared in the doorway.

"Good evening, Clovis," she said.

Clovis took a step toward her. "Good evening, Miss

Minton." She looked just as she had looked on the boat, sharp-faced and strong. He'd liked her from the start; she was fierce but she was straight, and for a moment he was sure she would be able to help him.

"Please take the boy out and order Furo to take him back to Manaus at once," ordered Mrs. Carter.

"Oh, not tonight," begged Maia. "Surely—"

"Tonight. I hope you are satisfied, making us use the boat and wasting fuel on a runaway boy."

Miss Minton gave Maia a quelling look. "That will do, Maia. Come along, Clovis. I'm really ashamed of you, putting the Carters to so much trouble."

Clovis shook off her arm and gave up hope.

"I'll come by myself," he said.

If Miss Minton, too, was his enemy, there was nothing to be done.

Left behind in the dining room, Maia was still on her feet.

"Please can I go to my room?" she asked.

"Certainly not. You will finish the meal."

Maia took a deep breath. "I feel sick," she said.

Mrs. Carter looked at her. She did indeed look very pale. Mrs. Carter weighed the possibility of a disgusting mess against her desire to punish Maia.

"Very well. You may go to your room. And stay there."

The two Englishmen had returned from upriver in a very nasty temper. They had spent two days on a boat with piglets and chickens and an old woman who was seasick even though the river hardly moved in the still heat. There were no bunks, only hammocks strung on deck, and Mr. Trapwood fell out of his in the middle of the night onto an inspector of schools from Rio who was not pleased.

Even worse had befallen Mr. Low, who had decided to have a swim when the boat stopped to take on more wood, and came out of the water to find a dozen bloodsucking leeches feasting on his behind.

And when they got to the Ombuda there was no sign of Bernard Taverner's son.

The interpreter whom Colonel da Silva had sent with them was very helpful. He went ahead to the chief of the Ombuda and greeted him in his own language and said that Mr. Low and Mr. Trapwood were important people who had come from Great Britain to search for a missing boy. But what he also said in a low voice was that these two gentlemen were being a great trouble to the colonel, who begged the chief and his friends to tell them some story about a lost boy which would keep them quiet and make them go away again.

The Ombuda chief and his friends were only too pleased to do this. They did not like Mr. Low and Mr. Trapwood, who had not brought any of the presents one usually brings when visiting a tribe—fishhooks, knives, and cooking pots—and they loved making up stories.

So they told them about an English boy, fair-haired and beautiful as the sun, who had been there, but had wandered away again.

"Where to?" asked the crows eagerly. "Where did he go?"

"In the direction of the Sacred Mountain," said the chief, pointing to the north.

"No, no, in the direction of the Mambuto forest," said his second-in-command, pointing in the opposite direction.

"Forgive me, Father," said the chief's young son, "but the boy went to the river." And he pointed somewhere different again.

"Ask them when this was," said Mr. Trapwood excitedly.

So the Indians and the interpreter talked among themselves and then they went to a hut on the edge of the clearing and fetched out an old woman.

The old woman wasn't just old, she was ancient, with arms and legs like sticks and not a tooth in her head, but when the chief explained what he wanted, she grinned happily and said yes, yes, she remembered the boy very well.

"His eyes were as blue as the blossom of the jacaranda tree, and his hair glistened like the belly of the golden toad that squats on the lily leaves of the Mamari River," said the old woman, who was having a good time. "His skin was as white as the moon in the season of—"

"Yes, but when? When?" interrupted the crows rudely. "When was he here?"

The old woman sat down on a tree stump and began to count. She used her fingers and her toes and then some pebbles on the ground, and the chief and his friends helped her.

Then she winked at the interpreter and said it had been fifty years ago.

"What!" shouted Mr. Trapwood. "Fifty years!"

She nodded and said yes, she was sure, because it was when she was a very small girl and still had all her milk teeth in her head, and the Indians nodded also and said yes, she had often told them of the lost boy who came when she was no higher than the tail of a swamp deer—and they led her back into the hut, patting her on the back while she giggled with glee.

So the crows had to give up, but they could not leave because the boat back to Manaus was not due for another two days, and they had a very uncomfortable time staying with the Ombuda, who drummed a lot and seemed to live mostly on nuts. That the tribe was sharing their food and shelter very generously did not, of course, occur to the crows, who had been brought up to think of the Indians as savages.

By the time they returned to Manaus, the Englishmen were not in very good shape.

"I've had enough of this," said Mr. Trapwood as they sat in their room in the Pension Maria overlooking the docks.

"So have I," croaked Mr. Low. "This business has got to be settled. The *Bishop* goes back in ten days' time and the Taverner boy is going to be on it."

"If he exists," said Mr. Trapwood gloomily.

"Of course he exists. You saw the letter."

"Well, why doesn't he come forward, or anyone else?"

"Do you think we ought to increase the reward? The old chap said we were to use our judgment."

"I suppose we might as well. After all, it's not us that's paying it. What we need now is a thorough house-to-house search of the buildings outside the city. If Taverner was a naturalist, he probably wouldn't live in the middle of town. And they may not have seen the notices out there."

"I'm sure that chap at the museum knows something," said Mr. Low moodily. "The one who said that Taverner didn't have a son."

Then the little Brazilian maid brought in their supper, which was the same as lunch and the same as breakfast—brown beans stewed with pigs' trotters. Mr. Low dug about in it gloomily, looking for bits of gristle, and Mr. Trapwood found a dead ant on his plate. It seemed to be a perfectly clean ant, but he gagged and pushed his plate away.

"This place is closer to hell on earth than anywhere I've been," he said.

On the morning after Clovis had been turned away from the house, the hairdresser came out from Manaus to do Mrs. Carter's hair. At first he was silent and surly, but when he found that Mrs. Carter meant to pay him at last, he cheered up and gave them all the news. The actors had all been thrown out of the Paradiso and had gotten hold of a van and were trying to get out of Brazil through Venezuela, where the British consul was supposed to be good-natured and inclined to turn a blind eye.

"But everyone thinks they'll be stopped at the border," said Monsieur Claude.

"Poor Clovis," said Maia when she heard this.

The twins shrugged. "He's only an actor," said Beatrice. "A vagabond. They're used to wandering about."

"Clovis isn't," said Maia, but she said no more about him. Since Clovis had been taken away by Miss Minton she had been quiet and subdued, scarcely speaking to anyone.

But the piece of news that interested the Carters most was that the reward for the discovery of Taverner's son had been doubled.

"It's forty thousand *milreis* now," said the hairdresser, crimping Mrs. Carter's curls. "They've put up notices everywhere."

"Imagine the dresses one could buy with that," said Beatrice.

"And the hats," said Gwendolyn.

"And the shoes."

"And the chocolates. Boxes and boxes of chocolates."

"You could buy something a great deal more useful than that," said Mr. Carter. The pair of glass eyes from Queen Victoria's piano tuner, for example; he had seen them in the catalog. Or he could pay off that shark Gonzales from whom he'd borrowed money and who was always pestering him.

"There's a new kind of wallpaper that stops insects from landing on it for twenty years," said Mrs. Carter wistfully. "I read about it at the dentist."

For a moment all the Carters stood with narrowed eyes, thinking of what they would do with so much money.

And on the following day, the crows arrived at the bungalow.

They had chartered a boat belonging to a wealthy merchant and landed at the Carters' jetty while the children were doing their lessons.

Mr. Carter was out bullying his workers somewhere, but when he saw the boat he came in quickly. Mrs. Carter brought Mr. Low and Mr. Trapwood into the dining room, where Miss Minton was giving the twins dictation.

"Fetch Maia," she ordered the governess. "These gentlemen want to question everybody."

The crows sat down, twitching their black trousers up at the knee so as to keep the creases in. They liked the Carters' dining room: the smell of Lysol, the shrouded windows. A decent British household at last. Maia was brought in. She recognized them at once, and the twins saw that she had turned pale.

Mr. Trapwood did not waste any time. "Some of you know already what I am going to say. We have come from England to find a missing boy—the son of Bernard Taverner. It is now very important that he is found and brought back before the *Bishop* sails. The reward for news of him has been doubled. Now I want you to think very, very carefully whether you have any idea of where such a boy might be hiding."

Maia looked up. *"Why* is he hiding? Why doesn't he come forward? Why doesn't he want to go back to England?"

The crows frowned. "Whether he wants to go back or not has nothing to do with it. The boy must go back, and at once. It is a matter of life and death."

"If we tell you something useful, will we get the reward?" asked Beatrice.

"Certainly."

The twins looked at each other. "We think Maia is hiding him," said Beatrice. "I had a toothache last night and I woke up and I saw her sneak out to that end hut where the rubber workers used to live. The one that was empty."

"We don't know for certain but that's what we think," said Gwendolyn.

"She goes outside sometimes when she's supposed to be in bed."

"No. Honestly. That's nothing to do with—" Maia had jumped up from her chair. "I don't know anything about the boy you're looking for."

"All the same, I think I might ask these young ladies to take us to the hut they describe. Have I your permission, Mrs. Carter?"

"Certainly. But if Maia has been deceiving us she will be most seriously punished."

Miss Minton had come to stand beside Maia. "If Maia has really been hiding someone she will certainly be punished. But I find this hard to believe."

"It isn't Bernard Taverner's son. Honestly—"

But it was too late. The crows had risen, and now everybody moved out of the bungalow, down the side path and toward the huts of the Indians. Furo and Tapi and old Lila were standing outside their door, looking on in silence.

Miss Minton had taken Maia by the arm, as if she expected her to run away. Her nutcracker face was closed and angry.

Mrs. Carter moved past the huts as if she were walking through an open drain, and the twins held their noses as they passed the potbellied pig.

"Please," began Maia, and stopped as Miss Minton's steely fingers dug painfully into her arm.

"Be quiet, Maia," she said.

The hut was locked, but that didn't help them. Mrs. Carter shouted to Tapi to bring the key, and Tapi disappeared into her hut. She was away a long time, but eventually, sulkily, she brought the key.

"Empty," she said to the crows. "Not inside. *Nada*. All gone away."

"We shall soon see," said Mrs. Carter, and took the key.

Maia bit her lip and stared at the ground.

The lock was stiff. "Give it to me," said Mr. Carter, taking the key from his wife. He fumbled for a while, then managed to turn it. The door swung open.

There was a loud screech, a flutter of black wings—and a trapped bird flew out, sending Mrs. Carter reeling backward.

Then silence. On the floor of the hut was an old blanket, a candlestick with a spent candle, and nothing else.

The hut was empty.

Nobody in the Carters' bungalow slept well that night.

The twins lay in bed thinking about the money that had escaped them.

"I was going to get that blue silk cloak in Fleurette's window." Beatrice sighed.

"It wouldn't suit you. The neck's too low."

They began to argue, but then remembered that neither of them could buy the cloak.

"All the same, I think Maia knows something. Did you see how worried she looked when they were opening the hut?"

"She's just the sort of person who would be on the side of a runaway. Look how she tried to shelter Clovis."

"But the Taverner boy isn't just a runaway. He's a criminal. He must be or they wouldn't be so keen to catch him."

"Well, I'm going to watch Maia. I don't trust her at all."

In their bedroom down the corridor, Mr. and Mrs. Carter, too, were thinking of all that could be done with the reward for the capture of Taverner's son.

"We could go back to England for a visit. I'm sure Lady Parsons would be pleased to have us to stay."

Mr. Carter did not answer. For one thing, he never spoke to his wife if he could help it, and for another, the last thing he wanted was to go back to England. He had left his job in the bank there in a hurry. Quite a big hurry. If he had stayed even a few days longer the police would have come for him, because he had borrowed money that did not belong to him. And out here he was getting behind again with certain payments. The forty thousand *milreis* would have helped to clear his debts. They wouldn't have cleared them all, but they would have helped.

Mrs. Carter was frowning, thinking of Maia. "I don't really trust that girl—and the governess favors her."

"Well, if you send her away we're done for," said Mr. Carter. "I owe that rogue Gonzales three batches of rubber and I haven't got one."

"How can that be?"

"You wouldn't understand," said Mr. Carter wearily.

He sighed and reached for the lamp, but Mrs. Carter got up once more and took her flit gun from under the bed. She was almost sure that she had heard something buzzing by the window.

Maia had put on her dressing gown and crept down the corridor to Miss Minton's room. She had brought her hairbrush, but the hundred strokes were just an excuse. She was perfectly capable of brushing her own hair, but she had a confession to make.

"But where can he have gone, Minty?" Maia asked after telling her unsurprised governess about Clovis. "The actors aren't here anymore and he doesn't know anyone else in Manaus. I'm so worried about him."

"He won't come to any harm," said Miss Minton, brushing steadily. "He's quite a sensible boy really."

But Maia could not see it like that.

When Miss Minton had taken Clovis to the boat, it was with the idea of telling Furo to take him to the Keminskys. She was sure now that Mr. Carter had never sent the cable to Mr. Murray, and she had hoped to ask Sergei's family to take Clovis in for a while. The Russians were well-known for their hospitality, and in the end surely the British consul would do something for the boy.

But Furo, with much hand waving, had explained that the Keminskys had gone away for two days to visit their farms in the north—and when she turned round Clovis had disappeared into the darkness.

Miss Minton had asked no questions—not even when she saw Maia creep back from the deserted hut which had housed the rubber gatherers: Till the Russians returned there was nothing she could do.

And now the boy had vanished.

The next day was a Sunday. On one Sunday in the month an English vicar came out to conduct a service in the next village upriver from the Carters' house. Mrs. Carter liked church. The twins in their pretty dresses were always admired, she heard other English voices . . . In England they had sometimes been allowed to join Lady Parsons in her pew. She had expected Maia to accompany them, but the girl looked peaked and wretched and had been sick in the night.

Mrs. Carter was displeased. "She seems to be making a habit of it. I hope it's not infectious," she said to Miss Minton, who shook her head. She knew exactly why Maia had been sick. She was worried about Clovis. She had been sick after she came across an Indian being flogged on Mr. Carter's orders.

"I think she needs a quiet morning by herself," said Miss Minton, and was told that it was her duty to accompany the twins.

"We don't want people saying we can't afford a governess," said Mrs. Carter to her husband.

So the family disappeared upriver in the launch. Maia noticed that it was not Furo who was steering the boat, but it was not till Furo came himself and beckoned to her that she allowed herself to hope.

"Come," he said, as he had done the first time, and Maia got up quickly and followed him. Her sickness had gone. She felt hopeful and excited. If this was a summons from Finn, perhaps he would know what to do.

This time she was not asked to put on a blindfold, and at this sign of trust her spirits rose still further. When they came to the green wall, she could make out the opening, now that she knew it was there. It wasn't much more than a change in the color of the green as the rushes took over from the undergrowth. She closed her eyes to protect them against the branches, and then they were through and she was in the lagoon again.

Even before she saw Finn, she felt as though she was coming home.

The dog wagged his tail, properly this time; nothing too gushing—he was not that kind of dog—but he remembered her.

She jumped out onto the jetty. Finn's hair was coal black, as it had been the first time she saw him, and he wore his headband; he was in his Indian guise again. But he looked relaxed and untroubled, and when she thought of the crows she found herself shivering.

"They've been at the Carters," she said. "The crows."

"I know."

Of course, he would know. He knew everything.

"And you've lost your little actor friend," he said, grinning.

Furo had paddled back to the entrance, and Maia followed Finn into the hut. He had a bowl of fruit on the table—avocados, prickly pears, nuts, a melon. Her mouth watered but she turned her head away, angry with Finn for speaking so carelessly of Clovis.

"Yes, I'm so worried about him. He came and the twins jeered at him and Mrs. Carter said he had to go back. But the actors had gone, so I hid him in the store hut. I thought I'd get Mr. Murray to pay his fare, but he hasn't. Then the crows came and they made me open the door—they thought it was you I was hiding—and he'd gone. Vanished."

"He'll be all right," said Finn.

His casual tone annoyed Maia. "That's what Miss Minton says, but *why* will he be all right? He's got nowhere to sleep and no money."

Thinking about Clovis and how she had let him down had brought tears to her eyes, and she brushed them away angrily. Clovis was her responsibility, not Finn's. Finn had troubles enough of his own.

But Finn had seen her distress. "Come and see the *Arabella*," he said. "I've cleaned the funnel. Walk carefully; there's some wet paint."

She followed him onto the little launch.

"Have a look under the awning," said Finn. "But don't make a noise."

She moved quietly forward. What strange animal had Finn brought aboard and tamed?

Someone lay sprawled out on the deck. He lay on his back, his limbs were thrown out loosely; he was so still that he might have been dead.

But he wasn't. He was deeply asleep. So asleep that even when Maia bent over him he did not stir.

"He'll sleep for a bit," said Finn. "I gave him something. He's a nice boy, but you're right: he does cry a lot."

"You mean you've drugged him?" Maia was shocked.

"It's only mashohara leaves," said Finn. "Old Lila used to give them to me in a drink. It's quite harmless."

But Maia was not altogether pleased. "You seem to know a lot about herbs and medicines—and dyes," she added, looking at Finn's hair.

"The Indians taught my father, and he taught me. It's how we lived partly, finding new medicines."

They went back and sat on the jetty, and he explained what he had done. "Furo told me that the crows were on their way, and he told me about Clovis being in the hut. He thought you'd get into awful trouble from the Carters. So I fetched him away in the night."

The dog lay quietly between them; two swallowtail butter-flies chased each other over the lotus leaves.

"Actually," Finn went on, "I've got an idea—I told you. I'll explain when I've woken Clovis." He looked up at the sun. "He'll be awake in half an hour. Better make some tea and serve it nicely. Clovis likes things properly done. Teacups with saucers and no bugs on the bread and butter."

Finn was right. Clovis woke up in exactly half an hour looking refreshed and well. He, too, liked the hut.

"I wouldn't mind living in a place like this," he said, helping himself to a biscuit.

"Well, that's a good thing," said Finn. "Because you're going to. For a few days. Till just before the *Bishop* sails."

Clovis looked up, his eyes full of bewilderment.

"I'll explain," said Finn. "I thought, you see, that you could take my place. The crows don't know what you look like—and they don't know what I look like. If Maia will do what I ask her, I think it could be done. Then you'll get safely to England and I'll get away."

Maia stared at him.

"But you can't! You can't send Clovis back to a *prison!*"

Finn was bent over the dog, steadily scratching the space between his ears.

"I think it's time I told you about Westwood," he said.

9

"IT MIGHT EASILY have been a prison," began Finn. "It had towers and a moat and battlements and it stood in acres of land ringed by a high stone wall stuck full of spikes."

But it wasn't. Westwood was a large country house—a stately home— which had belonged to the Taverners since the time of the Crusades. The head of the family was a stiff-necked, snooty landowner, Sir Aubrey Taverner, who brayed at people and spoke to the servants as if they were deaf.

Sir Aubrey's eldest son was called Dudley and he was exactly like his father: arrogant and snooty and certain that the Taverners were the most important people on earth. Dudley, too, shouted at the servants; he went off to his prep school without a murmur; he rode horses with large behinds; he shot things—and of course he was the apple of his father's eye.

The next child born to the Taverners was a girl whom they called Joan. She wasn't much good in some ways because only males were allowed to inherit Westwood, but all the same she was a true Taverner, with a voice like a foghorn. Joan bullied other children who had the bad luck not to be Taverners, and she, too, rode about on horses with large behinds, and Sir Aubrey liked her well enough.

But then came Bernard.

Bernard was the last of Sir Aubrey's children. His mother died soon after he was born, and he was a disaster. Bernard was afraid of loud voices. He was afraid of the dark. He was afraid of his brother, Dudley, who tried to make a man of him, and he was afraid of his sister, Joan, who threw him in the lake and held his head under the water to make him swim. When Bernard spoke to the maids, he did it quietly and he said "please" and "thank you"—and sometimes, though he was a boy and a Taverner, he cried.

His father, of course, was desperate. A boy like Bernard had never happened in his family before. He sent him away to the toughest school he could find, but though the teachers caned him even more than his father had done, and the boys did interesting things to him like squeezing lemon juice into his eyes and piercing the soles of his feet with compass needles, it seemed to make no difference. Bernard went on being quiet, and he went on being terrified of his family, and he went on saying "please" and "thank you" to the maids.

But there were some things Bernard was not afraid of. He was not afraid of spiders—when the servants screamed because there was a large one in the bath, it was to Bernard they went, and he would put a glass over it and let it out in the garden, admiring its furry legs and complicated eyes. He was not afraid of the adders that hissed on the moor. He *liked* the adders with their zigzag markings and flickering tongues. Bernard did not mind the rats in the cellars and he did not mind the horses.

He minded the people *on* the horses—his sister, Joan, with her braying voice and his brother, Dudley, with his whip—but if he met the horses quietly in a field he got on well enough with them.

It was one of the maids who showed him that there might be a way of escaping from Westwood. She was an ugly, gawky girl not much older than Bernard, and as much of a misfit among the servants as he was among his family. Bella was always reading the books she should have been dusting and was constantly in trouble, but she was the only friend Bernard had.

"There's people who make their living with animals," she said. "Naturalists they're called. You could be one of them."

"From then on my father knew what he wanted to do," said Finn. "He wanted to get as far away from his family as it was possible to go, and live with animals."

When you know what you want you usually get it. It took Bernard seven years, and all that time he said nothing to anyone, but saved every penny he could. He saved his Christmas money and he saved his pocket money. He never bought so much as a lollipop or a chocolate bar. And slowly, very slowly, his hoard built up. The maid who was his friend hid it for him in the cage of a stuffed owl in the attic, and all the time Dudley went on bullying him and his father went on beating him and his sister, Joan, went on jeering at him, but now Bernard had somewhere to go inside his head.

Then a month after Bernard's sixteenth birthday, Sir Aubrey came down to breakfast, and so did Dudley and so did Joan. They helped themselves to kedgeree and scrambled eggs and kidneys and bacon. Then Sir Aubrey rang for the footman to bring fresh coffee and said, "Where's Bernard? The wretched boy is late again."

But Bernard wasn't late—he was gone, and nobody from Westwood ever set eyes on him again.

He caught a banana boat bound for Brazil and traveled up the Amazon, and he was as happy there as he had been wretched in England. He'd been terrified of the butler, but alligators didn't trouble him. He made friends with the Indians; he found it easy to make a living as a collector. The only time he was unhappy and afraid was when he was asleep in his hammock and dreamed he was back in Westwood or at school. And when Finn was born, he decided to bring him up to love and respect the Indians, and never let anyone drive him back to his old home.

And so the years passed. Sir Aubrey wrote off his youngest son; he was probably in a gutter somewhere and serve him right. Dudley was the best person to inherit Westwood.

But then something awful happened. Dudley was killed in the hunting field. The horse was all right, and people were glad of that because it was a good horse, but Dudley wasn't. He broke his neck.

Sir Aubrey was exceedingly upset. Who would take over from him when he was dead and look after Westwood with its two lakes and its three woods and its farm, and who would give orders in the house with its forty-seven rooms?

He thought about this and then he decided that what mattered was that whoever it was should have the Taverner

BLOOD. Sir Aubrey was very keen on blood and always had been. His daughter Joan had it, of course, but she was married to a man called Smith and had already given birth to three daughters, one after the other, and daughters were no good. It was only males who could inherit Westwood.

Sir Aubrey decided to give her one more chance. Joan lived on the edge of the estate. If her fourth child was a boy, he would leave Westwood to him, though of course he would have to change his name to Smith-Taverner.

But it was not to be. When the midwife came out of Joan's bedroom and said, "It's another lovely little girl," Sir Aubrey was driven away from his daughter's house in a dreadful temper, and for weeks people were afraid to speak to him.

But then a brave old lady, a second cousin, came to see him and said, "Don't forget, Aubrey, that you still have another son."

"If you mean Bernard, he is not my son any longer. He was an ungrateful, cowardly scoundrel, and if he darkens my door again, I'll take my whip to him."

But the cousin said blood was blood and why didn't he try to find Bernard, and after a while Sir Aubrey saw the sense of this. Blood *was* blood; there was no getting round it. Better that Bernard should inherit Westwood than a total stranger.

Only where was Bernard? They put an advertisement in *The Times,* and a lot of other newspapers, asking Bernard Taverner to come forward and he would hear something to his advantage, but for a long time nothing happened.

Then, when they had almost given up hope, they had a letter from the editor of a magazine called *The Naturalist,* which was published in New York, and printed learned articles about animal and plants. This is what the editor wrote:

Dear Sir Aubrey,

I happened to see in The Times *of last October a request for information about Bernard Taverner.*

Taverner was a regular contributor to my journal, an outstanding naturalist and observer of wild life. I asked him for a piece about the manatee, a rare South American water mammal. Instead of his article I received this letter from his son which I enclose.

Dear Sir,

I am very sorry, but my father, Bernard Taverner, died two months ago. His canoe overturned in the rapids and he was drowned.

I am sending back the check you wrote him because it belonged to him and anyway I am too young to have a bank account.

Yours faithfully,
F. Taverner

Needless to say, this letter caused great excitement.

"By Jove, he had a son, then," said Sir Aubrey. "Well, our problems are solved. We'll send for the boy and train him up to run Westwood—it shouldn't take long to knock him into shape. No reason to suppose he'll be a namby-pamby like his father."

How to find the boy, though, was another matter. There was no address on the letter, and the only thing the editor knew was that Bernard's mail went to a post-office box in Manaus. *That's not where he lives, though,* he wrote. *He was always traveling. I believe he had an Indian wife.*

But this Sir Aubrey refused to believe. Instead he wrote two letters addressed to *The Son of Bernard Taverner,* one to the post-office box in Manaus and one care of the bank manager who had looked after Bernard's account. In both letters he explained what had happened at Westwood and said that the way was now open for Bernard's son to come back and take up his inheritance.

Finn received the letters and did not answer either of them. Instead he began to get the *Arabella* ready for her journey to the Xanti. Nothing Sir Aubrey had written made him feel that he could ever return to his father's home.

Sir Aubrey wrote again and sent a cable. Then, losing patience, he got in touch with the director of the firm of Wesley and Kinnear, Private Investigators, and asked them to send two of their best men out to the Amazon to find the boy and bring him back.

And two months later the crows arrived in Manaus.

In the hut beside the lagoon, Finn had fallen silent.

Then Clovis said, "Are you sure you wouldn't rather go back to be master of Westwood? Rather than—" He broke off as a capuchin monkey screeched suddenly in the trees.

"Rather than live like a savage?" finished Finn, grinning. "Yes. Quite sure."

Maia, too, had wondered. Sir Aubrey must be an old man by now; Finn would probably be able to stand up to him better than his father had done, and when he died Finn could take over and do anything he liked with Westwood.

"Let's get this clear," said Finn. "Whether you decide to help me or not, I'm never going back to Westwood. Never. And if the crows come here to this place I'll shoot them and go to jail. This was my father's sanctuary, and they're not going to set foot in it."

Maia and Clovis looked at each other. At times like this one remembered the Indian side of Finn.

"So how does it work?" asked Maia. "The crows find Clovis and think he's you?"

Finn sat with his hands round his knees, frowning as he thought. "I want them to find Clovis just before the boat sails, late on the night before, if possible. So that there's no time to trail him round Manaus—someone's sure to recognize him from the theater."

"Yes, but how?"

"They must know by now that I don't want to come to England. That I'm trying to hide until they've gone. So I will hide. Somewhere near the docks. But my hiding place will be betrayed. They'll hear that a boy is hiding and come to grab him in the night. Only it won't be me; it'll be Clovis. If Maia gets the timing right they'll find him just before the boat sails and take him straight on board."

"If I do what?"

"Betray me. Give me away by mistake. It's no good going to the police—they're on my side. You must let it slip to someone who is sure to go to the crows. Someone who'll do anything for money."

"Who?"

"Oh, for goodness' sake, surely it's obvious."

Maia nodded. "Yes," she said sadly. "The twins."

"I'll explain it all properly. It'll work, I promise you."

"Yes, but what will happen when they find out I'm not you?" said poor Clovis, who had turned pale.

"They won't. Not till you get to England. Not even then if you don't want them to. I'll give you a sealed letter saying I bullied you into taking my place. That I threatened you with torture. It takes six weeks to get to England—if you can hold out for another week or two at Westwood that will give me plenty of time to get away. By the time they find out, I'll be with the Xanti and you can go to your foster mother."

"Where is Clovis going to hide?" asked Maia.

"I've got a good place near the harbor, and absolutely safe. You will have to set it up because Clovis and I must stay here out of sight."

But Clovis was looking very doubtful. "What was the food like?"

"Where?" asked Finn.

"At Westwood. Did your father say?"

Finn shrugged impatiently. "No. But it'll be the usual British stodge, I expect," he said, looking at the bowl of fresh fruit he had picked that morning. "Steak and kidney pies and suet pudding and dumplings."

"Really? Suet pudding, do you think?" said Clovis wistfully. "My foster mother used to make them with treacle." He thought of the Goodleys, off to Colombia and Peru, if they weren't thrown in jail. "And it wouldn't be hot?" he said.

"No, it certainly wouldn't be hot. Westwood's in the north of England. They get a lot of snow."

"Snow," said Clovis, his eyes dreamy. "Not that I'd be staying." And then: "All right. I'll give it a try."

10

THE MANAUS MUSEUM of Natural History was very quiet this weekday morning. The boy who swept the floors was outside, weeding the flower beds, the porter dozed in his cubicle, and there were no visitors.

But in his lab behind the office, Professor Glastonberry was worrying about the giant sloth.

He often worried about the sloth. For the past year he had been putting the skeleton of the great beast together, and it was going to make a most impressive exhibit.

At least it should have.

For the truth was the skeleton was not complete. It was *nearly* complete but not quite. One rib was missing. The third rib on the left-hand side.

Professor Glastonberry had made a false rib out of plaster of paris and now he fitted it carefully into the breastbone, and it looked fine.

At least it did if you didn't know . . .

The trouble was that the professor did know.

He stood looking at his handiwork. The sloth on its metal stand seemed to fill the whole room.

He took the rib out. He put it in again. He sighed. A false rib was cheating.

But a missing rib was untidy.

At that moment he heard the creaking of the revolving doors and, peering out, realized that two people had come into the museum whom he recognized. The tall, thin woman who had been interested in Bernard Taverner's collection and the schoolgirl who had been with her: a girl with a lot of dark hair and intelligent eyes.

He came out of his office and said, "Good morning."

The tall woman smiled and at once looked less alarming. "This is Maia," she said. "She has come to make some drawings of birds' wings. May I leave her here to work on her own? I'll fetch her at three o'clock. I don't think she'll be any trouble."

"I'm sure she won't," said the professor. He was still holding the false rib and looked distracted.

"What a large rib," said Miss Minton.

"Yes." He took a deep breath and poured out the problem of the missing bone. "No one would know it was not the real one," he said.

Miss Minton looked severe. "*You* would know," she said.

The professor sighed. "That's what Taverner used to say."

"May we see it? The sloth?" asked Maia.

"Certainly."

He led them through his office and into the lab.

"It's not upside down," said Maia. "I thought sloths always hung from trees?"

"Not the giant sloths. They'd have splintered any tree they tried to hang from. This one would have weighed about four

"I think you should go and find the missing bone," said Miss Minton.
The professor stared at her. Was she serious?

tons when it was alive, but they've been extinct for thousands of years."

Once again the professor put the rib in and once again he took it out.

"What do you think?"

"I think you should go and find the missing bone," said Miss Minton.

The professor stared at her. Was she serious? Surely not . . .

"I'm afraid that's impossible," he said. "The original skeleton came from a cave near the Xanti River, miles away to the north. And I'm too old for expeditions."

"Nonsense," said Miss Minton. "Anyone who can walk can go on expeditions."

Then she took her leave and Maia said "good morning" to the stuffed Pekingese before she settled down at a table near the "Birds in Flight" exhibit, and began to draw. It was good to be in the museum again, and away from the Carters. Not just the Pekingese, but the Amazonian river slug, the lumpy manatee, the shrunken head, all seemed like old friends—and of course the Taverner Collection, which she now saw with new eyes. And as she drew, Maia tried to puzzle out the problem of her governess.

Maia had told Miss Minton that Clovis was safe with the Indian boy. Miss Minton had nodded, but she asked no more questions. It was strange how little she asked Maia about her comings and goings, when she pounced on every strand of unbrushed hair or a fingernail not scrubbed to cleanliness. Then, when Maia said she needed to go and work in the museum to finish her project on "Birds of the Rain Forest,"

Minty had done no more than raise an eyebrow and had gone about arranging it. She had even persuaded Mrs. Carter to let them go down on the rubber boat so as to give them more time in Manaus.

And why did Finn want to know Miss Minton's Christian name?

But she wasn't in the museum to think about Minty, or even to draw birds. She was here to do a job for Finn, and when she was sure the museum was empty she walked over to the door marked PRIVATE and knocked.

Professor Glastonberry came out at once. He really was a very nice man with his round, pink face and white fringe of hair.

"I'm sorry to disturb you again," said Maia, "but I have a message for you." And she handed him the note Finn had written in the hut.

The professor read it and looked at her intently. So she had found Finn and made friends with him. Not only that, but she wanted to help him.

"Yes," he said. "I see. You are a messenger and to be trusted. Come in."

He led her into his office and locked the door. Maia had never seen such a room. There wasn't an inch that wasn't covered in something: limb casts, snakeskins, jumbled bones . . . and books everywhere, even on the floor. But it was a friendly clutter, not like the mess in Mr. Carter's room.

"Sit down," he said, and moved a stuffed marmoset from a rickety chair. Then he read the note again. "I don't see why not. If it's just for one night. No, I really don't see why not."

"He said you knew a good hiding place. He said you showed it to him."

Professor Glastonberry smiled. He must have been close to sixty, but he looked like a pleased pink baby.

"Ah, he remembered, did he? Well, come along. If Finn says you're to be trusted, I'm sure he's right."

He took her into the lab and, for the second time, Maia was led to the giant sloth. But this time the professor put his shoulder to the heavy metal stand, which moved slowly to one side. On the wooden floor, grimed with dirt, Maia could just make out a square of darker-colored wood and an iron ring.

"It's a trapdoor," he said. "Goes down to a cellar and storeroom—but it's well ventilated. Got one high window. Best hiding place in Manaus, we used to say. Finn liked to play down there when he was little, while his father helped me."

Maia stood looking at the flight of steps which led into the darkness.

"Would you like to go down?" the professor asked.

"May I?"

"Of course. But you'd better have a light; there's no electricity down there."

He brought her a hurricane lamp and she climbed down. The cellar was huge and vaulted, with a recess at the back full of packing cases. Between the cases were exhibits which the professor had not had room for, or those waiting to be repaired. A beam of light fell on the red eyes of a moth-eaten puma. There were unstrung bows and painted shields, and a harpy eagle sitting on a lopsided nest. In a corner was a heap of round objects which might have been carved coconuts, but might also have been shrunken heads. But the floor was dry, and at the far end of the room, the high window gave a glimmer of light.

"It's marvelous," said Maia, coming up again. "No one could find you unless they knew."

The professor moved the stand back over the trapdoor. "I sometimes store Billy down there when the trustees come on an inspection. They don't approve of stuffed Pekingese in a serious museum."

"There's just one more thing," said Maia as the professor led her out of the lab. "Finn thought that we should—that I should—steal the spare keys, so that no one gets into trouble. Your staff or you if anything goes wrong."

"I doubt if anyone could do much to me," said Professor Glastonberry, "but it's true I wouldn't want my cleaners or my caretaker blamed."

"The trouble is," said Maia, looking up at him, "I haven't actually stolen anything before."

"There is always a first time," said the professor cheerfully. "The spare keys are hanging on that hook over there. And I'm going out in half an hour to have my lunch."

"There she is," said Mr. Trapwood, looking out of the window of the Pension Maria at the slender blue funnels of RMS *Bishop,* the sister ship of the *Cardinal,* which had just come into port. She would spend four days on the turnabout while the crew cleaned the ship, took on supplies, and had some time ashore. Then on Saturday morning she would set off again, to the mouth of the Amazon, across the Atlantic, and back to Britain.

The crows had been so sure of finding Taverner's son that they had booked a three-berth cabin for the return journey.

But they were beginning to give up hope. For it was clear that the wretched boy was deliberately hiding from them. A first people had tried to deny that Taverner had a son at all. Now, though, they were beginning to laugh behind their sleeves, and as the day for the detectives' departure grew closer, there were sly digs about the boy having outwitted them.

But why? The crows were *hurt*. They had come as bearers of good tidings to bring a savage jungle boy the news of his inheritance. They had been prepared to introduce him gradually to polite society—perhaps on the journey to teach him to use a knife and fork. Sir Aubrey had even given them some money to buy him clothes, in case he'd been brought up in a grass skirt.

And they had expected gratitude. It was only natural.

"Thank you, Mr. Low," the boy would have said, grasping them by the hand. And: "Thank you, Mr. Trapwood. You have saved me from a life of toil and darkness."

Instead of that, the boy was deliberately hiding and everyone in Manaus seemed to be helping him.

"We've got three more days," said Mr. Trapwood. "There's still a chance to flush him out."

"To carry him aboard by force if necessary."

"To get the bonus from Sir Aubrey!"

That was the most important thing of all. Sir Aubrey had promised them a hundred pounds each if they brought his grandson safely home.

"I still think there was something fishy about that pigtailed girl at the Carters' place."

Mr. Low agreed. "She had a shifty look. We'll have to keep an eye on her."

The crows were looking very much the worse for wear. Their black suits were dusty and torn; the maid at the Pension Maria had burnt every one of their shirts as she ironed them.

Mr. Trapwood's face was covered in lumps where the bites of the tabernid fly had gone septic, and both their stomachs had become boiling caverns of agony and wind.

"But we can still do it," said Mr. Trapwood, punching the table. "We'll try downriver this time. Those houses by the fishing place. The people there look poor enough; they should take some notice of the reward."

Mr. Low nodded and made his way stealthily toward the door.

"If you're thinking of getting to the lavatory before me, don't try," said Mr. Trapwood. "I'm going first."

"No, you aren't. I *need* it!"

"*You* need it . . . !"

Shoving and jostling, the two detectives raced each other down the corridor.

Professor Glastonberry, making his way up the hill to the café where he usually had his lunch, stopped, as he always did, by the bookshop in the square. It was run by a man who bought in books from all over Brazil, specializing in books about natural history.

In the window was a copy of *Travels in the Amazon,* by Alfred Russel Wallace, open at a beautiful woodcut of an Indian village.

He was admiring it when he realized that the tall, straight-backed woman who was also staring in the window was the lady who had left Maia in the museum.

"A beautiful book," he said, raising his hat.

She sighed. "Yes. Quite above my means, I fear."

"It is not a first edition," he said. "You might get it quite reasonably. I know the owner—perhaps he would put it aside for a while."

"Thank you, but he would have to put it aside for most of my life. My salary is not . . . princely . . . even when it is paid."

Both of them looked for a while longer at the book. Then Miss Minton gave her tight-lipped smile.

"I was dismissed once for reading," she said.

"Really?" The professor waited, but she said no more. "I left Maia working hard," he went on. "The caretaker promised to keep an eye on her."

Did she know what Maia was really doing in the museum? he wondered. Probably not, yet she didn't look like a person easy to hoodwink. As she bent down to pick up the basket with Mrs. Carter's shopping, he said, "Allow me."

She shook her head. "Thank you, but it's not heavy."

They began to walk toward the main street with its cafés and shops.

"I have been thinking about what you said—about the missing bone. Of *Megatherium*. The sloth, I mean."

"You have decided to go and look for it?"

"No, no. But Taverner was also against putting in a false rib. He was a good naturalist and a good man. I miss him."

"Yes. I can imagine that. Was it he who found the skeleton?"

"No. It was found many years ago. It went to a museum in Rio—too important for my little place—but no one had time to assemble it, so they sent it down to me. But Taverner knew the place it came from. Not only that—" He broke off. "His wife came from up there," he went on. "It's practically unexplored country."

"Did you know his wife?"

"Yes. She was beautiful and gentle. She died in childbirth because the English doctor wouldn't come out to an Indian girl at night. As you can imagine, it didn't make Taverner any more anxious to return to England."

They walked on for a while without speaking. Then the professor, blushing a little, for he was very shy, asked Miss Minton if she would care to join him for lunch. "It's only a little local café, but the food is good."

But as he had expected, she refused. "Thank you, I have some sandwiches."

But at the door of the café, Miss Minton was overcome suddenly by the glorious smell of real, strong Brazilian coffee.

"Perhaps a cup of coffee," she said.

It was a nice café, friendly and cheap, and it cost Miss Minton some effort not to allow the professor to buy her a dish of chicken and rice. "I lunch here most days," he said. "Since my wife died."

"Was that a long time ago?"

"Yes. Ten years now. I blame myself; the climate didn't suit her. I should have taken her back to England."

Miss Minton frowned. She did not approve of people blaming themselves for what was done.

"Are the caves difficult to reach? The ones where your sloth came from?" she asked.

"Yes. Difficult but not impossible."

"Did Taverner think there were more remains there? More bones?"

"He thought there might be. But that's neither here nor there. I shall be fifty-eight next year: an old man."

"That is the kind of remark I don't enjoy," said Miss Minton cuttingly, and picked up her coffee cup.

When she came back from the museum, Maia found the twins in an even worse mood than usual.

"What are those supposed to be?" Beatrice sneered, turning over Maia's drawings. "I can't make head or tail of them."

"I know. . . . " Maia sighed. "But birds are really difficult to draw."

"Well, why do you have to go and show off in the museum, then? I suppose you want everyone to say how clever you are."

"And you've got a mosquito bite on your forehead," said Gwendolyn. "It looks like the kind that goes septic."

"You've probably caught lice, too, on that Indian boat. You'd better not come near."

Maia said nothing and went to her room. She had stopped wondering what she had done to annoy them. But to tell the truth, the poor twins had just leaned something which upset them very much, and they had learned it from their mother.

"We don't like Maia, Mummy," the twins had said. "She's a prig."

"The way she goes on practicing the piano when she doesn't have to."

"And she flirts with the boys at the dancing class and shows off the whole time."

"And she's conceited about her hair. The way she brushes it and brushes it."

"And she sneaks off to talk to the servants."

Mrs. Carter sighed. "I know you don't like her," she said.

"We *hate* her," said Beatrice.

"When is she going *away* again?" wailed Gwendolyn.

"Oh, don't!" cried Mrs. Carter, caught off her guard. "Don't ever mention her going away. If Maia goes we are undone!"

The twins stared at her. Their small, round mouths hung open.

Mrs. Carter tried to pull herself together. "No, no, it's not as bad as that. But your father . . . there have been difficulties with the price of rubber . . . and so on. . . . Maia's allowance from her guardian is absolutely necessary to pay the bills."

"You mean she's staying forever and ever?" said Beatrice. "Just because she's rich and we're poor?"

"It isn't fair!"

"Now, please, girls. I'm sure your father will find a way round, and when he does we can send her away. But just for now please try to be nicer to Maia."

The twins shot her a furious look from under their pale eyelashes.

"We'll have to think of something," said Beatrice when they were alone again.

"We certainly will," said Gwendolyn.

"But if we get rid of her we won't be able to have any new clothes."

"Unless we can get hold of the reward for the Taverner boy."

"If we get that we won't need to see Maia ever again," said Beatrice gloatingly. "I still think she knows something. I'm going to watch her night and day."

"I'm going to watch her, too."

When she had first seen Finn's hut and the lagoon, Maia thought it must be the nicest place in the whole world.

Clovis did not think that at all. He liked being inside the hut, especially at mealtimes, but he found the surrounding jungle most alarming. The anteater lumbering down to drink like a gray tank sent Clovis rushing back indoors, and the chattering of the monkeys in the trees kept him awake at night.

Finn made him help with all the chores. Clovis had to keep the hut clean, scrub out the saucepans, and help get the *Arabella* ready for her journey. Clovis liked the hummingbirds; he learned to refill their bottles of sugar water, and he didn't mind painting the boat—he was used to painting scenery—but cleaning the bilges and burying the kitchen waste was not to his taste at all.

But if Clovis wasn't very good at rough work, he was absolutely first class at learning his lines. Every morning and every afternoon he sat down with the old red notebook in which Finn had written down all that his father had told him about Westwood, and when Finn tested him he found Clovis word perfect.

"There isn't very much," Finn had told him at the beginning. "Because my father never talked about Westwood if he could help it. And remember, they won't expect you to know anything—they probably think you've been brought up a savage. All the same, if you're going to stay for a week or two without being found out, it might help you to know a little."

So Clovis sat by the table in the hut, twisting a curl round his finger, and studied the notebook, and every hour or two Finn came and tested him.

"What does the front of the house look like?"

"It was built by Sir John Vanbrugh. There are two wings, an East Wing and a West Wing, and in the middle is a block with six stone columns where the main rooms are."

"What about statues?"

"There's a statue of Hercules strangling a snake in front of the West Wing and a statue of Saint George spearing a dragon in front of the East Wing."

"Now go through the front door. Think of yourself as coming back to where your father grew up. Think of yourself as Bernard Taverner's son," said Finn—and had to turn his face away as he remembered how good it had been really to be his father's son, and how much he missed him.

"You go into a Great Hall which is always cold, with a flagstone floor and a big oak chest into which Dudley shut your father for a whole night when he was three years old—" Clovis broke off. "Dudley is dead, isn't he?"

"Of course he's dead," said Finn impatiently. "That's what all the fuss is about. Go on. Go upstairs."

"There's a Long Gallery with a knight's armor, very tall, which used to shine in the dark. Once Dudley got inside it and made it raise its arm and a housemaid fainted. And there's a picture of a Taverner ancestor who went on the Crusades, with the head of a Turk impaled on his lance."

Clovis sighed. Westwood did not sound cozy.

"What about Joan?" Finn went on. "Remember she's your aunt Joan really. Where was her room?"

"On the next floor, overlooking the stables. The walls were completely covered with rosettes she'd won for riding—red ones and yellow ones and blue ones, and she had a fox's tail with dried blood on it nailed above her bed. Only it isn't called a tail, it's called a brush."

"And what was her nickname?"

"The Basher. Because she bashed people." He looked anxiously at Finn. "But she isn't there now, is she? You promised."

"No, of course not. She's married to a man called Smith and has four daughters."

But he could see that Clovis was looking far from happy, so he flicked over the pages of the notebook to find the few things at Westwood which Bernard had liked.

"What about the bluebell wood?"

"It's on the far side of the lake—not where Joan held his head under the water. On a slope down to the river. There was a pair of woodpeckers nesting there, and a badger burrow."

"And the garden?"

"There was a walled kitchen garden and the gardener was nice. He used to let your father pick strawberries, but he had a stammer and Dudley used to imitate him and—"

"Never mind Dudley," said Finn quickly. "He's dead. What about the other servants?"

"The butler was called Young, but he wasn't young. He was old, with liver spots on his hands, and everyone was scared of him. He got a maid sacked for reading the books in the library—the one who helped your father."

"And the dining room?"

Clovis rattled through every detail of the dining room. It always cheered him up thinking of English food and English meals.

But as often as he felt brave and forward looking, Clovis felt scared and told Finn he couldn't do it.

"I wish Maia would come," he kept saying, which annoyed Finn. Finn wished it, too. Till Maia came they would not know what had happened in the museum and whether their plan would work.

But when she did come, the next day, Finn saw by her face that all was well.

To get away from the Carters, Maia had needed to work hard at her pulmonary spasms. She had had a spasm at breakfast, wheezing and twitching, and another one in the drawing room when she was doing her embroidery. They were good spasms, she thought, but it wasn't till the third one, just before tea, that Mrs. Carter said icily that if her lungs were giving her so much trouble she had better go out.

Since it was raining—the heavy, dark rain that fell so often in the afternoons—she thought Maia might refuse, but she was out of the house in minutes.

And Furo, thank heaven, was in his hut and ready to take her to Finn.

This time the dog greeted her as a friend, placing his cold nose in her hand, and the happiness she always felt when she came to this place rose up in her.

"It's all settled," she said. "The professor was wonderful—he showed me everything. And I stole the keys," she added proudly. "At least I think I did, though he did tell me where they were, so that may not be proper stealing."

She handed them to Finn, hoping for praise, but he had obviously expected her to do what he had asked.

"Good. The trapdoor may be difficult to lift; we'd better take some oil. It's still under the sloth, is it?"

"Yes. And the professor is still worried about the missing rib. How's Clovis?"

"He's washing his hair. He's always washing it," said Finn gloomily. "I thought you might cut it for him."

"I've never cut anyone's hair before."

"There's always a first time."

Clovis came out of the hut then, with a towel round his head and very pleased to see Maia.

"She's done it," said Finn. "The hiding place is set up, she's got the keys. The boat goes at dawn on Saturday, so on Friday we'll get you settled there. We'll need blankets, a lamp, some food. I'm going to let everyone think it's me hiding there, even the Indians; that will make it safer. I'll tell them that the crows have heard about the lagoon."

But Clovis was looking definitely green. "How long do I have to be in the cellar?" he asked fearfully.

"Not even a whole night. The crows are due back on Friday afternoon; they'll come looking for you almost straightaway. You'll see it will work."

"Clovis, it's the best thing, honestly," said Maia. "The Goodleys have been turned back at the border. They've been locked up until they can sell their assets and clear their debts. They think you're staying with me, so they won't bother about you anymore."

"I suppose I could stay here," said Clovis doubtfully, looking round the hut.

"No, you couldn't," said Finn. "I won't be here, I told you. I'm setting off in the *Arabella*." He turned to Maia. "Come and see her," he said. "We've done quite a bit to her."

Maia followed him onto the launch. The rain had stopped. Finn had painted the floorboards and mended the awning. "She's almost ready," he said.

"Are you sure you can sail her alone? With having to get wood and everything?"

"Yes. I couldn't take you anyway," he said, reading her like a book. "I don't even know exactly where I'm going and you're a—"

"Don't say it," said Maia angrily. "Don't you dare say I'm a girl."

Finn shrugged. "All right, I won't. But it could be dangerous and I won't involve other people." He looked back at the hut, where Clovis was toweling his hair. "He's absolutely hopeless at the chores, but he's amazing at memorizing things. I reckon he knows everything about Westwood already. We did Sir Aubrey this morning—his eyes, his whiskers. An actor's training is not to be sneezed at." Then: "How long have you got?"

"Long enough to help you polish the funnel," said Maia, and took a cloth.

11

BY THE TIME Clovis had been in Finn's hut for three days, he knew Westwood by heart. He could go upstairs and downstairs, into the attics where the maid Bella had hidden Bernard's secret pile of money, and into the cellar where he had made friends with the bats. He knew the outhouse where Bernard had kept a pet rat and the tree to which Dudley and Joan had tied a little girl from the village and beaten her with willow twigs because she had been trespassing by the lake.

And he could imitate any accent.

"After he's been there a week, he'll be talking like Sir Aubrey or braying like Joan," Finn said to Maia.

The Goodleys had taught Clovis to fence, and he had been in so many plays set in grand houses that his table manners were excellent. If he got to Westwood, Finn was sure he could hold out for a little while. Finn had shown him a map of the north of England, and Clovis had discovered that the village where his foster mother lived was only thirty miles away, which had cheered him up a lot.

"But he's such a coward," Finn said to Maia. They were scraping the old paint off *Arabella*'s deck fittings, a job which Clovis did not care for.

"I don't think it's cowardly to be afraid of hiding in a dark cellar and waiting to be snatched by two horrible crows," said Maia.

Finn frowned. "You're always defending him," he said crossly.

"Well, he's alone in the world."

"So am I alone in the world," said Finn.

"No, you aren't. You've got Lila, who adores you, and Professor Glastonberry and the chief of police and all the Indians here. And when you get to the Xanti you'll probably have lots and lots of relatives. Aunts and uncles and cousins—and maybe grandparents, too. A huge family . . ."

"Do you think so? I hadn't thought of it like that." Finn did not look particularly pleased.

Maia nodded. "It's sure to be like that. Whereas Clovis and I don't have anybody."

"You've got Miss Minton."

It was Maia's turn to stare. Three months ago she hadn't known that Miss Minton existed. When she'd first seen her, she thought she was a terrifying witch. But now . . .

There was a pause. Then:

"And you've got me," said Finn.

Maia lifted her head and smiled at him. For a moment she felt completely happy. Then she looked at Finn's hand resting on the tiller.

"But you're going away."

"Yes," he said. "That's true. I'm going away."

• • •

Later that night, when Maia was back in the bungalow, and Finn was frying some eggs Furo had brought for their supper, Clovis said, "There's something I want to ask you about. When I was looking for Maia the first time, I asked for a place called Tapherini, or the House of Rest. Maia told me that that was what it was called and that Mrs. Carter had it on her notepaper. But no one had heard of it and they looked . . . sort of funny. And then the captain of the boat wouldn't put me down on the Carters' landing stage. He said it was a bad place. What did he mean?"

Finn sat back on his heels. He seemed to be wondering whether to speak or not. Then he said, "I'll tell you, but you must promise to say nothing to Maia." And he told Clovis what had happened when the Carters first came to the Amazon.

"They found an Indian longhouse by the river and some thatched huts back in the forest. The land and the houses belonged to the Tapuri, which is the tribe to which Furo and Tapi belong, but many of the Indians had left to find work in the town, and the elders of the tribe agreed to sell the land and the houses on it to the Carters.

"The price was agreed before witnesses. A proper ceremony took place and Mr. Carter signed the document to which the old chief put his mark. The Tapuri asked that the House of Rest, which was what the longhouse had been called, should be left standing, because a very wise medicine man had died there and his spirit still lived in the house and did not want to be disturbed.

"Mr. Carter agreed to everything. Good land by the river was hard to find since so many Europeans had come to Manaus to make their fortune, and the rubber trees in the surrounding forest were plentiful.

"The money was to be paid to the Indians in three lots. Mr. Carter paid the first lot promptly, in gold coins fetched from the bank, and the chief of the Tapuri thanked him and took his people to build themselves homes further up the river.

"A month later the chief's messenger came for the second lot of money and was sent away. Mr. Carter, he was told, was waiting for more gold to come from the bank in England on a special ship.

"The messenger went back into the forest and came again a month later. He was told that the ship with the gold on it had sunk in a storm."

And so it went on. The Indians began by being polite and ended up shaking their fists at the Carters. Those Europeans who knew what was happening went to the chief of police, who tried to force Carter to pay what he owed—but Carter always found an excuse not to do it. Not only that, but he broke his word to the Indians and pulled down not only the surrounding huts in the forest but the longhouse itself, and on the site he built his bungalow.

Mrs. Carter had Tapherini, or House of Rest, put on her writing paper—she thought it sounded good—but no one in Manaus ever called it that, nor would the Indian traders land on the Carters' landing stage but always, like the captain who had brought Clovis, stopped higher up. And the many decent Europeans who knew what had happened tried to have as little to do with the Carters as possible.

After this not many Indians would come to work for the family. Those who did, Furo and Tapi and old Lila, stayed for personal reasons—Lila because she wanted to be near Finn and his father; Furo because he was her nephew; Conchita and her husband, Manoel, because she had a crippled brother to support in Manaus; and Tapi's young sister, Unini, because she had lost her parents and looked on the Carters' servants as her family. When they worked in the house, they were unforgiving and sullen, and secretly they believed that one day the old medicine man's spirit, which had been disturbed and shamed, would rise up against the Carters, and the family would get what they deserved.

Clovis had been listening to Finn with a very worried face.

"But that's a sort of curse. Maia shouldn't live in a house that's been cursed."

"I know. But nobody has cursed Maia—nobody in the world would do that. And Furo and the others have promised to look after her. They absolutely promised."

"And you're not going to tell Maia?"

"No. Definitely not. She's got enough to put up with with those awful twins."

Mrs. Carter had at last arranged Maia's piano lessons with Netta's father, Mr. Haltmann. Maia went to his house before the dancing class while the twins were shopping with their mother, so she could enjoy it and not have to pretend that learning the piano was boring. If there was one thing the twins really hated, it was if Maia seemed to enjoy anything.

Mr. Haltmann came from Vienna and he was a first-class musician. He not only taught Maia the piano, he understood her need to learn the songs she heard everywhere: in the streets of Manaus, on the riverboats, in the huts of the workers.

"It is a rich land for music, Brazil. Everything flows into everything else. In one song you can hear the rhythm of the

Africans, the poetry of the Portuguese, and the sadness of the Indians."

He promised to look at the songs she had written down, and he suggested, too, that she have singing lessons and train her voice—but this she wouldn't do.

"My mother was a singer—she was wonderful, and I don't want to try and copy her," she said.

The other good thing which came out of her time with the Haltmanns was Netta's friendship. The Austrian girl welcomed her wholeheartedly; she had a litter of kittens in a basket, a basset hound with soulful eyes, and a baby brother as fat as butter. Netta walked with her afterward to the dancing class, and if Maia forgot to put on a gloomy face when she saw the twins sitting with their legs stuck out in the locker room, waiting to have their shoes put on, she was in trouble.

"What are you smirking about?" asked Beatrice now. "I suppose you're waiting for Sergei to ask you to dance."

The twins' plans for getting rid of Maia were not going well. They had been to her room and picked over her things, but Miss Minton had heard them, and since they themselves never went out of doors, it was difficult to spy on Maia properly. The notice of the reward for the capture of Taverner's son was still posted, but time was running out. Mr. Low and Mr. Trapwood were supposed to be leaving on the *Bishop* in three days' time.

But the twins had managed one trick. When they had arrived at their lockers, they had found invitations to a party at the Keminskys' on Friday night. It was Olga's birthday, and the Russians were going to celebrate in the grand manner.

Now they read them, holding them up in front of Maia and giggling.

"There doesn't seem to be one for you," said Beatrice.

Maia went to her locker, but there was nothing there. She tried desperately not to mind and failed. She had thought that Olga was as much her friend as Sergei. Not only did it hurt to be left out, but Friday was the night Clovis was to hide in the museum. For her to be in Manaus then would have been perfect if she was to betray Clovis to the twins.

And it would be a wonderful evening. The Keminskys were one of the richest families in Manaus. Sergei's father, Count Keminsky, owned huge plantations of rubber trees; he treated his workers well and the money flowed in—not only from rubber but from hardwoods and coffee and sugarcane. Maia had passed their house, a big mansion with pink walls and blue shutters and a garden full of flowering trees. There couldn't be anywhere better for a party.

All through the dancing class she waited and hoped, but no invitation came her way. Well, she wouldn't beg for one, and when Sergei came to ask her for the final polka, she refused and went early to the changing room.

Back in the Carters' bungalow Maia hid her feelings—at least she did from the twins and their parents. With Miss Minton she was not so lucky.

"Might one ask what's the matter with you?" asked the governess when they were alone. "And please don't say 'Nothing.' I hate wasting time."

So Maia told her. If she had expected sympathy she was very disappointed. "Really, Maia, you make me tired. Why don't you use your intelligence instead of your emotions? What do you really think happened to your invitation?"

"Oh, but they wouldn't—surely . . ."

Miss Minton snorted. "It's time you grew up and defended yourself. I'm not going to sort this one out for you. You do it yourself."

But before Maia could steel herself to confront the twins, Furo brought a message for her from the Keminskys' house. It was from Sergei, asking her to bring her Chopin mazurkas when she came to the party because Olga wanted to learn one to surprise her father.

"I think I won't say anything to the twins till we're getting ready to go," said Maia. "Then I'll surprise them."

Miss Minton nodded. "The dark blue taffeta?"

And Maia said, "Yes."

Finn's dog was called Rob, but no one used his name much. He was somehow all dogs rolled into one, with his trust and intelligence and faithfulness; and though he could hunt his own food and steady the canoe by putting his weight in the right place, he understood that when humans were upset one had to sit there while they pulled one's ears, or buried their faces in one's back, or even cried. A dog who will allow himself to be cried over is worth his weight in gold.

He had been Bernard Taverner's dog and now was Finn's, and other people did not interest him very much. But he was always very polite to Maia, and as she rubbed his back and said, "I don't know how I'm going to get the twins to do what I want," he caught the worry in her voice and did not move away, though he had heard some interesting noises in the bushes behind the hut.

"It's quite easy," said Clovis—and Maia looked up, surprised, for Clovis was not usually a boy who found things easy. "It's just acting."

"Yes, but I can't act."

"Anyone can act," said Clovis. "There are just a few tricks. Techniques they're called, but they're just tricks really."

They had just finished afternoon tea in the hut, which was Clovis's favorite meal, but when it was cleared he said, "Look. Watch me."

He went to the window of the hut and looked out, seeming to be interested in what he saw. Then he came back and sat down. After a while he got up and did the same thing. The third time Maia got up and followed him to the window.

"You see," said Clovis. "If you go to the window twice, the third time people will always follow you. It's the same when you're pretending to give someone the slip, but really you want them to come after you. Don't pause and look round furtively—just keep changing your pace. Sometimes dawdle, sometimes run . . ."

So while Finn checked the list of things that Clovis would need for his night in the museum, Clovis coached Maia in how to act the part of someone with a guilty secret. "Because they mustn't think I want to betray Finn," she said. "They know I wouldn't do that. They must think I've done it by mistake."

Just before Furo came to fetch Maia, Finn called her aside and took something out of the pocket of his trousers.

"Look," he said, and held out to her a beautiful silver pocket watch on a long chain. He clicked it open and showed her the initials *BT* engraved inside.

"Your father's?"

"Yes. He gave it to me on my last birthday. It was the only thing he brought from Westwood. I feel I ought to give it to Clovis. It would make them absolutely certain he was me."

"But your father wanted you to have it."

"Yes," said Finn, looking stricken. "But if it would help . . ." He shook his head. "Never mind, it's for me to decide."

Then Furo's canoe came through the reeds and Maia hugged Clovis and said good-bye. If everything went according to plan, he would be on the boat the day after tomorrow, and it was hard leaving him.

"But I expect you'll come to England, won't you?" Clovis said. He had given her the address of his foster mother. "I wish you were coming *now*," he said, and his eyes filled with tears.

As Finn helped Maia into the boat, he leaned forward and whispered in her ear. "Don't worry about Clovis," he said. "I'll see he's all right. I won't let him get too scared, I promise."

And Maia nodded and got into the canoe and was paddled away.

"That settles it," said Mr. Trapwood. "We're going back to the pension. We're going to pack. We're going to be on the *Bishop* first thing tomorrow. Sir Aubrey will have to send someone else out. Nothing is worth another day in this hellhole."

Mr. Low did not answer. He had caught a fever and was lying in the bottom of a large canoe owned by the Brothers of the São Gabriel Mission, who had arranged for the crows to be taken back to Manaus. His eyes were closed and he was wandering a little in his mind, mumbling about a boy with hair the color of the belly of the golden toad which squatted on the lily leaves of the Mamari River.

There had, of course, been no golden-haired boys; there hadn't been any boys at all. What there had been was a leper colony, run by the Brothers of Saint Patrick, a group of Irish missionaries to whom the crows had been sent.

"They're good men, the Brothers," a man on the docks had told them as they set off on their last search for Taverner's son. "They take in all sorts of strays—orphans, boys with no homes. If anyone knows where Taverner's lad might be, it'll be them."

Then he had spat cheerfully into the river because he was a crony of the chief of police and liked the idea of Mr. Low and Mr. Trapwood spending time with the Brothers, who were very holy men indeed and slept on the hard ground, and ate porridge made from manioc roots, and got up four times in the night to pray.

The Brothers' mission was on a swampy part of the river and very unhealthy, but the Brothers thought only about God and helping their fellowmen. They welcomed Mr. Trapwood and Mr. Low and said they could look over the leper colony to see if they could find anyone who might turn out to be the boy they were looking for.

"They're a jolly lot, the lepers," said Father Liam. "People who've suffered don't have time to grumble."

But the crows, turning green, thought there wouldn't be much point. Even if there was a boy there the right age, Sir Aubrey probably wouldn't think that a boy who was a leper could manage Westwood.

Later a group of pilgrims arrived who had been walking on foot from the Andes and were on their way to a shrine on the Madeira River, and the Brothers knelt and washed their feet.

"We know you'll be proud to share the sleeping hut with our friends here," they said to Mr. Low and Mr. Trapwood, and the crows spent the night on the floor with twelve snoring, grunting men—and woke to find two large and hungry-looking vultures squatting in the doorway.

By the time they returned to Manaus the crows were beaten men. They didn't care any longer about Taverner's son or Sir Aubrey, or even the hundred-pound bonus they had lost. All they cared about was getting onto the *Bishop* and steaming away as fast as it could be done.

12

"**S**TAY!" **SAID FINN** to his dog. "Stay and guard the hut."

The dog looked at him with despairing eyes and howled briefly.

"You heard me," said Finn. "Stay!"

Another howl; then the dog turned and threw himself down in front of the hut.

"Will he really stay?" asked Clovis.

"Of course. I won't be long." Finn was going to settle Clovis into his hiding place in the museum and then slip back to the lagoon.

It was already almost dark, but Finn knew the waterways that led to Manaus like the back of his hand. He was going to take Clovis in the canoe by the same route as he had taken Maia. There was plenty of time; Olga's party did not start for another couple of hours—and it was not till the party was in full swing that Maia was going to start working on the twins.

Finn had darkened his hair again; he wore his headband and a circlet of beads round his arm. Clovis was dressed in the cap and uniform of the cadets of St. Joseph's School in

Manaus. Finn's father had tried to send him there, but after the first week Finn had come home and told Bernard that if he wanted Finn to go back, he would have to handcuff him and drag him there by the hair.

If anyone caught a glimpse of them in the backstreets of Manaus as they made their way to the museum, they would think it was a boy from the college being taken back to school by his Indian servant.

"Right. I think we've got everything: the keys, a lamp, your satchel, the money so you can get to your foster mother. No, wait. There's something else." Finn felt in his pocket. "Here, I want you to have this." And he handed him Bernard Taverner's watch on its silver chain.

Clovis stared, turned it over. "I can't take this. It's your father's, isn't it?"

"Yes. But if you're going to be me, you'd better have it," said Finn, and turned away quickly, for it was far harder than he had expected, giving away the watch he had seen so often in his father's hands.

They pushed the canoe off and Finn began to paddle out of the lagoon. The dog howled again, but he did not move, and then they were through the rushes and on their way.

It was a silent journey. If they had to speak they did it in whispers. Finn stopped where he had dropped Maia the first time they met and tied the canoe up to a tree. He would make his way back as soon as Clovis was safe in the hiding place.

They waited for half an hour, till it was entirely dark. There was no moon, and no street lighting, in the small lanes along which Finn led Clovis.

As they came to the back door of the museum, they heard the sound of dance music coming from the Keminskys' house.

The party had begun.

Maia had said nothing to the twins about the party till it was time to get dressed. Then she disappeared into her room and came out in the last dress the matron of the school in London had bought with her before she went away: a dark blue rustling taffeta with a very full skirt and a row of tiny pearl buttons on the bodice. Miss Minton had brushed out her waist-length hair and left it loose—and for a moment she almost forgot the job that faced her in the Keminskys' house.

Then she and Miss Minton knocked on the twins' door.

"I'm ready," Maia said.

The twins stared at her.

"But you're not going."

"Oh yes I am. Sergei wrote to me. Miss Minton's going, too—to keep Mademoiselle Lille company and help out. He said his father would send a boat for us if we couldn't go with you."

The twins glared and tried a different tack.

"You're too skinny to wear a low neckline."

"And your hair will get in a mess."

"Shall I braid it again?" Maia asked Miss Minton, and her governess pursed up her mouth and said, "No."

The twins were dressed in their favorite party pink; rather a *fleshy* pink, which was perhaps a pity because their short necks coming out of a double row of ruffles made them look a little like those hams one sees on butchers' slabs near Christmas. They wore several bracelets, so that they tinkled as they walked, and they had had an accident with their mother's scent. Beatrice had taken some and sprinkled it behind her ears and then Gwendolyn had tried to take it from her and the stopper had come off, so that both of them smelled violently of "Passion in the Night."

Mrs. Carter did not mean to stay behind in the bungalow. She had invited herself to play bridge in the club in Manaus. Mr. Carter came out to say good-bye, holding a small box containing the eye of a murderer who had been hanged in Pentonville Prison. It had arrived that morning and excited him very much.

"Very nice," he said absently, looking at Maia's dress, and was glared at by his wife. "The twins, too . . . very fetching"— and he hurried back into his study.

It was nine o'clock before the Carters' cab drew up at the Keminskys' house. There were Chinese lanterns strung between the trees; the air smelled of orange blossom; music streamed from the windows.

Maia had never been in such a sumptuous house. The walls were hung with rich tapestries and paintings of Russian saints framed in gold. Tubs of white lilies and crimson poinsettias were massed on the sides of the staircase; hundreds of wax candles glittered in the crystal chandeliers.

Sergei and Olga now came running out to greet them.

"You look like a beautiful wave with your dress and your hair," said Olga, touching the blue taffeta, and Sergei said she must hurry because they were going to play a polonaise next. "And we're good at polonaises, aren't we?"

Then the count and countess came out of the drawing room to greet them. The count looked like a picture from a book about the Russian steppes, with a high-necked embroidered blouse, wise, dark eyes, and a black beard. The countess was a beautiful, untidy woman who wore a priceless emerald pendant slightly askew over her dress and enfolded Maia in a warm embrace.

"The children have told me so much about you," she said, and held out her arms to the twins, who backed away. The twins did not get hugged. They always made that clear from the start.

Mademoiselle Lille came to lead Miss Minton away, and soon the party was in full swing.

Afterward Maia thought what a wonderful evening it would have been if she had been just an ordinary guest with nothing to do except enjoy herself. The Keminskys were the most amazing hosts—rosewater was served to the dancers in crystal goblets; in the dining room the food laid out on a white damask cloth was like food in a fairy tale—Russian piroshkis, rare Brazilian fruits, a three-tiered cake for Olga's birthday— and the count had found proper Gypsies to play for them.

But Maia was working to a timetable. Clovis would be safe in the museum by ten o'clock. The crows were already back in the Pension Maria. Between ten and dawn the following morning, when the *Bishop* pulled up her anchors, she had to betray Clovis's hiding place to the twins.

And she had to make sure that they would act.

If only everyone hadn't been so nice to her, whisking her off to dance, to drink lemonade, or go into the garden. Not just Sergei and Olga and Netta; everyone.

But at least it wasn't difficult to keep track of the twins. If she couldn't see them in their flesh-pink dresses or hear the tinkle of their bracelets, she could smell them, for they still moved in a cloud of their mother's "Passion of the Night."

Ten o'clock struck on the big grandfather clock in the hall. Time to begin.

Maia excused herself from the next dance and went to the big window which looked out toward the docks.

The twins, who were not dancing, watched her.

Maia came back, circled the floor once with a Brazilian boy, then stopped and went back to the window.

The twins were still watching her. Oh please, let Clovis be right, she prayed.

For the third time she turned to go to the window, and yes, Clovis was right. The twins followed her.

"What are you looking at?"

Maia swung round, startled. "Nothing . . . I mean . . . I just wondered when the *Bishop* is sailing. It is tomorrow morning? They haven't put it off?"

"Yes, it is. Why do you want to know?"

"I don't really . . . I just wondered. Mr. Low and Mr. Trapwood are going to be on her, aren't they? They're definitely going back to England?"

The twins exchanged glances.

"What does it matter to you?"

"It doesn't." Maia was beginning to look very flustered and guilty. "It doesn't at all."

She made her way slowly to the door and left the room, allowing herself only one anxious glance at the twins. Don't keep turning round, Clovis had said; don't overdo it.

Beatrice and Gwendolyn were now definitely suspicious. "Do you think she knows where the Taverner boy is after all?"

"If she doesn't, why is she so jumpy?"

"There's still time for the reward."

"I'm not going to let her out of my sight," said Beatrice.

"And I'm not either," said Gwendolyn.

Maia had paused on the landing. The Keminskys had placed an icon there, a holy picture with a lamp burning underneath.

The picture was of Saint Theodosius, a very thin saint with huge black eyes. Maia had never prayed to a Russian saint before, but as she heard the twins coming, she fell to her knees.

"Please," she gabbled aloud. "Please keep him safe. Please don't let the crows find his hiding place before they sail. *Please*."

The twins had stopped on the stairs to listen. Now, as Maia got to her feet, they followed her downstairs and into an empty cloakroom where the children had left their outdoor things when they arrived.

Careful not to look back, Maia went to her bag. As well as her hairbrush and her shoes, she had hidden a packet of nuts and a sandwich wrapped in greaseproof paper. She took them out.

"Who are they for?"

Beatrice had come up behind her. Now she wrenched her arm back and Maia dropped the nuts.

"You'd better tell us."

"No one . . . For me." Maia was getting more and more flustered.

"Don't be silly. The house is full of food. You were going to give them to someone, weren't you? The boy you're hiding."

"No. *No*. Oh please . . ."

Beatrice had taken Maia's arm and was twisting it.

"You're hurting me. Stop it."

There wasn't any need to act now. Beatrice was really hurting her. And now Gwendolyn took her other arm and jerked it back.

"Let me go!"

"Not till you tell us where he is. Not till you admit you know."

Real tears came to Maia's eyes as the twins, one on either side, yanked her arms still farther back.

"It's only . . . oh please . . . You don't want him to be caught—he doesn't want to go back to England. He's only a boy and he's so afraid."

The twins gave grunts of satisfaction. They had caught her out!

Two more savage yanks, then Gwendolyn took hold of a handful of Maia's hair and twisted it away from her scalp.

"Quick, where is he? If you don't tell us we'll really hurt you."

"And scratch your face, so that your precious Sergei won't want to look at you again."

Maia gulped, sniffed. It wasn't difficult. The twins, when in an evil mood, were surprisingly strong.

"If I tell you will you let me go?"

"Yes. Unless you lie to us."

"He's in the museum . . . in the Natural History Museum, but please, please don't give him away! He's not a criminal and—"

"Whereabouts in the museum?"

The door was thrown open and Sergei stood there. "What are you doing? How dare you! Let her go!"

The twins dropped Maia's arms. Then they ran out past Sergei, leaving him alone with Maia.

"They're fiends, those girls!" he said, putting an arm round Maia. "What was it about?"

"I can't tell you, Sergei, but it's all right, trust me. It really is all right."

"I'll kill them," muttered Sergei through clenched teeth. "I'll really kill them."

But when he went to look for the twins, they were nowhere to be seen.

13

THE TWINS, IN their flesh-pink party frocks and satin shoes, had run out into the street. They panted across the square, turned down a side road, and as they ran they quarreled.

"We can't go and see those men without Mummy," said Gwendolyn.

"Yes we can. I know where the Pension Maria is. It's quite near."

"But it's down by the docks. There are awful men there. I'm not going without Mummy," said Gwendolyn obstinately.

"All right, then, we'll get her. But don't blame me if she tries to get half the reward."

"She won't. We wouldn't let her. It's for us and no one else."

A man came out of his house and stood by his garden gate.

"You see, he wants us for the White Slave Traffic," said Gwendolyn, and tried to run faster.

The man, who had come out to walk his dog, crossed the road, but the twins did not stop till they reached the club where their mother was playing bridge.

. . .

"Right, that's it," said Mr. Trapwood. He shut the lid of his suit-case. "In another couple of hours we can go on board."

He looked longingly at the lighted ship, ready for her start at dawn. She looked so clean, so nice, so British. . . .

Mr. Low came to stand beside him. "Decent bunks, decent food, people speaking English. You can't believe it."

But in spite of the relief of being on the way home, the crows were broken men. Mr. Low was still feverish, Mr. Trapwood's insect bites had spread in an infected mass over his face and neck, and neither of them could keep down their food.

It wasn't being ill, though, that worried them the most. It was failure. They would go back with an empty berth in their cabin and a sad story to tell Sir Aubrey.

"He'll probably hire some other detectives and send them out. He won't give up so easily," said Mr. Low, moving back to the bed.

"It's The Blood," said Mr. Trapwood gloomily. "The aristos are like that when it's The Blood they're dealing with."

Minutes later, the pension bell pealed loudly down below. Then the maid came up and knocked on the door.

"There's three ladies to see you," she said.

And before the crows could ask any more, the door was thrown open and Beatrice and Gwendolyn, followed by their mother, came excitedly into the room.

"We know where he is! We know where the Taverner boy is hiding!"

"We know for sure!"

The crows, who had been lying weakly on the bed, sat up. Their eyes glinted. They were changed men.

"Where? Where?"

Beatrice said, "If we tell you, are we sure to get the reward? As soon as you've found him?"

"Of course."

"All of it?"

"Yes, yes . . ."

"He's here in the museum. The Natural History Museum, just down the road."

Mr. Low was hitching up his suspenders, fetching a coil of rope. Mr. Trapwood was strapping his pistol underneath his jacket. They were not surprised; they had suspected Glastonberry all along.

"We want to see you catch him."

"No!" Mrs. Carter spoke sharply to her girls. "There may be a struggle. Or violence."

"That's true enough." The crows were buttoning up their jackets. "You just go back home; we'll see you get the money."

"The address is Carter, Tapherini, Rio Negro. I'll write it down for you," said Mrs. Carter.

"But send it to Miss Beatrice and Miss Gwendolyn," said Beatrice. "Send it to us."

"It'll go to the police station; you can fetch it from there," said Mr. Trapwood, patting the bulge inside his jacket. "How do you know he's in the museum?"

"Maia told us. We made her. We twisted her arm till she did. We knew she had a secret."

The crows nodded. The dark girl with the pigtail. There'd been something fishy about her from the start.

"Now ladies, if you just go home, everything will be taken care of, and I assure you that your reward is safe."

• • •

The museum, of course, was locked, but it was not difficult to find Professor Glastonberry's house. It was a modest bungalow in a quiet street lined with palm trees. The crows rang the bell, then thumped on the door, then rang again.

After a long time the door was opened, and an old woman peered through a crack.

"We want Professor Glastonberry. At once. Fetch him."

"*Nada*," she said. "Nothing. No here."

"Yes, he is. You're lying."

The crows pushed her aside. The professor's house had a small study, a sitting room, and a bedroom with an empty bed.

"Where is he? Tell us at once!" They shook her roughly by the arm. "Where?"

"Is in Obidos. Fetch *bichos* for museum."

"Well, find his keys, then."

"No keys."

"Don't lie to us."

The crows were losing their tempers.

"No lies," she said. "Professor has keys on himself."

"We're wasting our time," said Trapwood. "Come on; we'll go to the police. They'll force open the door."

At the police station there was only the glimmer of a light in one window. The crows thumped on the door, shouted, banged on the glass. At last a very young man, his uniform unbuttoned, came out yawning.

"You must open up the museum at once," shouted Mr. Trapwood. "The Taverner boy is hiding there."

"Eh?"

"The museum. You must open it quickly," squeaked Mr. Low.

The policeman shook his head. "Colonel da Silva no here."

He yawned again and tried to go back into his office, but the crows pushed him aside.

"Show us where your tools are. For entering a building."

"What is tools?" asked the befuddled young man.

But the crows were already rampaging through the building, opening doors, peering in cupboards . . .

"Here—these'll do. A chisel, a crowbar . . . and this metal rod. We can use it as a battering ram."

"Right."

Ignoring the young policeman, who was shouting and waving his arms, the crows ran out into the street.

The outer door of the Museum of Natural History was massive, but the crows were no longer the ill and feeble men they had been an hour ago. They were men of steel now that they were so close to success.

They chiseled and they prized, they cursed and they sweated, and presently the hinges broke and they were through.

"Find the lights," ordered Trapwood.

Mr. Low bumped into an anaconda, stumbled over a case of coatis, and found the switch.

The whole world of the rain forest appeared before them: coiled snakes, crouching monkeys, huge caimans with bared teeth. It all looked very different at night.

"He might be anywhere."

They began to search.

"Come out, Taverner, we know you're there!"

"Your time's up, boy. We won't hurt you."

"You'll be all right with us."

They went on shouting and searching—behind a case of capybaras, under a bench holding an aquarium of piranha fish, on the top of a cupboard of pelts . . .

Nothing.

They went into the second room, and the third. Then up the stairs to grope among the throwing spears and necklaces of teeth . . .

Still nothing.

Downstairs again, into the professor's office and his lab. Nothing except an eerie skeleton on a metal stand.

"Get the girl. The pigtailed girl. We'll force her to tell us."

"All right."

Mr. Low made for the door.

The yellow eyes of a snarling jaguar stared at Mr. Trapwood. He didn't much like the idea of being in the museum alone.

"No, wait. I'll come with you. We may have to bring her by force."

Miss Minton was behaving oddly. She had taken no steps to follow the twins and had prevented Sergei from doing so. Instead she was watching Maia, who was pretending to enjoy the party and not making a good job of it. Maia's color was high, she was obviously upset, but Miss Minton did not go to her; she just watched.

She had been watching now for several days.

The children were not dancing any longer. They were falling on the food. Maia did her best to eat—she had never seen such exotic dishes—but she could hardly swallow anything. What was happening in the museum? Sergei had interrupted the twins before she could tell them about the trapdoor under the sloth. Poor Sergei, who had only wanted to help and protect her, and who now looked at her, angry and bewildered, not enjoying his own party as he should.

What was happening? Had they found Clovis yet?

In the entrance hall there was a disturbance. One of the maids was arguing with two grim-faced, black-clad men, who now pushed her aside.

"We want the pigtailed girl who lives with the Carters."

"Maia, she's called."

They opened the doors to various rooms while the servants tried to stop them. Then the door of the dining room.

The only pigtailed girl was a very small blonde sitting on the lap of her governess so that she could reach the table. Maia sat bent over her plate. She had arranged her loose hair so as to partly hide her face, but it didn't help her. The crows knew her at once. "That's her—over there. You, girl, you're to come with us."

"No."

Maia had risen and was holding on to the side of the table.

"If you don't, we'll have to use force."

Sergei got to his feet, prepared to do battle. Then a bony hand descended on Maia's shoulder.

"I think you had better go with these gentlemen and tell them what they want to know," said Miss Minton. She turned to the crows. "I shall, of course, accompany her."

"No, Minty, please! I can manage by myself!"

"You must let me be the best judge of that. Come along, Maia."

By the time they got to the museum, Maia did not have to act her panic. There was no chance to explain anything to her governess; if Miss Minton told the crows that Clovis was not Finn Taverner, all her work would be undone. If only there was a moment to explain before the trapdoor was opened.

But there wasn't.

"Right. Now. Where's the boy?"

Maia was acting again. "Don't make me tell you, please. He's my friend. And he begged me not to let you take him back."

Miss Minton said nothing. She looked grimmer than Maia had ever seen her. There was no help to be expected there.

"Look, we've got no time to waste. And we've got a gun." Mr. Trapwood patted his chest.

"Shoot me, then," said Maia. "You can shoot me before I'll betray—"

"That's enough, Maia. You're being hysterical. Tell these gentlemen what they want to know and then we shall go home."

"I don't want Finn to—"

"Finn. Is that his name?" said Trapwood. "Yes, that sounds right. The letter was signed 'F. Taverner.' Come on, then."

"He's in the cellar," Maia's voice was very quiet. She turned her head away.

"Where's that? How do you get down there?"

"There's a trapdoor. It's under the giant sloth. The skeleton. In the lab."

The crows barged ahead, holding Maia by the arm, and Miss Minton followed. Still no chance to warn her governess.

They reached the sloth. "There, look. You can see the handle," said Mr. Low.

Mr. Trapwood pushed him aside and caught the edge of the stand with his arm.

The sloth crashed to the ground.

Miss Minton and Maia cried out, seeing the jumbled bones.

"There it is! Come on. Heave!"

Mr. Trapwood heaved. The door creaked slowly upward. . . . And out of the dark hole there sprang, not a cowering, frightened boy, but a furious, thrashing figure. A boy with black hair and a headband who charged at the two men, shouting and jabbering in an Indian dialect. The crows tried to grab his arm—and missed. The Indian boy ran past Mr. Low, but was tripped up by Mr. Trapwood and stumbled, cursing in his strange babble, screaming like a trapped animal.

Maia gave a moan of despair and stood there, her hand over her mouth. What was Finn doing here? What had gone so terribly wrong? And where was Clovis?

The crows wrestled with Finn. Two to one; a gun against bare fists. But as they fought the boy, trying to pinion him, they were aghast.

So this was the heir to Westwood—a savage, babbling away in an unearthly tongue! No wonder he had been afraid to take up his rightful place in England! He probably lived in a tree.

Maia's eyes never left Finn. He was still hoping to escape, she could see that. If he could get out into the street, he might have a chance, but not here. He fought like a demon; once he managed to free himself, but Mr. Low caught his leg while

Mr. Trapwood hit him on the side of the head with the butt of his pistol.

"Now, now, boy, we're not here to hurt you."

But the wild boy didn't understand. He went on struggling and fighting and shouting in his ghastly tongue. They'd have to tie him up to get him on the boat. And what would Sir Aubrey say? If ever there was a hollow victory, this was it.

Miss Minton, all this time, had been standing stock-still, looking at the Indian boy with a strange expression on her face. Now she walked carefully to the edge of the open trapdoor and looked down the flight of steps leading into the darkness.

Miss Minton waited. She was staring intently at the back of the cellar and the pile of packing cases.

Then she said loudly and clearly, "Come out, Finn Taverner. Come out and be a man."

Among the packing cases something stirred. A glimmer of light fell on fair hair. A boy straightened himself and stood up.

Miss Minton continued to stare down into the murk.

"You heard me, Finn," she said—and the crows turned, amazed. "The mantle of the Taverners has fallen on your shoulders. It is time you faced your destiny."

Clovis looked up and saw the upright figure of Miss Minton, standing above him. She had always made him feel brave—and now he forgot that an hour before he had been overcome with terror and begged Finn not to give him up to the crows.

Clovis straightened himself. He squared his shoulders. He tossed back his curls. Then slowly, with immense dignity, he climbed the cellar steps.

"Unhand my servant, please," he ordered the crows. "As you see, *I* am Finn Taverner."

"Unhand my servant, please," he ordered the crows.
"As you see, I am Finn Taverner."

The crows let go of the Indian. They stared at the golden-haired youth who had appeared at the top of the cellar steps. The boy's breeding showed in every movement; he was an undoubted and true aristocrat. Here before them was The Blood which Sir Aubrey longed for, and they were filled with joy.

The boy now addressed his servant. "You have served me well, Kumari," he said—and every word was crystal clear; the words of a perfect English gentleman, speaking slowly to a foreigner. "Now I give you your freedom. And with it, this token of my thanks."

And out of the pocket of his tunic he took a watch on a long chain which he handed to the Indian.

"But, sir," said Mr. Trapwood, who had seen the glint of silver. "Should you—"

"I am a Taverner," said Clovis. "And no one shall say that I am not grateful to those who have served me. And now, gentlemen, I am ready. I take it you have reserved a first-class cabin for me?"

"Well," began Mr. Low.

Mr. Trapwood kicked his shin. "It shall be arranged, sir," he said. "Everything will be taken care of."

"Good. I should like to go on board immediately."

"Yes, sir, of course. If you'll just come with us."

Clovis bowed to Miss Minton, then to Maia. His eyes were dry and his dignity was matchless.

Then he followed the crows out of the museum.

14

COME AND SEE her," said Finn. "Come and see your namesake."

He got into the canoe beside Maia and Miss Minton and paddled round to the side of the *Arabella,* so that Miss Minton could see the name painted on the bows.

Miss Minton put up a bony hand to trace the letters. For a while she was silent. Then she said, "It's a better name for a boat than for a governess. Or a housemaid."

She sniffed and felt for her handkerchief, the same one with the initial A on it that she had lent to Maia in the cab—and once again Maia thought what an idiot she had been not to guess what Finn had guessed so quickly.

"He said if he got away and got himself a boat he'd call her after me," Miss Minton went on. "I didn't help him all that much—he'd have done it anyway—but he never forgot a promise."

They were in the lagoon. It was the day after Clovis had sailed on the *Bishop.* The twins and Mrs. Carter had gone to church. But when Miss Minton had shown Mrs. Carter the mysterious bruises on Maia's arm, she had gotten permission to keep her at home—and as soon as they were safely away, Furo had come to fetch them.

Back in the hut, Finn began on the questions.

"How did you know? How did you know who I was as soon as you saw me come out of the trapdoor in the museum?"

"You're so like your father. The eyes, the way your voice is pitched. He wasn't much older than you are now when he ran away from Westwood. And I knew he'd married an Indian woman and had a son; we kept in touch. So when I saw that the crows had caught you, I realized your plan had gone wrong."

"You mean you knew what we were planning?" said Maia— not at all pleased.

"More or less. Your acting skills are not very great," said Miss Minton, "And as a liar you are bottom of the class. I made friends with old Lila, and when she realized that I knew Bernard, she told me about this place. But you seemed to know what you were doing, so I left you to it."

"We did know what we were doing," said Finn. "But Clovis just went berserk when he got down to the cellar. Some skulls came tumbling out of a packing case, and he saw these eye sockets staring at him. Then he fell over a throwing spear and the lamp kept going out. There was a weird moaning noise, too—it was only the water pipes—but he got hysterical and said he felt sick and he couldn't go through with it. I suppose it was sort of stage fright— he really thought the crows were going to hurt him. I'd promised Maia I wouldn't let him get too scared, so I stayed. I meant to make a dash for it when the crows opened the door and lead them away from him. When the sloth fell over he thought it was a bomb!"

"Poor Clovis," said Maia.

"She's always sticking up for him," said Finn.

"Still, he gave a fine performance at the end, you must admit," said Miss Minton.

Then they asked her about her time at Westwood.

"I was just a housemaid," she said. "No one called me Arabella—the butler wouldn't permit it. I was always Bella, except to Bernard."

And she told them what had happened after Bernard left.

"You can't imagine the uproar. Everyone was stamping about and shouting, but they were angry, not sad. Then very soon after that the butler found me reading in the library—no one read the books at Westwood; I was meant to be dusting them, not reading them—and I was dismissed. It was the best thing that ever happened to me. I remembered what Bernard had said—that I should go away and get an education. He said there were colleges where you could study at night and earn your keep during the day. So I went to London and I did just that. It took me six years to get a degree, but I did it." Miss Minton looked away and permitted herself a smile, for she had gotten not just a degree but a First, which no one had done in that college before.

"So then you became a governess," said Maia.

"Yes. But Bernard wrote to me, and his letters made me want to see the place where he was so happy. I tried hard to save enough for the fare, but I never succeeded—and then this job came up with the Carters. Just two weeks after I accepted it, I heard that Bernard had died—the letter came back with a blue cross and 'deceased' on the envelope. It was a fearful shock. Then, when I came out here and guessed what the crows were up to, I kept my eyes open. I knew how Bernard felt about Westwood and that he would hate his son to be dragged back there against his will."

"Well, thank goodness you did," said Finn.

But Miss Minton now wanted to see the animals that Bernard had written about.

"Does the anteater still come?" she asked. "And the capuchin monkey?" And Finn said yes, and showed her everything—the hummingbird bottle, the place where the turtle hauled out of the water—while the dog padded between them.

"I see why he was so happy here," she said. "It's a wonderful place."

"Yes, but Finn's going away. In the *Arabella*," said Maia. "He's going a long, long way," and Minty frowned at the sadness in her voice. "And he won't take me."

"No, of course not," said Miss Minton. "That would hardly do."

Maia looked up into her face. "Wouldn't you like to go on a great journey? Find a place no one knew about?"

"What I would like has nothing to do with it. I have my living to earn, and you must get an education."

But even though she knew that Finn would not take her, Maia was hungry for all the details of his journey.

"What if they aren't there anymore?" she wanted to know. "The Xanti?"

"Then I'll go on till I find them," said Finn. "They have to be somewhere."

Miss Minton was silent. It wasn't strictly true—tribes had been wiped out by illness, or fighting, or been kidnapped. She could not be happy about a boy of his age making such a journey alone, but she had no power to prevent Finn from living his life as he wished. Maia was a different matter. She was wholly responsible for keeping Maia safe, and it was out of the question that the girl should be allowed to go.

It was as they came away from the lagoon in Furo's canoe that Miss Minton suddenly told Furo to stop. A breeze had sprung up, and as the leaves of a tall broad-leafed tree blew to one side, she had seen on its trunk a large and most exquisite butterfly.

Miss Minton did not chase butterflies, but this one was so enormous and so beautiful—and so still—that she clambered out of the canoe and went to look.

"My goodness!" she said.

The butterfly was still because it was dead. Dead, but perfectly preserved in the web of a large spider who had left it there, and would probably come back and eat it later.

Very carefully, Miss Minton took the butterfly from the tree, using her handkerchief so as not to touch it directly, and carried it back.

"Oh!" said Maia. "I've never seen anything like that!" And even Furo shook his head.

The brilliant yellow and black of the wings ended in two long tails, like the tail of a swallow.

"It looks special, doesn't it?" Maia went on. "Professor Glastonberry will know what it is."

Miss Minton nodded, trying not to feel excited. "It is most unlikely that it will turn out to be anything unusual," she said firmly, but Maia saw her looking at the creature lying on her lap again and again.

In Manaus it quickly got about that Finn Taverner had been snatched by the crows and taken on board the *Bishop*, and that it was the Carter twins who had betrayed him.

The reaction of almost everyone was anger. Anger with the crows, anger with the twins.

Colonel da Silva was particularly upset. All the trouble he had taken to lead the crows astray had come to nothing. He felt he had failed his old friend Bernard, and he was going to miss Finn.

"I'd better go and see what's to be done about the *Arabella*," he said to his second-in-command. "And all Taverner's things. The dog'll go wild, I imagine; he can fend for himself." He sighed. "I'll go next week—the Indians will see that no one steals anything. And if those wretched Carter twins come again to ask about the reward, send them away with a flea in their ear. The boy hasn't been gone three days. Nasty, moneygrubbing little worms!"

And he turned aside and spat out of the window, a thing he hadn't done since he was a young cadet and thought spitting was the thing to do.

Professor Glastonberry had had trouble with the exhibits he was supposed to collect in Obidos and had been late coming home. It was therefore not till nearly a week had passed that he came back to the museum and found that his first caller was Miss Minton.

Miss Minton had been very distressed when the sloth came crashing to the ground, and although they had been able to right the skeleton before they left, there had been no time to examine it.

Now she knocked on the door of the lab and found the professor standing by it with a worried look.

"I came to ask if there had been any serious damage. We never thought the crows would be so violent."

"No. None of the bones are broken—the backbone's been dislodged, but I can fix that."

He went out to shut both the lab door and the door of his office. Then he said, "I'm not quite clear what happened. They say that Finn's been caught and dragged back to Westwood. But surely Maia wouldn't have given away his hiding place?"

"No, it wasn't like that. Or only in a sense." And she told him the whole story: about the children's plan, the way it had nearly gone wrong, and the happy ending.

The professor was delighted. "Good, good. So Finn is safe! And of course I should have guessed that you were Bella— Bernard spoke of you as the only friend he had as a boy. Finn's keeping out of the way, you say?"

"For the time being—till Clovis is safely out to sea. Then he'll sail off in the *Arabella,* and I'm afraid Maia's going to be upset. She has a great thirst for adventure."

"And you? Do you have a thirst for adventure?" the professor asked.

"Who doesn't?" said Miss Minton, and shrugged. Then she took out the box in which she had packed the butterfly. "I wondered if you knew what this was."

Very carefully, the professor lifted the layers of cotton wool. "Good heavens—don't tell me you've found a Hahnet's Swallowtail!" He took the box over to the window. "But you have! And perfectly preserved!"

Miss Minton explained about the spiderweb.

"I could get you a good price for it if you wished to sell it. They're very rare. I know a collector in Manaus who's been wanting one. Or I could buy it for the museum. But you'd get a better price from him."

"What sort of a price?"

"In English money, about eighty pounds."

Miss Minton stared at him. "But that's almost half my yearly wage!"

"Well, that's what it's worth. More if you sent it to England. After all, Taverner lived by collecting and selling the things he found, and he's not the only one."

Miss Minton was silent, looking into the future. Could it be that a door had opened for her? She would never leave Maia, but one day . . . Was it possible that she could escape from the drudgery of teaching children like the twins?

The professor, watching her, decided to strike while the iron was hot.

"I have to go to lunch now," he said. "I know you don't care for foreign food, but if you wish I could give you a list of the things that are worth collecting. Some of the plant resins are very valuable—and you don't have to go after them with a net!"

"Did I say I didn't care for foreign food?" said Miss Minton huffily. "I don't remember saying it. In fact, I didn't say it."

Up in the bungalow, the twins thought of nothing but the reward. When would it come, what would they do with it, how could they stop their parents from trying to get a share? Maia heard them still whispering about it when they went to bed. Sometimes their voices rose and they seemed to be on the edge of a quarrel, but then they made up again because they saw themselves as standing alone against the world.

"And as soon as we get it we can get rid of Maia."

That was the other thing they whispered about. They had

gotten rid of Miss Porterhouse by accusing her of stealing their things, and they had gotten rid of Miss Chisholm by telling their mother that she had been seen in Manaus with MEN.

They'd have to think of something different for Maia, but they would do it, and once Maia went, Miss Minton would go, too, and they would be free.

And while the twins quarreled about the reward, Mr. and Mrs. Carter quarreled about Maia's allowance.

"I tell you," said Mr. Carter, "I have to have this month's allowance for Maia. It's no good you hanging on to it like you did last month."

"Well, you can't. The twins need new dancing shoes—and the dentist says they should have braces on their teeth. You know how expensive that is. You don't want your daughters to grow up with crooked teeth, do you?"

"If all I had to worry about was my daughters' teeth, I'd be a happy man. That swine Lima has walked out on me—my own agent! If he gangs up with Gonzales I'm finished."

"Perhaps if you didn't spend our money on those ridiculous glass eyes, you wouldn't be so hard up."

"Let me tell you that my collection is worth more than anything else in this house."

"Well, why don't you sell it, then, and pay your debts? You know I only agreed to have Maia because of the money she brought. It's I who have to put up with her, not you—you hardly see her. You hardly see your own daughters. And anyway I've ordered a new cockroach killer. They're sending it out from the army and navy stores in London and it's expensive."

"Cockroach killer! I've never heard of anything so ridiculous. Just throw benzene over them and set them alight."

"Really, Clifford—no wonder you can't run a proper business. Benzene indeed! I shall have to write to Mr. Murray and ask him for more money for the girl. She's not worth keeping for what I get."

She broke off because Maia had come into the room, carrying her dancing shoes, to say that the launch was ready to go to Manaus.

Maia had heard the quarrel—their angry voices echoed through the bungalow. It was a long time since she had thought that the Carters had taken her in because they wanted her, but knowing that she would still be living with these people after Finn had gone was hard to bear.

Two hours later she was playing the piano to Mr. Haltmann and had forgotten her misery. She was getting on well, but the best part of her lesson came at the end when Haltmann made her sing. She still wouldn't listen when he suggested that she have her voice trained, but she asked him about the Indian tribes—had their songs been collected, could she get hold of them?

"I mean the Indians that live in tribes in the forest, not the ones near the towns."

"A few of them have been collected," he answered. "Only a very few—and there is much work to be done there. But you would find these songs very different and not at all easy to write down."

"But it could be done?"

"Yes . . . with patience and a good ear." He smiled at Maia's eager face. "And you have both, I think?"

At the dancing class everyone knew that Finn Taverner had been caught by the crows, that the twins had betrayed his hiding place, and that he was on his way to England and the dreaded Westwood.

Everyone was sorry and no one would speak to the twins—not that they noticed. Even before the news of the reward, the twins had lived in a world of their own.

Sergei was not there—his father had taken him on a journey upriver—but Mademoiselle Lille had brought Olga.

The Keminskys' governess had come with red-rimmed eyes and the news that her father had died back in France, and that she was sailing home on the next boat to Europe.

"I am thinking," she whispered to Miss Minton as they sat and watched the children dance, "why don't you come and take my job? The Keminskys are excellent employers—well, you have seen."

"Yes, I can imagine no one better to work for," said Miss Minton. "But I couldn't leave Maia."

"Perhaps they would have Maia also. The children are very fond of her—Sergei in particular."

"When do you leave?"

"In two weeks. My poor mother is quite distraught."

"I'll think about it. Thank you," said Miss Minton.

But she doubted whether Mr. Murray would give permission for Maia to go to live with an unknown family of Russians. She would say nothing to Maia—there was no point in raising her hopes.

Though Finn had made it clear that he would not take Maia with him, she could not stop dreaming. It seemed to her that there could be nothing better than to travel on the *Arabella* on and on and on. . . . To wake at dawn and cook breakfast over a

Primus stove and watch the herons and cormorants dive for fish . . . to feed logs into the firebox and smell the woodsmoke as they caught . . . And then to chug up the still, dark rivers with the trees leaning over to give shade, or across the sudden white-water lagoons where the water was milky in the sunlight.

This was what she had imagined that evening in the school library, sitting on top of the ladder and reading about the treasures that the Amazon would pour into the lap of those who were not afraid.

But she had not then imagined Finn. Finn was obstinate; he could be bad-tempered and curt and he was far too full of his own opinions—but she had fallen into friendship with him as surely as the soppy older girls at school had fallen into love. And now he was going, and Clovis had gone, and she would be left alone with the twins.

At first, hoping that Finn would change his mind and let her come, she had worked extra hard helping him with the *Arabella*, but after a while she became so interested that she helped for its own sake.

"Have you got any books about boats?" she asked Minty.

"One doesn't learn about boats from books," said Miss Minton, but she found a manual about the maintenance of steam launches in the secondhand bookshop in Manaus.

"What do you think they'll be like, the Xanti?" Maia asked Finn, and he shrugged.

"My father said they were the kindest people he'd ever met. And they knew everything there was to know about healing. I'd like to learn that from them. After all, three-quarters of the medicines we use come from plants, and most of them come from the forest here." He hesitated. "I thought maybe one day I could become a doctor, but not the kind that just gives people pills."

Maia nodded. Finn would make a good doctor, she could see that. "Did he say if they had any songs?"

"They'll have songs all right. All Indians sing, especially when they're traveling."

Maia sighed. She wanted to learn about the songs like Finn wanted to learn about the plants.

But it was hopeless. "It's too dangerous," was all Finn would say, and that was that. She tried to put it out of her mind, but she couldn't. There were girls at school who wanted to ride, and others who wanted to go on the stage, and there was a girl who had made a terrible fuss till she was allowed to learn the oboe—not the flute, not the clarinet, it had to be the oboe. They knew that these things were for them; and Maia knew that boats were for her. Boats, and going on and on and not arriving unless one wanted to.

When they weren't working on the boat, Finn took her into the forest. He showed her which nuts to pick and which to avoid, how to get fruit down from the high branches and how to walk quietly, picking up her feet higher than usual, not thumping and blundering about. Once he brought down a paca with his bow and arrow.

"They're good to eat," he said. "You have to be able to kill for food if necessary"—and he waited for Maia to make a fuss, but though she turned pale when the little rodent twitched on his arrow, she said nothing. He showed her how to make body paint from urucu berries, and how to fetch water from the river without getting scum into the kettle—and the more she learned the more she wanted to learn, and the more she dreaded the day of his departure.

But he wasn't gone yet. Not quite. She could still come into the lagoon and hear him whistling as he did his chores. And she would have been very surprised if she had known that Finn, too, was fearful of the parting and of making the journey by himself.

Then just two weeks after the *Bishop* had left Manaus, the liner came out of the maze of waterways at the head of the Amazon delta and headed out for the open sea. Even if Clovis had been found out, there would be no chance now of sending him back before they reached England.

"There's no point in waiting any longer," said Finn. "The boat is as ready as she'll ever be. If we clear the reeds away, she'll just get through."

We, thought Maia bitterly. Obviously he expected her to help him clear the passage out of the lagoon, and then he'd wave good-bye and she'd never see him again.

"If it had been the other way round, I'd have taken you," she said.

"I suppose you think that makes it easier for me," said Finn angrily.

"I wasn't trying to make it easier for you," said Maia, and stalked away.

But Finn did not go immediately. It was as though the *Arabella* wasn't so sure she wanted to go adventuring after her quiet time in the lagoon. First they found a small leak through the hull under the floorboards, and then Finn dropped the washer for the valve which regulated the amount of steam to go into the boiler. He didn't just drop it, he dropped it into the deepest part of the lake, and though he and Maia dived for it again and again, they couldn't find it. Furo went into Manaus to get a replacement, but before they could put it in, another week had passed.

It was harder for Miss Minton to get away to the lagoon. When she did manage it, she bullied Finn about *Caesar's Gallic Wars*.

"Those legions are never going to get across the bridge at this rate," she said, looking at the book, still open at page fifty-seven. But when she had finished lecturing Finn about the importance of Latin to someone who wanted to collect plants, she lent a hand with the chores, scrubbing the floor of the hut to whiteness.

"Having been a housemaid always comes in useful," she said.

One afternoon when the children were on their own, they saw that the macaws on the tree that guarded the entrance had flown up, squawking.

But it was not Furo come to fetch Maia. It was Colonel da Silva with his second-in-command, come to take charge of Bernard Taverner's possessions.

"*Dios!*" he said paddling up to the hut. "What is this?"

So Finn explained, and when he had finished the colonel was laughing so much he looked as if he was going to fall into the water. The idea of the crows bringing a penniless actor to Westwood was the best thing he had heard in ages. "And you, *senhorita*," he said to Maia. "A heroine no less."

He told them that instructions to pay out the reward for Finn's capture had been telegraphed from the *Bishop,* so Mr. Trapwood and Mr. Low could have no suspicion that they did not have the right boy.

• • •

Then came the day Maia had dreaded. The last of the provisions were loaded onto the *Arabella*—manioc flour and dried beans and oil for the Primus stove and gifts for the Indians.

That night Finn came to say good-bye to Furo and the others.

"You're to look after Maia," he told them. "Promise me you will not let any harm come to her."

And Furo, who had been sulking because he, too, wanted to go with Finn, gave his promise, as did Tapi and Conchita. Only old Lila was inconsolable, weeping and rocking back and forth and declaring that she would be dead before he returned.

Watching from her window, Maia saw him come out of Lila's hut, and for a moment she thought he was going to leave without saying good-bye. Then he walked across the compound and stood under her window and she heard him whistle the tune that he had whistled on the night she came.

Blow the wind southerly, southerly, southerly,
Blow the wind south o'er the bonny blue sea. . . .

She ran outside then and hugged him and wished him luck, and she did not cry.

"You're not to spoil it for him," Minty had said, and she didn't.

But when he had gone, she stood for a long time by the window, trying to remember the words of the song. It was a song begging the wind to bring back someone who had gone away in a ship, but she did not think it ended happily.

Well, why should it? Why should the wind care if she never saw Finn again?

15

SIR AUBREY HAD sent the carriage to the station. He himself was going to wait for his grandson in the drawing room.

If it *was* his grandson.

Clovis sat between Mr. Trapwood and Mr. Low. The crows were going to hand him over personally before returning to town.

It was cool. It was, in fact, very cool with an east wind blowing off Westwood Moor, and Clovis drank in the air with relief. No sticky heat, and no insects. He was in England at last.

They had driven for at least twenty minutes down an avenue of lime trees. Clovis could see the glimmer of water between the coppices. That must be the lake where the Basher had held Bernard's head under water.

Then suddenly the carriage curved round a bend and Westwood lay before him.

It was exactly as Finn had described it: an East Wing, a West Wing, and a block in the middle—but it was very large: larger than he had been able to imagine.

For a moment Clovis found his stomach lurching. The crows were easy to hoodwink; they had fawned on him all through the journey and spent their spare time in the bar. But Finn's grandfather would see through him; he was sure of that.

They passed the fountain with the person on it who was strangling a snake. He seemed to have lost his head, which was a pity. Then the carriage stopped outside the main entrance.

And Clovis saw a crowd of people massed on the stone steps which led to the front door! There were women in blue aprons, women in black dresses, men in livery and overalls and tailcoats . . .

Of course! The servants all lined up to greet him!

Clovis's panic grew worse. He hadn't realized that there could be so many servants in the world. Then he remembered that this had happened in *Little Lord Fauntleroy* when Ceddie arrived from America, and in a play called *The Young Master* when the lost heir returned to his home.

The coachman opened the door. Mr. Low and Mr. Trapwood waited respectfully for him to get out first.

Clovis squared his shoulders. He took a deep breath as he had always done before he went onstage, and moved forward.

And upstairs, in the drawing room, Sir Aubrey put his telescope to his eye.

When the boat docked at Liverpool, the crows had stopped at a gentleman's outfitter and bought a tweed suit and cap for Clovis—the best that the shop could supply. Now, as he peered through the eyepiece, Sir Aubrey saw a handsome lad, blue-eyed and sturdy, who carried himself like a prince. The boy shook hands with the butler, the housekeeper, and the cook,

*The boy shook hands with the butler, the housekeeper,
and the cook, exactly as he should....*

exactly as he should; then, at the top of the steps, he turned and thanked the lesser servants for their welcome before following the butler into the house.

And Sir Aubrey's heart leaped. He had been worried, no good denying it—Bernard might have produced anything—but this boy looked splendid. He would not chatter to the servants as his father had; he was gracious but he kept his distance.

In the hall the steward waited to show Mr. Low and Mr. Trapwood into the office. The crows had hoped to be asked to stay to supper, but Sir Aubrey did not dine with detectives. However, they were paid off and got their bonus, along with a glass of beer, before they said good-bye to Clovis and were driven back to the station for the London train. The butler (who was not the old one who had sacked Bella but a younger man with black hair) now led Clovis past the chest into which Dudley had locked Bernard, past the knight in armor out of which Dudley had jumped, and the picture of the man with the Turk's head impaled on a lance. Then he knocked on a heavy oaken door, announced, "Master Taverner, Sir Aubrey," and withdrew.

Over what seemed like acres and acres of rich dark carpet, Clovis looked at Sir Aubrey Taverner—and Sir Aubrey Taverner looked at him. Clovis saw a stout, red-faced man with a white mustache and bushy eyebrows. He was leaning on a stick, so Clovis thought he must have gout; everyone older than fifty seemed to have gout in the sort of plays Clovis had acted in, and he decided to be very careful and not bump into him.

Sir Aubrey, on the other hand, saw the grandson of his dreams. Clovis's eyes were very blue, his hair was thick and golden; he bowed low over the hand stretched out to him. (The Goodleys had been very keen on proper bowing.)

"Well, my boy, here you are at last. What made you hide away so long?"

Clovis had thought of the answer to this one.

"Because I was afraid I was not . . . worthy to fulfill my role." He looked at Sir Aubrey to see if he had overdone it, but he hadn't.

"Nonsense. You'll soon learn, my boy." And then: "You're not at all like your father. Not at all."

"I believe I take after my mother, sir," said Clovis. Since he had never seen his mother, who had dumped him in an orphanage as soon as he was born, he felt quite safe in saying this.

"All the same, you remind me of someone. Now, who can it be?"

Clovis waited nervously.

Then: "I know," said Sir Aubrey. "Yes. Your great-great-uncle Alwin. He was an admiral in Nelson's navy. Went down with his ship at the Battle of the Nile. There's a portrait of him in the gallery. I'll show it to you later."

Clovis then asked what had happened to the head of the man who was strangling a snake and Sir Aubrey said that Dudley had blasted it with a shotgun.

"He was after some poachers," he said, and fell silent, looking very sad. "Splendid chap, Dudley. Ask anyone."

Clovis said that he had heard from his father how strong Dudley was, and tried to think if he had heard anything nice about Dudley, but he hadn't. Fortunately, since Sir Aubrey was looking very upset, the butler announced Mrs. Smith and her three older daughters. The youngest daughter, Prudence, was still in nappies and did not go out to dinner.

Again Clovis had no difficulty in recognizing Mrs. Smith as the Basher, and her daughters as the ones who were no use to Sir Aubrey because they were the wrong sex.

"How do you do, Aunt Joan," said Clovis, smiling winningly and hoping that the Basher had settled down since her marriage.

"Well, you led us quite a dance," brayed Joan, and introduced her daughters.

The girls were very thin and frail with straight fair hair and woebegone expressions, like banshees. Hope, who was eleven, had buckteeth, Faith, who was nine, had trouble breathing through her nose, and Charity was so frightened of her mother that she stammered, but they were nice girls all the same.

All three of them looked anxiously at Clovis. Their mother had said that one of them would have to marry him when they grew up so that their family could get a share of Westwood. The girls knew that Bernard had been mad and had run away from home and talked to housemaids and to rats, so the idea of marrying his son made them feel very frightened. But now, as Clovis smiled and shook hands with them, they felt better. He did not look like a boy who ran away from home and talked to housemaids.

The butler now announced that dinner was served. Clovis offered his arm to the Basher (which he knew was correct because of all the plays with dinner parties that he had acted in), and they crossed the gallery and went down the great carved stairway to the dining room.

As soon as he saw the table with its snow-white cloth and smelled the faint, warm smell of fresh rolls and roasting meat, Clovis knew it was going to be all right. He remembered the

Hotel Paradiso and all the other places where he had eaten vile food, and a smile curved his lips that made his face look very beautiful. Even his foster mother couldn't have cooked a better meal. The asparagus soup was delicate and creamy, the roast beef was brown and crisp on the outside and just a little pink in the middle, the potatoes melted in the mouth. And for dessert, they had bread-and-butter pudding with dollops of cream. . . .

Clovis ate, and as he did so he decided he could probably hold out for a week, or even two, before he gave himself up. Finn would be glad of the extra time, and it would be a pity not to stay for the other things: ginger pudding, and boiled mutton with capers perhaps . . . and there'd be proper crackling on the pork.

As for the little banshees, when they returned home they, too, were satisfied.

"I wouldn't mind marrying him," said the eldest, Hope.

"I wouldn't either," said Faith.

"Nor me," said Charity. "I w-wouldn't . . . mind, too."

Then they sighed. "Mother will tell us which one it's going to be," said Hope. "As long as it's not Prudence."

Prudence was still in nappies and far too small to be in the running, but she had curls and a dimple and her sisters hated her.

As for Clovis, he lay freshly bathed in a linen nightshirt between cool and spotless sheets. No mosquito netting, no fly-paper, no beetles . . . yes, he would definitely hold out for at least a week. He had promised Finn and he would do it.

But Sir Aubrey was not yet in bed. He had limped up to the Picture Gallery at the top of the house and stood for a long time looking at the portrait of Alwin Taverner in his naval uniform.

Really, the likeness was extraordinary! The nose, the eyes, the mouth, the way his hair fell over his forehead—all of it was the same as in the boy who had come today.

It happened sometimes that a likeness skipped a few generations and then showed up stronger than ever, thought Sir Aubrey. That was the amazing thing about The Blood.

16

FINN HAD BEEN gone three days, and life in the bungalow seemed even more dismal than when Maia first came.

Miss Minton saw that lessons went on, but though Maia worked as hard as she had done before, she did so without joy. She didn't want to *read* about plants and animals any longer, she wanted to find them. She wanted to be out there in the forest starting a real life, and much as Miss Minton loved books, she understood her.

The weather, as the dry season got under way, became even hotter. In her room, Miss Minton took off her corset and put it on again. Not because she was afraid of Mrs. Carter, but because she knew that British women did not throw off their underclothes—and because she had told Maia not to make a fuss when Finn went away. If Maia could behave well over the parting, she could behave well about the heat rash spreading up her back.

Meanwhile she watched Maia carefully, because there was no doubt that the Carters were becoming very strange indeed. As Mr. Carter's business went from bad to worse, he spent more and more time in his study, peering at his glass eyes—and since his own family would not look at them, he called in Maia.

"Look at that one," he said to her. "It's the left eye of a tramp found dead in a ditch on Wimbledon Common. Look at the way those blood vessels are painted! You wouldn't imagine a tramp could afford an eye like that."

"Perhaps he was a very important person before he became a tramp," suggested Maia—but the eyes were beginning to get into her dreams.

Mrs. Carter had set up what she called her "larder" in a cupboard in the hall, but it was not a larder to store food. Instead of bottles of plums or pats of butter, the shelves held flasks labeled POISON, and masks for protecting the face, and rubber gloves. There were glass jars of chloral hydrate, and spray cans with nozzles, and a new very large bottle labeled COCKROACH KILLER—KEEP AWAY FROM FIRE.

"We'll be safe now," she told the girls. "No creepy-crawlies will get past us now."

She had also started to talk to the picture of Lady Parsons on the wall of the drawing room.

"You were right," Maia heard her say to the lady's fierce, red face. "I should have let Clifford go to prison instead of bringing him out here. Look what we have come to!"

And one morning Maia came into the drawing room and found the portrait wreathed in red ribbon.

"I hope you haven't forgotten that today is Lady Parsons' birthday," she said to the twins. "Do you remember when she allowed you to share her cake?"

"Yes, Mama, we wouldn't forget."

"What kind of cake was it?" asked Maia. She had spoken without thinking, wanting to be polite. There was certainly nothing she was less interested in than the cake which Lady Parsons had shared with Beatrice and Gwendolyn when they were still in England.

The twins glared at her. Lady Parsons was *theirs*. Maia had no business even to ask.

"It was a sponge cake with pink icing," said Mrs. Carter.

"No, it wasn't, Mother. It had white icing," corrected Beatrice.

"No, it didn't. It was covered with marzipan and grated chocolate," said Gwendolyn.

They went on arguing, but Maia had forgotten them again, following Finn in her mind.

Where was he? Did he have enough wood for the firebox? Were his maps accurate? Did he miss her at all?

Finn did miss her—she would have been surprised to know how much. He had never sailed the *Arabella* alone for any distance and it wasn't as easy as he'd hoped. While she was under way he managed well, but when it came to anchoring in the evening or setting off at dawn, he would have given anything for another pair of hands. Not any pair of hands—Maia's. She had obeyed his orders quickly but not blindly; he had learned to trust her completely.

And she was nice. Fun. Quick to catch a joke and so interested in everything—asking about the birds, the plants. This morning he had found himself starting to say, "Look, Maia!" when he saw an umbrella bird strutting along a branch, and when he realized that she wasn't there, the exotic creature, with its sunshade of feathers, had seemed somehow less exciting. After all, sharing was something everyone wanted to do. He could hear his father's voice calling, "Look, Finn, over there!" a dozen times a day.

But his father was dead and he had left Maia, and suddenly being alone, which he had always enjoyed, turned into loneliness, which was a very different thing.

He had anchored close to a sandbank, a beautiful place sheltered by large-fronded palms, and found a nest of turtle eggs. A shoal of black-banded fishes glided past the boat; he had caught some earlier, using pieces of banana to bait his line, and they made a delicious supper. He had hardly touched his stores, and the *Arabella* was going steadily.

"What's the matter with me?" said Finn.

He was doing what his father had suggested. He was going to see the Xanti, but now he wondered what it was all about. They were just as likely to put an arrow through him as to welcome him with open arms.

The dog, who had been curled up on the foredeck, thumped once with his tail, then got to his feet and offered him a wet nose for comfort.

"It's all right," said Finn to his dog. "It's all right, Rob."

But there was more to his unease than loneliness. He knew he could not have taken Maia; he had no idea how the journey was going to end, and in any case Miss Minton would never have allowed her to come.

All the same, he felt he should not have left her. He remembered Clovis saying, "But Maia shouldn't live in a house that's been cursed."

Only that was silly. He had told Furo and the others to look after her and they had promised.

It was that other side of him, the Indian side, which went in for rubbish like premonitions and inklings, and things you felt without knowing why. Suddenly furious with himself, Finn crawled to his haversack, turned up the lamp, and took out *Caesar's Gallic Wars*.

"After marching from the country of the Menapii . . ." he translated. And became an ordinary English schoolboy doing his homework.

When Finn had been gone for nearly a week, the Great Event which the twins had been expecting actually happened. Colonel da Silva arrived in the police launch, bringing the reward for the capture of Bernard Taverner's son.

He brought it as he had promised, in Brazilian notes so that it could be divided into two equal parts, but he warned the twins to get it into a bank as soon as possible.

"If you don't have an account your parents could bank it for you."

But the twins did not mean to do that. As da Silva left, they were already counting out their separate heaps on the dining-room table.

Twenty thousand *milreis . . . each.*

For a short time Beatrice and Gwendolyn were perfectly happy.

Miss Minton and the professor had become friends. He had taken the butterfly she had found to the collector in Manaus, who had paid her. He had also lent her a collecting tin and

some preservative, and though so far she had not found anything else worth selling, she was secretly proud of having
become a naturalist.

Because Maia now had lunch with the Haltmanns after her
music lesson, Miss Minton lunched with the professor in the
little café he had shown her. But being friends did not mean
blabbing out one's troubles, and Miss Minton was slow to share
with the professor her anxieties about Maia. It was only when
he particularly asked about her that she said, "I'm not happy
about the way things are going at the Carters. The twins are
bullying Maia more openly now and their mother seems to live
in a fantasy world. She talks to the portrait of Lady Parsons and
sometimes I'm afraid she—"

But Miss Minton stopped there, not liking to admit that her
employer was possibly losing her mind.

"They will have anxieties about Mr. Carter's business," said
the professor. "I understand that Gonzales is baying for Carter's
blood. He certainly seems to owe enormous sums of money.
Isn't there anywhere else that you can take Maia?"

Miss Minton hesitated. Even to the professor she preferred
not to reveal her plan before she was sure it could be carried
out. "I've written to Mr. Murray," was all she said.

She then asked about his work, and he sighed deeply. "Carruthers is dead," he said, and his large, pink forehead creased
into lines like a mournful pug's.

Miss Minton waited. She didn't think she had heard about
Carruthers.

"He was a brilliant man, knew more about extinct animals
than anyone I know, but they hounded him."

"Who hounded him?"

"The 'proper' scientists. You should have seen what they wrote about him in the papers. 'An unrealistic dreamer, a man who let himself be led away by myths and stories—always searching for the impossible . . .'"

"What was he searching for?"

The professor put down his fork. He seemed to be looking into the distance. Then he said, "The giant sloth."

"The bones, you mean? The skeleton? Like your rib?"

"No, the beast itself. He was convinced it wasn't extinct. The natives have always had stories about it—they call it the *Maupugari* . . . a great creature with reddish hair which walks on its curved claws. You get sightings of it every so often." He sighed. "It was Carruthers who got me interested in sloths—we were friends in Cambridge. And now . . ."

"How did he die?"

The professor shrugged. "He was searching somewhere in the Matto Grosso and got a fever. It's not so difficult to die out here. Personally I think they broke his heart."

Miss Minton waited while he dabbed his eyes with his handkerchief. Then she said, "Perhaps it wasn't such a bad way to go. Still working, still searching . . . Better than dying in a hospital with strangers."

"Yes. Yes, you're right. But I wish . . ."

Something now occurred to Miss Minton. "You don't think he was right, do you? That the sloth is not extinct. You don't agree with him?"

The professor blushed. "No, no," he said. "It's most unlikely." But he didn't meet her eyes.

Miss Minton now gathered up her belongings. "I have to fetch Maia from her piano lesson," she said.

But when she left the restaurant, she did not go straight to the Haltmanns. She crossed the square, turned down the street to the Keminskys' mansion, and asked to speak to the countess.

The professor was right about Gonzales. He arrived at the Carters the next day, along with two unpleasant-looking henchmen.

Gonzales was a Brazilian who had traded in the Amazon for many years. He was not a nice man, but he dealt fairly in business and Mr. Carter had now exhausted his patience.

Mr. Carter took him into the study, but the walls were thin and it was almost impossible not to hear what Gonzales was saying.

"I've had enough," he said in Portuguese. "Either you let me have what you owe me in full, or I will take legal action."

Then Carter's voice, low, whining. "I only need a few more weeks. They're bringing in a big batch of rubber from the north of the estate. It will fetch a good price."

"That is not what I have heard," said Gonzales.

The voices went on for a while longer: Gonzales's loud, Carter's a low mumble. Then Gonzales threw open the door, bowed to Mrs. Carter, gathered his henchmen, and was gone.

For two days after Gonzales had come, Mr. Carter tried to sort out his papers and his bills. He even went out into the forest, a thing he did not often do, to encourage those workers who were still with him.

But then a little packet came from England, with the greatest prize he had yet seen: a double set of navy-blue eyes.

"They're from a captain in the French army. He was blown up in a battle. Look how they match—it's incredible!"

And he disappeared again into his study and wasn't seen except for meals.

Mrs. Carter had started to write to Lady Parsons in England, covering the paper with her hand when anyone came into the room. She wrote several of these letters and tore them up. But in the end she was satisfied with what she had written, and posted the letter herself in Manaus.

As for the twins, their happiness did not last long. At first they made lists of what they would buy: the dresses, the shoes, the hats, the boxes of chocolate. If Beatrice decided to order a flounced party dress in pink organdy, Gwendolyn decided to order one in blue. When Beatrice thought she would buy some proper scent, Gwendolyn said she was sick of boring lavender water and said she would have some, too.

"You don't have to copy me," said Beatrice crossly, and Gwendolyn looked at her blankly. The twins had always copied each other.

Mrs. Carter had asked them to share some of the money with their parents.

"Your father is having a hard time, girls. I think it would be kind to let the whole family join in your good fortune," she said.

But the twins absolutely refused.

"It's ours. We need it. We don't want Maia to have money and not us. We want her to go."

So now the twins became suspicious, first of their mother, then of the servants.

"They're always hanging about," they said fretfully.

This was true. Tapi and the others, remembering their

promise to Finn, took every chance they could to see that Maia was all right.

Hiding their money became the most important thing to the twins. At night, Beatrice hid her banknotes in an old doll's carriage which she kept by her bed. Gwendolyn slept with hers under her mattress.

They took the money with them to the lavatory, they brought it into the dining room when they were doing their lessons.

By now they had stopped planning how to spend the money. They just wanted to look at it and count it and gloat over it.

From being suspicious of everyone else, the twins became suspicious of each other. They suspended a piece of cotton between their beds so that one of them couldn't creep out at night without waking the other. Then Beatrice developed a septic throat and couldn't go to the dancing class, and Gwendolyn wouldn't go without her in case her sister stole the money while she was away.

But what worried Maia was not the way the twins behaved. The twins had always been odd. What worried her was the feeling that Minty was hiding something from her. That her governess had a secret.

A few days after Gonzales's visit, she knocked on Miss Minton's door and opened it, to find her kneeling on the floor putting books into her tin trunk.

She looked up quickly and shut the lid, but for the first time Maia felt she was interrupting something private.

"I'm putting some of these away. I've found some ants in the Shakespeare."

"They must be really tough ants," said Maia, "to hold out against Mrs. Carter's sprays."

"Ants *are* tough," said Miss Minton, and changed the subject.

But Maia continued to feel uneasy, for she had the feeling that what Miss Minton had been doing was *packing*.

Oh Finn, thought Maia, I know I should be glad you're free and happy, and I *am* glad. Only I really don't know what to do here anymore.

But Finn wasn't happy. Both he and the boat seemed somehow sluggish, and he couldn't quite get rid of the knot in his stomach.

He had moored by a huge dyewood tree. The water flowed quietly in a deep channel; nowhere better could be found.

So why? He'd had his supper of beans and roasted maize; the deck was piled with chopped wood; the dog had gone ashore to find his own supper and came back with a smug expression and blood on his jaws.

Everything was fine.

A group of howler monkeys came swinging through the trees, making their evening racket, half screech, half laughter, and stopped when they saw the *Arabella*.

Perhaps I should have gone to Westwood, thought Finn. "They'd have knocked all this rubbish out of me. Foreseeing disasters . . ."

What did he think could happen to Maia in the Carters' bungalow? The whole point about the Carters' bungalow was that nothing happened in it. It was the most boring house in the world—and the Indians had promised to look after her. "No harm will come to your friend," Furo had said.

So why did the unease get worse all the time?

He remembered saying good-bye to Maia. She had come out of the house in her dressing gown; she ran so lightly, but when he'd hugged her she felt wonderfully solid.

No, Maia would be all right.

"I'm not going back," said Finn aloud. And in the trees, the monkeys threw back their heads and roared.

17

ONE OF THE things Clovis had been most afraid of was being forced to ride. He had seen the horses in the stables, and they looked large and twitchy. If Sir Aubrey put him in the saddle, Clovis meant to confess straightaway and take the money Finn had given him to run away to his foster mother.

But the week after he arrived at Westwood, Sir Aubrey asked Clovis to come into the library because he had some bad news for him.

"Now I want you to be brave about this, my boy. I want you to take this like a man and a Taverner."

Clovis's heart began to thump. Could someone have died—Maia perhaps, or his foster mother—and if so, how did Sir Aubrey know? Or was it just that he had been found out?

"I won't hide from you the fact that the Basher—your aunt Joan, I mean—disagrees with me. She was all ready to teach you. She had picked out a fine mettlesome filly to start you on; nothing sluggish or second rate. A real Thoroughbred. You'd be going over jumps in a couple of weeks. But I'm afraid I cannot allow it."

"Can't allow what, sir?" asked Clovis.

"Can't allow you to ride. Can't allow you to go on a horse.

You can imagine what it cost me to come to this decision; the Taverner children have always been up in the saddle from when they were two years old. But after Dudley's terrible accident . . ." Tears came into Sir Aubrey's eyes. He turned away. "If there was anyone else to inherit Westwood, I would let you take your chance, but with Bernard and Dudley both gone . . ." He pressed Clovis's shoulder. "You're taking this very well, my boy. Very well indeed. You're taking it like a man. I confess I expected arguments, even tantrums."

"Well, it *is* a disappointment," said Clovis, wondering whether to break down and cry, a thing all actors learn to do at the drop of a hat. But in the end he just gave a brave gulp instead. "I had, of course, been looking forward. . . ." He looked out of the window to where the Basher, mounted on a bruising chestnut, was galloping across a field. "But I do understand. One must always think of Westwood."

Sir Aubrey nodded. "You're a good lad. Of course no one will ever take Dudley's place, but . . ." He took out his handkerchief and blew into it fiercely. "There's another thing. About your schooling. Bernard was very weedy about his school, but then Bernard was weedy about everything. All the same, I think you're a bit old to be sent away now. Boys usually leave home at about seven or eight, you know, and you'd feel out of it. So I'm going to engage a tutor for you. He'll come next month when you're settled in."

"Thank you, sir," said Clovis. And then: "I'm afraid I'm not very clever."

Sir Aubrey looked shocked. "Good heavens, boy, I should hope not! The Taverners have never been bookish. Except your poor father, and look what happened to him."

Clovis went downstairs and out into the garden, where the little banshees were waiting for him to play ball with them. If he didn't have to ride, maybe he could hold out another week or two before he confessed. The idea of confessing was nasty; not just because everybody would be so angry with him, but because Sir Aubrey would be disappointed. He'd obviously mellowed a lot since Bernard was a boy. Old gentlemen did that, Clovis knew, at the end of their lives.

It was while they were having lunch that Clovis decided he would find a way of visiting his foster mother in the next few days. She would know what to do for the best. And he wanted to make sure that she was still there, in her cottage on the village green, before he gave himself up.

The butler took away Clovis's pudding plate and filled it up with a second helping of apple crumble. The way the young master enjoyed his food gave great pleasure belowstairs. It was a pity that the cook was engaged to be married and would soon be leaving.

Mrs. Bates, Clovis's foster mother, lived in the end cottage of a row of small farm cottages on Stanton Green. Her husband had died even before she took in Clovis, but she was thrifty and hardworking, and though she had to go out to work in some of the big houses in the neighborhood, she kept her house and her garden spotless.

Clovis had come by bus. Sir Aubrey had given him a ten-shilling note for pocket money, so there was no need for him to use the money Finn had given him.

As he crossed the green, it seemed to Clovis that nothing

had changed. The well was still there in the center of the common, and the old oak tree, and some boys were kicking a football on the grass. He had been gone four years; they were too young to remember him.

But when he knocked on the door of the cottage and opened it, Mrs. Bates went red and then white and hugged him while the tears ran from her eyes.

"Jimmy," she kept saying. "Well, well, you're back, Jimmy! And how you've grown. And my, don't you look well, and so smart! So those Goodleys did right by you after all!"

"Well, not exactly. The company folded up, so I came back."

"Aye, and don't you speak nicely. Oh, I can't believe it! I was thinking as how I wouldn't ever see you again. Sit down, boy. There's some scones in the oven. They'll be done in a jiffy. And there's some buttermilk fresh from the cow."

While she spoke, he looked round the room. He'd been Jimmy Bates, and then Clovis King, and now was Finn Taverner—but here nothing had changed. The cross-stitch sampler was still above the mantelpiece, the brass kettle was on the hob, there was a pink geranium on the windowsill. But everything looked smaller, and . . . poorer, somehow. Had things been hard for his foster mother? Her apron was neatly darned, but there seemed to be more darns than cloth. And had the rug always been so threadbare? "Have you been all right, Mother?" he asked her.

"Oh aye, times aren't easy, but I do some cooking for people in the village and I manage, with the garden and all. Oh yes, I manage fine."

She went to the oven and took out the scones.

"Well, now," she said, putting out the butter and the home-made strawberry jam. "You start talking, boy. You start right from when those Goodleys took you away. I want to know everything."

So Clovis began. He told her about the years of traveling, the discomfort, the low pay—but also some good times at the beginning when the Goodleys had made a pet of him, and he'd enjoyed acting. "I sent you some postcards, but they'd never remember to let me have stamps."

"I just got the one," said Mrs. Bates. "Oh, I did miss you, Jimmy boy."

"And I missed you," said Clovis, biting into a scone. The scones at Westwood were very good, but these were better.

And then he told her about his last voyage out to the Amazon, about meeting Maia and Miss Minton, and about the disaster of the *Lord Fauntleroy* matinee.

To Mrs. Bates it was like a fairy story. "Go on. Go on," she kept saying.

So Clovis went on to what had happened with Finn at the lagoon, and the plan they had worked out to set Finn free and get Clovis back to England.

But now poor Mrs. Bates began to be very muddled and very upset.

"You mean you're pretending to be someone else?"

"Well, that's what actors do," said Clovis.

"Yes, but everyone knows it's only pretense." She shook her head. "You mean at Westwood they think you're the heir? And they're still thinking it?"

"Yes. But I know I'll have to confess."

"Of course you will, Jimmy. You couldn't live a lie. That grand place—I've heard it's splendid. You must tell them straightaway. And of course you can come here. Times is hard, but we'll manage."

"Thank you," said Clovis.

He looked round the cottage again. Funny how small it was. He'd wanted so much to be back here when he was with the Goodleys, but now . . .

But he knew his foster mother was right. He would confess. He'd do it the very next day.

But finding a time to do it was not easy. The next day Sir Aubrey was shut up with his bailiff, and the day after that he was driven into York for a checkup with his doctor.

But on the third day after Clovis had seen his foster mother, Sir Aubrey suggested a little walk round the park. He took his stick and a pair of binoculars and put on his deerstalker hat, and they set off.

"Time you got to know the estate," he told Clovis.

But before they crossed the courtyard, Sir Aubrey stopped by the statue with the severed head. He touched the neck stump with his stick, then ran it over the battered forehead and nose of the head lying on the ground.

"Something I wanted to ask you, my boy," he said. "About this statue. Could you leave the head the way it is after I go? Because of Dudley. Something to remember him by?" He sniffed and blew his nose.

"After you go, sir?"

"After I pop my clogs. Turn up my toes. Die, you know, what. When everything in the place is yours."

Clovis took a deep breath. Now was the time. He couldn't go on with this lie.

"Actually, sir," he began, "I've got something to tell you." He flushed, but went on resolutely. "You see—"

A thunderous, braying voice interrupted him. The Basher, mounted on an enormous black horse, came galloping across the Home Paddock toward them. Behind her, looking cold and worried, came the three banshees on their ponies.

"Came to ask the boy to tea," brayed the Basher. "The girls want him to play charades."

So that was the end of the first confession.

The next time he was alone with Sir Aubrey was after dinner, when they were served coffee in the drawing room.

The fire was drawing nicely; Sir Aubrey looked sleepy and amiable. Perhaps he wouldn't be *too* angry?

"Sir Aubrey, I've got something to tell you."

"Grandfather. Told you to call me Grandfather, boy."

"You see there's been a mistake—a muddle. The crows—I mean Mr. Trapwood and Mr. Low—thought I was someone else and—"

He began quickly to tell his story, looking down at the fireside rug. When he had finished he lifted his head, waiting for the explosion.

Sir Aubrey lay stretched out in the chair; his arm hung limply by his side and from his chest there came a deep and rumbling snore.

He hadn't heard a word that Clovis had said.

Clovis almost gave up after that. Only the thought of what his foster mother would say if he did not tell the truth kept him going. And at the beginning of his third week at Westwood, he managed it.

He was with Sir Aubrey in the picture gallery. The old man often took him there, and in particular he liked to stand Clovis next to the portrait of Admiral Sir Alwin Taverner in his cocked hat and point out to Clovis how alike they were.

"Look at the nose, boy—the way it turns up, just like yours." Or: "See the cleft in the chin—exactly the same."

This time Clovis felt he couldn't stand this, and before Sir Aubrey could take him to see a picture of what was supposed to be another of his great-great-uncles, he took a deep breath and began.

"Sir Aubrey, I have to tell you—"

"Grandfather," interrupted the old man. "I've told you to call me Grandfather."

Clovis was getting desperate. "Yes, but you see you're not really my grandfather. There's been a mistake. I'm really—" And this time, very quickly, he managed to tell his story.

Clovis had often imagined what would happen after he owned up and told the truth. He had imagined Sir Aubrey ragingly angry or icily cold or even *hurt*.

But never in his worst nightmares had he imagined anything as terrible as what happened next.

18

THE TWINS STILL hadn't decided how to spend the money, and they still wouldn't take it to the bank. They had sewn two calico pouches to keep it in, which they wore round their necks even when doing their lessons. The pouches came down quite low over their stomachs, and every so often they patted them to make sure the money was still there.

"Like kangaroos with indigestion," said Maia.

But what upset Maia was the way Miss Minton was behaving. She had taken to going off on her own, and when Maia asked her where she was going, she gave answers that weren't answers at all.

And *had* she been packing her trunk?

The twins, of course, missed no chance to taunt Maia.

"Your precious Minty's got a secret, and we know what it is," jeered Beatrice.

"But we aren't going to tell you," said Gwendolyn.

"Only you needn't think she's going to stay with you."

Even so, it wasn't till Minty lost her temper with the twins that Maia realized that something was seriously wrong.

They were doing an English exercise in Dr. Bullman's book.

"Beatrice, can you give me an example of alliteration?" asked Miss Minton.

"No, I can't," said Beatrice.

"What about you, Gwendolyn?"

Gwendolyn shook her head. "I can't either."

Miss Minton's corset was troubling her, but she kept her patience.

"Read what Dr. Bullman says again, Beatrice. At the top of the page."

"'All . . . it . . . eration is the use of words beginning with the same letter, or contain . . . ing the same letter. . . .'" She stopped and patted her pouch. "I don't know what that means."

Miss Minton, who had explained twice, explained again. "Suppose you say 'In a summer season when soft was the sun—'"

It was at that moment that Mrs. Carter entered the dining room.

"Well, Miss Minton," she said. "How are the girls getting on? It's nearly time to send a report to Dr. Bullman. I hope you have it ready."

Miss Minton looked at Beatrice, who was yawning, and at Gwendolyn, who was scratching her ear.

"No, Mrs. Carter," she said. "I do not have it ready. What's more, I am not prepared to send a report unless the twins start to work properly. Ever since the reward came they have been impossible to teach. I think you had better write the report yourself."

And while Mrs. Carter gobbled with anger, Miss Minton got up from her chair.

"There will be no more lessons today, girls," she said, and swept out of the room as though she was a person with rights and not a governess.

Maia had been in the dining room, fetching more paper, and heard everything. She could not help being pleased, but she was scared, too. What if Mrs. Carter sent Minty away?

The next day was Miss Minton's afternoon off. Mrs. Carter tried to stop her going, but Miss Minton said she had business to attend to in Manaus.

"You'd better be careful, Miss Minton. I have dismissed governesses for less impertinence than you have shown in the last few days."

"I did not mean to be impertinent," said Miss Minton, but at lunchtime she was seen getting on the rubber boat, bound for town.

"Is everything all right, Minty?" Maia asked before she left.

"Everything is fine," said Miss Minton. "Or rather it will be. Keep out of the way of the twins till I get back."

But she had explained nothing.

Supper was never a cheerful meal in the House of Rest, but that day it was like eating in a graveyard. Then, halfway through the meal, Tapi came in with a letter brought by a special messenger who had vanished back into the dark.

"Gonzales!" said Mr. Carter in a low voice, and took it into the study.

The letter was as bad as Carter had feared. Settlement day was tomorrow; he would meet Carter in his office by the docks. If Carter couldn't pay, Gonzales was going to send in the bailiffs.

"Bailiffs!" cried Mrs. Carter, when her husband at last told her the truth of what was happening. "Those dreadful people who take everything away! But they can't!"

"Unfortunately, they can," said Carter. "Don't you remember in Littleford . . ."

Mrs. Carter began to sob. "Oh, not again! Not again! The disgrace . . ." She gave a sudden shriek. "Lady Parsons's portrait—they mustn't have that. I'll hide it first thing in the morning," she said wildly.

Mr. Carter gave her a look. "That's not worth much, but my collection . . ."

The twins, hearing raised voices, came down the corridor. "What's the matter? What's happened?" they wanted to know.

"Nothing, girls, nothing. It's bedtime." Mrs. Carter looked at the pouches round their necks. Tomorrow she would *force* the girls to take the money to the bank. And once the reward was safely deposited, the bank manager would help her work on the twins; it was ridiculous that they should keep it all when the family was in such trouble. "And don't sleep in those things," she went on. "They could strangle you."

Maia had gone to her room. She went to light her oil lamp but found that it was gone and only a single candle in an old brass candlestick stood by her bed. She went down to the twins' room and, as she had expected, found that they had "borrowed" her lamp.

"It's just for tonight," said Beatrice. "We need one each for what we've got to do. Anyway, everything in this house belongs to us really."

Maia was already in bed, trying to read by the light of the single candle, when there was a knock on the door and Tapi came in. She was dressed in her best clothes, but she looked worried.

"We go to a wedding. A big wedding with dancing and eating. We must go because is Furo's brother and he angry if we not there."

"It sounds fun, Tapi. I hope you enjoy it."

"Yes. We all go—my sister, Conchita, Manoel, old Lila, too. She not want to go but she must."

Tapi sighed. There had been a furious row earlier when Lila said she could not go—none of them could go because they had promised to look after Maia—and Furo had said if they did not go, his brother would start a feud which could last for years.

In the end Lila had given in and now they were all setting off in the canoe for the long journey upriver to the village so as to be in time for the celebrations, which began at dawn.

"But you be very careful, yes? And Miss Minton she back soon. Here . . . is for you."

And Tapi took a bunch of bananas and a mango from the basket and laid them on Maia's bed.

It was strange with the Indians gone. No sound came from the huts; they had even taken the little dog.

Maia looked at the clock. The last boat should be in soon. She would stay awake and say good night to Miss Minton.

But she must have dozed off. When she looked again it was nearly ten o'clock. She hadn't heard anyone come in, but Minty could move very quietly when she chose.

Maia got out of bed. The house was silent and dark. She took her candle and knocked on Miss Minton's door.

No reply. She knocked again. Then she pushed open the door and went in.

The room was empty. Miss Minton's bed had not been slept in. But there was something else—something that frightened Maia badly.

Miss Minton's trunk was gone.

Back in her room, Maia told herself not to be silly—but the fear would not go away. Miss Minton's trunk was like . . . well, it was part of her. Hardly a day passed when she did not pick a book out and read Maia a passage or show her a picture. If the trunk was gone, then surely it meant that the twins were right and Minty had left her?

The more she thought about it, the more likely it seemed. Miss Minton being angry with the twins, standing up to Mrs. Carter, going off when she was told not to.

Minty no longer cared what the Carters thought of her because she was going away.

Not since the news of her parents' death had Maia felt so wretched and alone. She tried to tell herself that Minty would not leave her, but lying there in the darkness, she failed. After all, Finn had left her—people did go away. Her parents had done it, too. They had gone to Egypt and left her at school.

And now Minty. . . .

After another hour of tossing and turning, Maia went to the washstand and took two aspirins. Then she took a third for good measure, and at last she slept.

And she slept deeply. . . .

An hour later Beatrice woke and felt under her pillow for the pouch with the money in it, then remembered that she had hidden it under her clock, temporarily.

When she had borrowed Maia's lamp, it was with the plan of finding an even safer place for the money somewhere in the house while everyone else was asleep. But now she had a brilliant idea. She put a match to the lamp, which flared up, leaving a stench of paraffin.

"Wake up, Gwendolyn," she said, shaking her sister by the shoulder. "Listen, I've thought of a way of getting rid of Maia."

Gwendolyn, half asleep still, said: "What?"

"We'll hide our money in Maia's cupboard in the dining room—the one where she keeps her books. We'll hide it in the one she's always reading—the one with the picture of a sloth. Then, in the morning, we'll scream and say our money's been stolen and make everybody search . . . and it'll be found with Maia's things. Mummy will have to send her away, then."

Gwendolyn wasn't sure. "Suppose Maia gets up before us and finds it. She might steal it."

"She won't wake before us; I'll set the alarm. You'll see, it'll work."

"Why don't you just hide *your* money in Maia's books."

"Don't be so feeble. It's got to be both of us. Come on."

So Gwendolyn lit her lamp and the girls blundered about, trying to remember where Gwendolyn had put her pouch the night before and bumping into things.

"I put it in my underclothes drawer," said Gwendolyn. "I know I did, but it isn't there."

"No, you didn't—you put it in your shoe bag."

"No, I did *not*—"

But now, in her room down the corridor, Mrs. Carter woke up. She could hear the girls. What on earth were they up to? She put on her slippers and made her way to her daughters' room. On the way she saw two large, brown beetles which narrowly missed her foot.

"Cockroaches," shrieked Mrs. Carter, and ran to her "larder" to take down the can of Cockroach Killer.

She sluiced it over the tiles where she had seen the beetles and hurried on to the twins' room, the can dribbling in her hand.

"What on earth is it? What's the matter?"

Now it was Beatrice who couldn't find her money. "I put it under the clock and it's gone. Gwendolyn has stolen it."

"No I haven't, you lying little grub. You put it in your sewing basket."

"Mind the lamp!" shouted Mrs. Carter as the girls began to fight. She grabbed for the lamp by Beatrice's bed, and as she did so, the top came off the can of Cockroach Killer and a sticky stream of black liquid poured out over the burning wick.

There was a loud whooshing noise and a tongue of flame shot up. Mrs. Carter tried to put out the lamp and knocked it over. It was already too hot to touch. A curl of flame licked the sheets on Beatrice's bed. The stream of Cockroach Killer was like a channel of fire which moved to the second bed.

Beatrice screamed as her nightdress caught at the hem, and Mrs. Carter tried to beat out the flames with a pillow.

"Out, girls . . . out. Not the window, the door. Hurry, hurry."

But they could hardly see now for smoke. The second lamp, in the path of the fire, had exploded. And now the curtains were alight!

"What's happened? What's the matter?"

Mr. Carter had come running down the corridor, coughing. Now he opened the door, and the draft sent the flames up to ceiling height.

"Push them out at the front," he yelled. "I'll go back for Maia."

He turned and stumbled back down the smoke-filled corridor. But he did not go to Maia's room. He did not even try to. Instead, he groped his way into his study and began to tear open his cabinets.

"My collection," he muttered. "My collection . . ."

And his hand fastened on the velvet box of eyes just as he slid to the ground, overcome by the smoke and flames now rolling and licking through the bungalow.

19

MISS MINTON WOKE in a four-poster bed and found herself staring at a picture of a Russian nobleman on a sleigh being chased by wolves.

She was lying in a spare bedroom in the Keminskys' house. Her head ached, for she was not used to wine, and a lot of it had been drunk the night before at Mademoiselle Lille's farewell party. The Keminskys' governess was returning to France on the following day, and Miss Minton had agreed to come and work for the Russian family and teach Olga and Maia.

In spite of her aching head, Miss Minton was content. Maia would be happy here in this easygoing and friendly house, away from the ill temper of the twins and their parents' strangeness. She had said nothing to Maia till Mr. Murray had given his permission, but yesterday his cable had come. He had not only agreed to let Maia go to live with the Keminskys, he had arranged to send Maia's allowance direct to Miss Minton at a different bank. It seemed that the British consul had already warned the old lawyer that the Carters were in trouble.

Miss Minton got up and dressed. Downstairs in the breakfast room, the countess was sitting over a big samovar, pouring out glasses of steaming Russian tea. Olga was beside her and got up to curtsy, but Mademoiselle Lille was still in her room.

"She is having breakfast in bed—she is a little . . . tired after last night," explained the countess.

Miss Minton smiled. Mademoiselle Lille was probably *very* tired: she had been so sad about leaving the Keminskys that she had comforted herself with an amazing amount of wine.

Nothing less like breakfast at the Carters could be imagined. The light, luxurious house, the friendly servants, the Keminskys themselves. Sergei had already left; he now went to the cadet school in Manaus. To teach only Maia and Olga would be a delight.

"But I must hurry back," said Miss Minton now. "I don't like to leave Maia too long with the twins. Professor Glastonberry has kindly agreed to store my trunk, so Maia and I will be able to come down on the rubber boat next week."

"No, no—my husband will send a boat for you," said the countess.

Miss Minton had not planned to spend the night at the Keminskys. Mademoiselle Lille had begged her to stay for her farewell party, but Miss Minton had stood firm until the count had pointed out that if she stayed, she could sign her contract with his lawyer the following morning, naming her as their new governess.

Knowing how little the Carters were to be trusted to pass on messages, Miss Minton had sent the note for Maia to Furo, and one of the count's servants was ordered to take it to his hut.

Good news, Miss Minton had written. *I'll tell you everything in the morning. I'm staying overnight at the Keminskys' because I have some business to see to in the morning. Tell the Carters I'll be back at midday, but tell them nothing else!*

Furo would make certain that Maia got the note. She had seen how the Indians guarded Maia since Finn went away.

She was rolling up her napkin when there was a commotion at the door, and the count, who had been supervising the loading of one of his ships, came quickly into the room, followed by Professor Glastonberry, already badly out of breath.

The count went straight to his wife and spoke hurriedly in Russian, but Miss Minton had caught the word "Carter" and risen to her feet.

"Oh, my dear." The countess turned to her. "It's bad news, I'm afraid. There has been a fire in the Carters' bungalow. The house is destroyed, but everyone has been rescued, I understand. They have been taken to the Municipal Hospital."

Miss Minton was already by the door. Every trace of color had vanished from her face.

"The count's carriage is waiting to take us to the hospital," said the professor.

Miss Minton turned to the count.

"Thank you," she managed to say, before she followed the professor out into the street.

The twins were crying. Their beds in Ward C of the hospital were close together because the ward was very full, and they lay on their sides facing each other, and gulped.

"It's gone. It's just gone!"

"All of it's gone. There's nothing left, not a single *milreis*."

The nurses had at first been very kind. Neither of the girls was badly hurt. Beatrice's hair was singed, and she had a small burn on her leg. Gwendolyn had fallen on the gravel path as she ran out of the house and had sprained her ankle. But there was always shock and smoke inhalation to consider, and for a while a nurse sat by their beds and tried to comfort them.

"Your mother's safe; she's going to be all right. She's in the next ward. You can go and see her."

But the twins were not crying for their mother.

"It's our money," sobbed Beatrice.

"The money for the reward. Twenty thousand *milreis* each—and it's all burnt!"

"Perhaps you will get it again, from the insurance?"

But the Carters, of course, were not insured, and the twins went on sniveling till the nurse became impatient and walked away.

Mrs. Carter was in the next ward. Her arm was bandaged and she had inhaled a lot of smoke. Even so, she found time to complain about the way the hospital was run, the lack of hygiene, and the patients whose young children were allowed to visit them and ran all over the ward.

"And there's a fly on my water jug," she said fretfully. "Two, in fact."

She was still complaining when a smartly dressed Englishman came to her bedside. He was the British consul's assistant.

"Mrs. Carter, the consul has asked me how we can help you return to England. There seems to be little future for you here."

"You mean you'd pay our fares?"

"For you and your daughters, yes. Do you have anyone you could go to in England? Relatives or friends?"

Mrs. Carter frowned. She did not actually seem to have any

friends. Then her face cleared. "Lady Parsons, in Littleford. She would take us in, I'm sure. She is my mother's cousin . . . well, almost. Her address is Grey Gables, The Promenade, Littleford-on-Sea."

The young man wrote this down. Then he said, not meeting her eye, "Your husband won't be returning to England, just yet, I'm afraid." And as gently as he could, he told her that when he came out of the hospital, Mr. Carter faced a trial and possible imprisonment for fraud and embezzlement. Just as he had cheated the bank in England, so had he done out here. It wasn't only Gonzales to whom Mr. Carter owed more money than he could ever hope to repay.

Miss Minton ran up the hospital steps, and the professor, mopping his brow, ran behind her.

"The Carter family," she said at the desk. "The girls from the fire. Where are they?"

"Ward C," said the receptionist, and they hurried up two flights of stairs.

The twins were still whimpering, but they stopped to stare at Miss Minton.

"You're not badly hurt, I understand," she said. "I hope you're not in pain."

"Our money's gone." Beatrice sniffed.

"Yes. But you might have lost your lives." And then: "Where's Maia?"

The twins shrugged. "Daddy went back to find her. We don't know where she is. She didn't come in with us."

Miss Minton's heart began to pound. The professor put a hand under her arm. "I'll go and ask the sister."

He made his way down the corridor and came back with a set face.

"She said there were only the two girls and their parents in the ambulance. She didn't know there was another girl."

Miss Minton took a deep breath, trying to steady herself.

"But Mr. Carter went back for her, the twins say. She *must* be here."

The sister had come out of her office to join them. Now they all hurried to the men's ward.

Mr. Carter's burns were serious. His hair and eyebrows were singed, his face was swollen, both arms were bandaged. He lay still with his eyes closed. But Minty had no thought to spare for him.

"Mr. Carter, where is Maia? Your daughters say you went back for her. Did you bring her out safely?"

"I . . . tried . . ." lied Mr. Carter. "I went right to her door, but it was impossible. An inferno . . ."

Miss Minton swayed. "I am not the kind of person who faints," she said as the sister moved toward her.

But there she was wrong.

20

FOR A FEW hours the bungalow had been beautiful. Orange and crimson and violet flames lit up the night sky; showers of golden sparks flew upward as the fire danced and played on the dying house.

Then it was over, and there was nothing left—only gray ash and those strange objects which survive disaster. The nozzle of a flit gun, a splintered washbasin . . . and in what had been Mr. Carter's study, a single eye, cracked by the heat, staring creepily at the heavens.

So when Finn sailed back down the Negro at dawn, he saw no flames and heard no roaring as the house was destroyed. Everything at first seemed to be as it had always been: the big trees by the river, the huts of the Indians, the Carters' launch riding at anchor.

Then the dog, standing beside him, threw back his head and howled.

"What is it?" asked Finn.

But now he, too, smelled the choking, lingering smoke.

And as he sailed toward the landing stage, he saw it—the

space, the nothingness where the Carters' house should have been. Not even an empty shell. Nothing.

He had thought that the news of his father's death was the worst thing that had happened to him, but this was worse, because he was to blame. If he had taken Maia as she had begged . . .

He was shivering so much that it was difficult to steer the *Arabella* to the jetty and make her fast. There was no point in searching the ruins; it was so obvious that no one could survive such a blaze.

But there was one last hope. The huts of the Indians had been spared. Perhaps they had gotten Maia out; perhaps he would find her sleeping there.

He pushed open the door of the first hut and went inside . . . then the second and the third. They were completely empty. Even the parrot on his perch had gone, even the little dog. A broken rope in the run outside showed where the pig, terrified by the flames, had rushed back into the forest.

There was no doubt now in Finn's mind. They had let Maia burn and fled in terror and shame.

What would it be like, Finn wondered, going on living and knowing that he had killed his friend?

The howler monkeys had been right to laugh when he said he wasn't going back. He had turned downriver again almost at once to fetch Maia, and he had made good time, traveling with the current—but he had come too late.

Finn went outside again and stood on the square of raked gravel that had been the Carters' garden.

His mind seemed to have stopped working. He had no idea

what to do. Should he go in to Manaus and see if he could find anything out—from the hospital perhaps?

After a while he found himself walking back along the river path to where he had left the *Arabella*. As he came to the fork in the path which led back into the forest, the dog put his head down excitedly into a patch of leaf mold. Finn pushed him aside and saw a smear of blood . . . and then a little way off, another . . . and another.

He almost fell over her, she lay so still, hidden in the leaves and creepers, almost as if she had burrowed into the forest to die.

But she was not dead. She lay stunned, still in her night-dress, breathing lightly with closed eyes. The blood came from a gash in her leg. He could see no burns on her skin. She must have fainted from loss of blood.

Then, when he said her name, she opened her eyes. One hand went out to his sleeve.

"Can we go now?" she whispered.

And he answered. "Yes."

Maia opened her eyes and saw a canopy of trees and, shining through the topmost leaves, a high, white sun.

She could smell the rich, heady smell of orchids and hear a bird whose single piercing cry came clearly over the puttering sound of an engine.

Then the overhanging trees disappeared. She was looking up at a pale, clear sky, and the light was suddenly so dazzling that she closed her eyes for a moment, because she did not want to wake up or to stop. She wanted what was happening to her to go on and on and on.

She was lying on a groundsheet on the bottom of a boat. They were moving steadily through the water, not fast, not slowly; the perfect speed to lull her back to sleep. She was covered by a gray blanket. She pushed it off and saw that her leg was bandaged. It throbbed but not unpleasantly . . . it seemed to belong to someone else.

She closed her eyes and slept again.

When she woke once more, it was to find that something was resting against her side, snoring gently: a dog the color of dark sand . . .

So then she turned her head and saw behind her Finn, sitting quietly in the stern, with his hand on the tiller—and knew she was on the *Arabella* and safe.

It was the Indian side of Finn that had taken over when he found her in the wood. That managed to carry her to the landing stage and lay her down in the *Arabella*. That bandaged her leg and made her swallow one of his bark potions, and then cast off, telling her to sleep and sleep and sleep . . . Sometimes the European side of him protested and told him that he ought to take her to the hospital for proper treatment.

But he took no notice; he knew now what was best for Maia, and he was right—for now, as she woke beside the dog, she was herself again. The fear and exhaustion had gone from her face.

"I'm hungry," she said, and smiled at him.

She had escaped through her high window; the gash on her leg was made by the broken glass as she scrambled through. The doors were already smoldering when she woke.

"I don't remember much after that. It was the smoke, I think. I know there wasn't anyone in the huts."

"Why not?" said Finn fiercely. "They promised they'd look after you."

"There was a wedding—an important one. They all went. And Minty, she went somewhere, too," said Maia. "She's left me."

"No."

"What do you mean, no? She wasn't there—she didn't come back from her day off."

"Maybe. But she won't have left you. That isn't what will have happened. What about the others?"

"They escaped. I saw the river ambulance take them away, but I hid. I couldn't bear to be with them anymore. They were all quarreling and screaming. So I hid in the trees. I didn't notice my leg at first, but then . . ." She shook her head. "But it doesn't matter, Finn, none of it matters, because you came back."

They set a course back up the Negro, then turned into a smaller river, the Agarapi, which flowed northwest to the lands where the Xanti had last been seen.

It was a beautiful river. They traveled between small islands where clumps of white egrets roosted, or clouds of tiny pearl-gray bats flew up from fallen logs. What amazed Maia was how varied the landscape was. Sometimes they sailed through dark, silent jungle where all the animals were out of sight in the topmost branches. Sometimes the river wound through gentle countryside, almost like England, where swamp deer grazed in grassy clearings. Once they passed into a patch of scrubland and saw a range of bare, brown hills in the distance before they plunged into the rain forest again.

"If this is the 'Green Hell' of the Amazon, then hell is where I belong," said Maia.

She was completely happy. When she took the bandage off her leg she found a mulch of some strange green mold, which Finn had put there, and beneath it, a wound which was almost healed.

"You really ought to be a doctor," she said. "Or a witch doctor perhaps?"

"It's often the same thing."

She had cut the bottom off a pair of Finn's trousers and borrowed one of his shirts—and Finn had pilfered a roll of cotton, meant for the Indians, from which she'd made a kind of sarong for when she was in the water. The nightdress she had escaped in had been torn up for cleaning rags.

Everything she owned had been destroyed in the fire, and she missed nothing except her toothbrush. Scrubbing one's teeth with twigs was not the same.

She trusted Finn completely. If he said a pool was safe to swim in, she dived in without a second thought, and the dreaded piranha fish did not tear at her flesh, nor did a caiman come at her with snapping jaws. If he told her a mushroom was safe to eat, she ate it.

"My father had this thing he used to say to me," she told Finn. "It was in Latin. *Carpe diem.* 'Seize the day.' Get the best out of it, take hold of it and live in it as hard as you can." She pushed back her hair. "After he died, and my mother, I couldn't do it too well. There never seemed to be a day I wanted to seize all that much. But here . . ."

"Yes, some places are right for you. Your mother was a singer, wasn't she?"

"Yes. But she never made a fuss about it. I never remember her saving her voice for the performance or gargling with eggs and all that stuff. She'd just sing—in the house, in the garden, anywhere."

"Everyone says you ought to get your voice trained," he said, and frowned because if she had a future as a singer, perhaps she shouldn't be taking off into the unknown.

She shook her head. "I'm all right like this."

"But won't you miss music?"

"There's always music. You just have to open your mouth."

They'd stopped to make a fire in a little bay and cook the fish they'd caught earlier.

"You had good parents," said Finn.

"So did you." She steadied the pan on the flames and poured in the oil. "Do you think there'll be someone in the Xanti who'll remember your mother?"

Finn blew on the embers. "I don't know. We may not find the Xanti," he warned her.

Maia shrugged. "It doesn't matter. But if we do, will they accept me? I don't have any Indian blood."

"If they don't, we won't stay. I wouldn't let anything happen to you. I've got my gun."

"I'm not scared," said Maia. And she wasn't. She'd been scared of the nastiness of the twins and of being shut up in the Carters' bungalow, but she wasn't scared of traveling through unknown lands with a boy hardly older than she was herself. She thought perhaps she wouldn't be scared of anything ever again if she was with Finn.

They did not hurry. Their route led to the west, and the forests of Japura, and each night Finn laid out such maps as he had, and the notes his father had given him. One thing stood out. In a fork of the river was a small island with a jacaranda tree standing between two tall kumu palms. If they found this marker they were in Xanti country—but how far or how near it was they did not know.

All the same, they stopped again and again. Finn wanted to collect the plants he knew he could sell, and he was teaching Maia. He climbed to the top of the leaf canopy and came back with clusters of yellow fruits which could be boiled up to treat skin diseases. He found a tree whose leaves were made into an infusion to help people with kidney complaints and brought back a silvery fern to rub on aching muscles. Most of these plants had Indian names, but as they sorted their specimens and put them to be dried and stored in labeled cotton bags, Maia learned quickly.

"You'd be amazed how much money people give for these in the towns," said Finn.

But not everything he collected was for sale. He restocked his own medicine chest also. And every day he bullied Maia about taking her quinine pills.

"Only idiots get malaria in the dry season," he said.

"I think I ought to cut my hair off," said Maia, one morning, as she tore yet another tooth out of Finn's comb.

"No. That's a bad idea."

Maia looked up, surprised. "But you wanted Clovis to cut his hair."

"That was different."

They talked of Clovis often, and it was Finn, now, who wondered if they had been fair to him. "He's either shut up in that awful place or he's confessed and been thrown out."

"Well, at least he's in England, and that's what he wanted."

But she could see that to Finn, who was afraid of nothing else, Westwood was still a dread.

"And if he's been thrown out, it will all start again, I suppose," he said. "More crows. More hiding."

"Well, they won't find us here," said Maia.

They were anchored between two islands in a kind of cave made by the overhanging branches of a pono tree. A pair of otters had been diving round the boat; the frogs started up their evening croaking.

It had been a magical day; they had seen a family of terrapins sunning themselves, and a pair of harpy eagles. There'd been a gentle following breeze to help them, and the rain that sometimes came down even in the dry season had held off.

"You know you said you used to wake up every morning in the lagoon when your father was alive and think, 'Here I am, where I want to be.' Well, that's how I feel when I wake up on the *Arabella.*"

Maia did not care whether they found the Xanti or not. It was not about arriving for her, it was about the journey. Even the sadness about Minty deserting her had gone.

For Finn, who had almost kidnapped her, there were moments of anxiety. He should have told someone that Maia was safe, instead of taking her away without a word, but gradually he stopped worrying and gave himself up to the journey.

And if Maia knew deep down that she would not be allowed to sail away forever up the rivers of the Amazon, she managed to forget it. She sang as she worked and when Finn whistled "Blow the Wind Southerly," she smiled, because she had been wrong to be cross with the wind. The wind had brought him back, and she was content.

And when Finn complained at the end of a day that they had not come very far, she said, "What does it matter? We've got all the time in the world."

Which is not always a clever thing to say.

21

MISS MINTON WAS staying at the Keminskys'. She had lost everything in the fire except her trunks of books, but with her butterfly money she bought the few things she needed. Because the Keminskys had been kind to her, she was determined to do her duty, so each morning she taught Olga and helped the countess with her letters.

The rest of the day she searched for Maia.

It was now a week since Maia had vanished. Miss Minton had always been thin, but now she looked like a walking skeleton. When she passed through the streets, people turned to look at her anguished face.

The Carters' servants—Tapi, Furo, and the others—had not returned. When they had news of the fire, old Lila had fallen ill with a raging fever, certain that they had killed Maia by leaving her, and they had gone farther into the forest to search for a medicine man who could cure her.

But Miss Minton went to talk to the Indians living along the riverbank and by the docks; she searched the ruins of the bungalow again and again. She questioned the river patrols, and the people who came in on the ships, in case Maia had lost her memory and wandered off.

Many people helped her. The Keminskys—Sergei in partic-ular—the chief of police, the Haltmanns, Madame Duchamp from the dancing class, and the children who studied with her. In the short time she had been in the Amazon, Maia had made many friends.

But the person who stopped Minty from losing her reason was Professor Glastonberry. Every morning he left the museum in charge of his assistant and searched for clues.

The professor alone was certain that Maia was not dead.

"There are almost always . . . remains," he said, "when some-one burns to death."

"You mean . . . bones . . . or . . . teeth?" asked Miss Minton.

"That's what I mean," said the professor firmly.

He worked with the chief of police and the count. He spent hours at the docks, and at least twice a day he came back to see that Miss Minton had eaten something, or even slept.

But when a week had passed, Miss Minton gave up hope. She had as good as killed Maia by deserting her. Now she must cable Mr. Murray and tell him that Maia was dead.

She had put on her hat to go to the post office when the Keminskys' maid showed in the professor.

As soon as she saw his face, Miss Minton reached for a chair.

"Is there—" she began.

"Yes, there is news. A man in a trading canoe on the Agarapi saw the *Arabella*. And he was certain that two children were aboard."

Miss Minton looked round the Keminskys' drawing room

as though she would find there the powerful boat she needed, ready and waiting.

"I must go at once, she said.

"*We* must go at once," said the professor.

The countess begged her to wait for her husband's return. "He could find you a good boat and a crew."

But waiting was something that Miss Minton could not do.

"I'm going to buy some supplies and a few things Maia might need," she said to the professor. "I'll meet you at the docks in an hour."

But when they reached the harbor there was no boat to hire and no one to help them. It was midday; everyone had gone home for lunch, and for the afternoon sleep which followed it.

"Well, we shall have to steal one," said Miss Minton.

Then they saw a boat they knew. The Carters' launch, the spinach-colored boat without a name. Gonzales had brought it down after the fire to sell and help clear Mr. Carter's debts.

"No one will miss it for a few days," said Miss Minton. "And if they do, it doesn't matter." She looked at the professor. "Can you manage her?"

"I expect so," said Professor Glastonberry. He sighed, but he didn't try to stop her. It would have been like trying to stop an avalanche. "There seems to be enough wood stacked up for now."

Miss Minton had already picked up her skirts and jumped aboard. Now she took up the boat hook and waited while the professor fed the furnace with wood and the engine spluttered slowly to life.

"If we find Maia," said Miss Minton as they set off, "I swear I'll give this boat a proper name."

. . .

The journey they took up the Negro and into the Agarapi River was very different from the dreamy voyage Finn and Maia had made the week before.

"Faster—can't we go faster?" Miss Minton kept saying.

When their supply of wood ran low, she jumped ashore, grasping the machete which Furo had left with the other tools, and slashed her way through the undergrowth as though she had been born with a knife in her hand.

Everything she had forbidden her pupils to do, she did herself—thinking gloomy thoughts, going off into black daydreams. One minute she thought that Maia had died in the fire, and the child seen on the *Arabella* was an Indian girl to whom Finn had given a ride. The next minute she thought that it had been Maia, but that she had now drowned, or had reached the Xanti, who had killed her.

"You couldn't blame them if they'd turned savage," she said, "the way some of the tribes have been treated."

"Yara was a very gentle soul," said the professor. "Finn's mother."

"That was *then*," said Miss Minton.

The professor left her alone and gave his mind to the boat. The launch was larger and faster than the *Arabella,* but this only meant that she needed more wood. He had taken off his shirt; his chest was covered in soot, his face was crimson from the heat, but he pushed the boat on like a mad magician.

But when Miss Minton tried to make him sail on through the night, he put his foot down.

"It's dangerous and foolish," he said. "If we run aground we'll never get her off."

So Miss Minton lay down in the cabin and the professor lay down on the deck, and as soon as the first light came, Miss Minton made black coffee so strong that it almost took the roof off their mouths—and then they were off again.

"I was an idiot," she said, sitting in the stern with her hand on the tiller. "I should have stayed with Henry Hartington, who pushed puppies through the wire mesh of tennis courts. Or Lavinia Freemantle, who plucked the wings off butterflies. Goodness knows, I've had enough awful children to look after. But Maia . . ."

They saw things the professor would have loved to stop for: a deserted hummingbird nest with two eggs no bigger than peas, a scarlet orchid which was new to him—but Miss Minton could not bear him to halt the boat. Even if a giant sloth with long red hair had come lumbering down to the water's edge, she would have insisted on going on.

But he did not let everything pass.

"Do you have to go on calling me Professor Glastonberry?" he complained when they had traveled for three days.

Miss Minton was steering, looking for signs of sandbanks or submerged rocks.

"I don't know your Christian name," she said.

The professor blushed. "It's Neville," he admitted.

Miss Minton turned to look at him—oil-stained, unshaven, dripping with sweat—and woke up to what he was doing for her.

"What's wrong with Neville?" she said.

After that she became calmer and more sensible. She opened some of the tins they had brought and made proper meals. She even allowed herself to see the beauty of the river and remembered how once she had hoped to make a living as a naturalist.

"You won't lose your job because of this," she asked, "going away so suddenly?"

The professor shrugged.

"Probably not. But if I do it doesn't matter much. I'd have to retire anyway in a couple of years and I have a bit of money saved." He put another log of wood into the firebox. "I used to go on trips with Taverner sometimes. I could make a living like this . . . it's not just collecting—people pay good money now to be shown the wildlife." He stared out over the water. "It was what I meant to do when I came out here, but my wife didn't care for traveling."

They turned into the Agarapi and soon afterward saw a great snake, endlessly long, rustling through the leaves and dropping down into the dark water.

"An anaconda," said the professor.

"Is it dangerous?" asked Miss Minton.

"Not to us," said the professor. "It's a good omen—the God of the Water making himself known."

"Then perhaps we'll find her," said Miss Minton under her breath.

"What do you mean to do with Maia when you do find her?" the professor asked that night.

"Take her back to the Keminskys and never let her out of my sight again," said Miss Minton.

"She may not find it easy."

"Why on earth not? The Keminskys are the kindest people in the world."

"Yes. But she has tasted freedom."

"That's neither here nor there," snapped Miss Minton, whose corset was sticking to her back. "I've tasted freedom, too," she found herself saying. "But I have to go back and so does she."

Now they had to remember the route Finn had meant to take, but lack of sleep and anxiety were beginning to make them clumsy. And there was another worry: the draft of the Carter boat was greater than that of the *Arabella*. What if the river became too shallow for them to go on?

By the fifth day Miss Minton had secretly given up hope and even the professor stopped trying to be cheerful.

Then, just a week after they had set off, they rounded a bend and heard the barking of a dog.

The children turned and saw the spinach-green boat coming toward them.

"Oh no! Not the Carters!" said Maia. She looked round desperately for somewhere to hide. "If I ran off into the jungle . . ."

But it wasn't the Carters. In a way it was worse, because from the woman who now rose from her seat in the stern, she would not have tried to hide or run away.

"You're mad!" shouted Miss Minton across the narrowing gap between the boats. "You're completely mad, Maia. What do you mean by this?"

Then she disappeared into the cabin, where—for the first time since Maia had been lost in the fire—she burst into tears.

But the relief of seeing Maia safe soon took a different turn. On board the *Arabella* she complained about Maia's tangled hair, her bare feet, her strange clothes. She had brought a toothbrush—even a hairbrush—but as she said, it would take days to get Maia to look civilized again. She berated Finn for taking Maia off, she inquired nastily about his Latin, and wanted to know how often they took their quinine pills. By the time she had finished nagging and finding fault, Maia was almost ready to wish that Minty *had* deserted her.

Later the children went over to have supper on the Carters' launch. The professor, who turned out to be an enthusiastic cook, had opened a tin of corned beef and made a splendid hash with wild onions and peppers.

Finn, who had always admired the professor, had brought over some specimens for him to identify—and it was now that they heard what had happened to the Carters.

"It's rather an amazing story," said Miss Minton. "Lady Parsons actually cabled and offered them a home! You can imagine how pleased the twins were—going off to live with a proper lady!"

Maia was surprised. "She always seemed such a fierce person in the painting—that square face, and her choker of pearls."

"Well, she's certainly done her duty," said Miss Minton. "They sailed just before we came away."

"Did Mr. Carter go, too?" asked Finn.

Miss Minton shook her head. "He has to stay in the hospital for a while. He's probably sorry, because what faces him when he comes out will not be pleasant." And she explained about the trial and what would happen if he was found guilty.

But soon the talk turned to the Keminskys.

"I'm sorry you never got my note that night," said Minty. "I was arranging for us to go and live with them. You'll like that, won't you?" she asked Maia.

Maia was silent, looking down at her plate.

"Of course she will," jeered Finn. "Sergei will be able to kneel at her feet like a person in a book."

Miss Minton quelled him with a look. "The Keminskys have been kindness itself. They've prepared a room for Maia at the top of the house with a view of the river."

But Maia did not want to look at the river; she wanted to *be* on it. The grand house, the rich food, the Russian babble meant nothing to her now. She wanted to be with Finn, and free. . . .

"Do I have to go back?" she asked quietly.

"Yes. First thing tomorrow morning," said Miss Minton. "Bring your belongings as soon as you've washed."

Knowing it was her last night on the *Arabella,* Maia fought against sleep. She must remember it all—the lapping of the water against the side of the boat, the white moths, the fireflies . . .

Finn, too, was awake. "When we're grown up I'll come back for you, I promise. No one can stop us then."

But she wasn't grown up and nor was he, and Finn was going on alone. The professor had tried to persuade him to come back with them, but Finn only said, "I promised my father I'd go and find the Xanti. I promised."

Now, though, lying in the dark, he realized how much he hated the idea of going on by himself. He wasn't afraid exactly; he knew he could do it—but it suddenly seemed utterly dismal to go on without his friend.

"We could still run away into the forest," said Maia.

But Finn said no. "Minty really cares about you. The professor told me she nearly went mad when she thought you'd been killed in the fire. You can't play tricks on her—or on him. They're good people. It's just . . . oh, why can't grown-ups understand that we might know what is right for us just as well as they do?"

The children slept at last, but on the boat without a name, Miss Minton lay awake.

After a while she got up and went out onto the deck. Everything had turned out as she had hoped. She had found Maia, and Maia was safe and well. Not only safe and well, but happy—at least she had been. Finn, too. They had kept the boat tidy, labeled their specimens properly, taken their quinine. Bernard would have been proud of his son.

So why did she feel so . . . uncomfortable?

Behind her the professor stirred in his sleep.

"Are you awake?" she asked him.

He opened his eyes. "I am now," he said.

"I need to talk to you," Miss Minton said. "I'll go and make us some tea."

The children slept late, and washed and dressed almost in silence. Both of them were afraid to speak. Maia packed her belongings in an old canvas bag and stroked the dog.

"I'll come over in a minute and say good-bye," said Finn.

The Carters' boat was ready to leave, breakfast tidied away, ropes coiled. The professor was sorting out the firebox and feeding in fresh logs. Miss Minton, sitting in the stern, had a parcel wrapped in burlap on her knees.

"I'm ready," said Maia, trying to keep her voice steady. She mustn't cry. Above all, she mustn't sulk. "Finn's coming over to say good-bye."

"No need," said Miss Minton.

"He'd like to."

"All the same, there is no need."

Maia looked at her governess. Miss Minton seemed differ-ent. . . . Softer? Rounder? More at peace?

"Why?" she asked. "Why is there no need?"

"Because we're coming with you. We're going on. Get back on the *Arabella* and tell Finn we'll follow three lengths behind."

As Maia turned to go, hardly believing that there could be such happiness, she heard a loud splash. Miss Minton was leaning over the side, watching the parcel she had held on her knees floating away downriver.

"What was that?" asked Maia.

Miss Minton straightened herself.

"If you *must* know," she said, "it was my corset."

22

Now, Beatrice!" boomed Lady Parsons. "How often have I told you that Kiki's jacket must be buttoned up right to his little neck? You don't want the little doggy to catch a chill, do you?"

Beatrice glared at the shivering animal, standing on the hall table getting ready for his afternoon walk.

Beatrice did want him to catch a chill. She wanted him to catch a chill and then pneumonia and then die.

But she said nothing and did up the top button of the tartan waistcoat that he always wore for his afternoon walk, since he did not have enough hair, or enough sense, to keep warm.

"Now the lead," ordered Lady Parsons, and Beatrice fetched the lead and clipped it on while Kiki snapped at her fingers.

"There you are, my little treasure," said Lady Parsons to the dog. And to Beatrice: "Now you're to take him at least three times up and down the Promenade; I shall *know* if you've only taken him twice because Mrs. Tandry will be looking out of the window. And he must *not* be allowed to sniff at other dogs."

It was a gray, windy day; the waves beat drearily on Littleford's gravel beach. But there was nothing to be done. Since they had arrived in England, Beatrice had to walk Kiki every afternoon and Gwendolyn had to walk him every morning.

While Beatrice tugged the little dog sulkily along the windswept beach, Gwendolyn was in the pantry pouring boiling water into Lady Parsons' stone hot-water bottle, ready for Lady Parsons' afternoon sleep. When she had finished, she carried it upstairs to the big bedroom with its Turkey carpet and lace-covered tables, and the pictures of Sir Hector Parsons, who had been shot by mistake in Kenya while trying to shoot lions. If she hurried downstairs now, she could get half an hour to look at a comic she had found in the kitchen drawer before it was time to lay the tea.

"Gwendolyn!" came Lady Parsons' angry voice from her bedroom. "Come back here at once! How many times have I told you that the bottle *must* be wrapped in my shawl. Do you want me to burn my feet?"

Gwendolyn did want it, she wanted it just as much as Beatrice had wanted the little dog to get pneumonia, but after nearly a month in Lady Parsons' house she knew she was helpless. The Carters were penniless; there was nowhere else to go.

"I hope I don't have to tell you which of my shawls the bottle must be wrapped in?"

"No, Lady Parsons. It's the violet crocheted one in the second drawer down."

"Well, if you know, why don't you do it straightaway?" said Lady Parsons. "And tell your mother to hurry up with turning the collar on my blue velvet. I'm going to wear it for my bridge party tonight."

But as the girl left the room, Lady Parsons leaned back on her pillows with a satisfied sigh. The girls were slow and they were stupid, but they could be trained and so could their mother. She had been right to take them in.

Lady Parsons was a widow and rich. She was also quite amazingly miserly. Saving money was a passion of hers, and when she could see her bank balance swelling she felt a deep happiness that nothing else could give her.

Her husband had left her Grey Gables, which was definitely the largest and showiest of all the houses on the Promenade. He had left her a big garden and a gazebo and her private bathing hut on the Front. She was a healthy, middle-aged woman who could do anything she liked, and that was exactly what she did. She *saved*.

When she first read the letter from Mrs. Carter telling her that Clifford was in trouble again and that they were penniless, Lady Parsons had been annoyed. What did the Carters' difficulties have to do with her? Mrs. Carter might be her second cousin twice removed, but that didn't give her the right to bother her.

But then Lady Parsons had a brilliant idea. Her personal maid—the one who helped her to dress and did her hair and kept her clothes in order—was getting old. She would sack her, and she would also sack the paid companion who came to take the dog out and wind her knitting wool and read to her. And she would train the Carters to do the work! Not only would this save two whole wages, but there would be no need to give the Carters free time or Sundays off, which servants always seemed to want these days.

(As for Mr. Carter, who was on his way to prison in Brazil, he would, of course, never be mentioned nor allowed to darken her doors again.)

So far the plan had worked well. She had made a sitting room in the basement where the family could sit when she didn't want them, and sometimes, when she drove out, she took Beatrice and Gwendolyn, or their mother, up beside her in the carriage so that her friends could see how kind she had been to take them in.

"Aren't you grateful to dear Lady Parsons?" the friends would say as she stopped the carriage to bow to them, and the twins would grit their teeth and say yes, indeed they were. But the moment they got home, they were set to work again.

The jobs she found for them were endless. They had to match her embroidery wool, bring up her breakfast tray, and feed Kiki on steak cut exactly into half-inch cubes. They were sent to the shops in all weathers, mostly to the chemists, to fetch medicines for whatever she thought might be wrong with her. They had to tidy her underclothes drawer and hook up her bust bodice, and Mrs. Carter had to darn Lady Parsons' stockings and take up her hems and trim her hats.

At night the Carters were so tired that when a black beetle walked across the floor of their basement sitting room, Mrs. Carter did not even trouble to get the spray from the pantry.

One of the jobs the twins hated most was reading aloud. They were poor readers, they read slowly and stumbled over words, but since Lady Parsons used being read aloud to as a way of getting to sleep, she did not mind. Beatrice had to read the whole of Ivanhoe, and Gwendolyn read a different Library Romance each week, without taking in a single word.

And at breakfast they read aloud from the newspaper— which was how they found out what had happened to Maia and Miss Minton after they left.

Beatrice was reading out the Society Pages and what King Edward was doing that evening, when she saw something on the opposite page, which printed the foreign news.

She stopped reading, gaped, then read with her finger under the lines to make sure she had read properly.

"Well, has the cat got your tongue?" asked Lady Parsons sharply, looking up from her coddled egg.

But Beatrice was so startled that she just went on goggling at the article. Then she said, "It says here that Maia and Miss Minton and that fat professor have vanished in the jungle. Maia went off with some boy or other in a boat, and Miss Minton and the professor went after them to bring her back, and now everyone has disappeared. Please, Lady Parsons, I must show this to Mama and Gwendolyn."

Beatrice did not often run, but she ran now, holding the newspaper and taking no notice of Lady Parsons' bleats.

Mrs. Carter read the whole article aloud. It seemed that Maia and Miss Minton had been missing for some weeks, and a search party had been sent out to look for them.

The part of the country in which they were last seen is still inhabited by savage tribes, some of them cannibals, not to mention jaguars, pit vipers, caimans, and other dangerous predators. It is feared that some serious harm may have befallen the party.

"So she did survive the fire," said Mrs. Carter. They had left Manaus when Maia was still missing.

"Well, it serves her right if she gets put in a cooking pot— she always liked the Indians better than anyone else."

"Now Beatrice!" said Mrs. Carter. "You mustn't say such things."

"Well, we won't *say* them," said Gwendolyn. "But nothing can stop us *thinking* them."

And all that day, as they gave the dog his worm powders and ironed Lady Parsons' handkerchiefs and sewed the pom-poms back on her bedroom slippers, their small, tight mouths would suddenly curve into a smile.

"It may be awful here, but at least we won't get eaten," said Beatrice.

And Gwendolyn agreed.

23

MAIA HAD NEVER had any sisters or cousins, but she had them now. Her day in the Xanti village began with the three girls who were closest to her in age, pulling her out of sleep and down to the river for a swim.

The swim did not have much to do with striking out over the water, nor with serious washing. It was about splashing and ducking each other and pretending to have been attacked by electric eels—and afterward it was about chasing each other through the trees and combing each other's hair and persuading Maia that she needed a bead anklet.

Then it was the turn of the babies, who were brought down to the edge of the stream and doused with water from hollowed-out calabash shells while they screamed at the top of their lungs. Maia had a pair of babies that were her special charge—tiny, big-eyed creatures who turned into thrashing demons when she tried to make them clean.

When she got back with the babies, Miss Minton was usually at work on her English–Xanti dictionary, but today she was surrounded by a group of women begging her to do her imitation of a person with a stomachache.

"STOMAK-AKE," they chanted, because that was their favorite. When she needed a word for her dictionary and couldn't make the Xanti understand, Miss Minton took to acting. They had enjoyed her horribly snapping teeth when she wanted the word for "alligator," and they were impressed when she pricked herself with a needle to get the word for "blood." But the one they liked best was definitely the one where she rubbed her stomach and doubled up with pain and groaned.

Yet when Miss Minton, soon after she arrived, was struck by one of her blinding migraine headaches, there had been no need for her to act. The women found her leaning against a tree with her eyes shut and came back with a disgusting, dark green brew of bitter leaves which she forced herself to drink—and in a few hours she was herself again.

The Xanti village was not the dark huddle of huts in the gloom of the forest that Maia had expected. It was in a clearing open to the sky. At night they could see the Southern Cross, and stars so bright they seemed unreal, and by day the sun shone down on the compound where the children played and animals wandered.

Nearly all the children had pets: a little boy with a crippled foot had a huge bird-eating spider with a jungle vine tied round its middle, which he led along like a dog. One of the chief's nephews owned a golden tamarin, a monkey so small that it could be covered by a human hand. Tame macaws and parrots and hoopoes flew onto people's shoulders and off again, driving Finn's dog to despair.

By the time the sun was high and everyone was wandering about, eating breakfast, Professor Glastonberry appeared. The Xanti had woven palm-leaf shelters for their guests, but he pre-

"STOMAK-AKE," they chanted, because that was their favorite.

ferred to sleep on the Carters' boat with the *Arabella* moored beside him so as to watch the boats and his collection, which was growing fast.

After breakfast the women usually went to their work, weaving hammocks or pounding manioc roots into flour or making baskets—but Maia did not have to join them. She was allowed to go to the musicians. There was a man who played a tiny, three-holed flute made out of the bones of a deer, and another man who had a hollowed-out palm trunk which made a noise like a tuba. . . .

Maia was learning to play the little flute, and the men sang for her—all the Xanti did, she begged so hard. They sang their work songs and their feasting songs because they understood that Maia needed to know about songs like Miss Minton needed to know about words, and Finn needed to know about the plants they used for healing.

And it was now that Maia saw what Haltmann meant when he said that she would find the purely Indian music very different, and not at all easy to write down. The songs were wild and strange, and often seemed to have no tune at all—and yet the more she heard them, the more she liked them.

But they wanted a fair exchange. "SING, Maia" was heard as often as "STOMAK-AKE." Maia had begun by singing funny songs for the children because she knew how much the Xanti liked to laugh. But it was the old folk songs that they liked best; sad songs in the minor key in which lovers were separated, ships sank, and people wept by open graves.

By midday the Xanti were usually asleep again in their hammocks or under the trees, and Maia and Finn would wander off to a cool part of the riverbank, keeping a wary lookout for Miss Minton, who might suddenly decide they should do some mental arithmetic or Latin verbs.

"You know I told you what my father said you had to do—'seize the day,'" said Maia. "Well, it seems to me there's no point in doing that here. You don't have to seize it. They *give* you the day."

Finn spent much of his time with the old chief and the men who surrounded him. Because he had spoken a few words of Xanti before he came, Finn learned quicker than the rest of them. The chief was not a fierce warrior with feathers, as Maia had expected; he was more like a headmaster, and from time to time he would come out of his hut and lecture the Xanti about what they should do—especially the women, who were supposed to work harder and get up earlier to bathe. Often he came out with his arm round Finn's shoulder. He had known Yara, and remembered her.

Finn was quieter here, thought Maia, not always working out how to get to the next thing and the next, and he watched the women carefully as they prepared the food, or fetched water from the river, or hoed the little gardens they had made on the edge of the clearing.

"My mother must have done all those things," he said. "I wonder if it was hard for her to leave her friends."

In the afternoons there was usually an expedition into the forest to collect plants and berries. Maia could never get over how quiet the Xanti were, how careful of the land. They treated every clump of trees or trickle of water as though they were old friends. They could walk barefoot over thorns and through swamps and piles of leaves which might easily have concealed a snake, but somehow they knew that it didn't.

"They have wise feet," the professor said.

But the professor was not often able to go into the woods for an afternoon. When he first came he had drawn a giant sloth on the packed sand—a terrible creature with long hair and fearsome claws—and the Xanti said, yes, yes, they knew of such a beast. They had their own name for it, and soon everyone was roaring frightfully and lumbering about and waving their dangerous claws.

They said it lived in caves on a ridge of high ground upriver, and after that the professor's life was no longer his own. By midday, every man who could be spared, and some who could not, had piled the deck of the Carters' boat with logs and was waiting on board to show him the way. To travel on the "fire boat" after a lifetime of paddling canoes was the best thing they could think of.

They did not find the giant sloth—it took them many days even to find the caves—but they found other things: fossilized fishes and strange stones and the seeds of a flower that blossomed only once in twenty years . . . all of which the professor stored away.

Then one day as they were exploring an outcrop of rock, they saw, caught on a jutting piece of stone, a tuft of reddish hair—and close by, what seemed to be two large claw marks in the hard sand.

The Xanti went wild. The professor tried to calm them, knowing how many tests and measurements had to be carried out still, but at that moment he would have given anything to be with his friend Carruthers, who had died still believing in the existence of this elusive beast.

And that night when they got back to the village, there was

a party. The Xanti were not warriors. They did not fight battles with other tribes, and when danger threatened they simply disappeared into the forest, often staying away for weeks. But when special food was needed they could use their bows and arrows with fearful skill, and now the hunters set out and returned with two wild pigs, a brocket deer, and a pair of plump bush turkeys.

The Xanti were very fond of parties. They liked everything about them. They liked painting their faces in interesting ways, they liked making ornaments to wear; they liked feasting and dancing . . . and they very much liked getting drunk on the beer that the women brewed from manioc roots.

Miss Minton had at first tried not to come to the parties, and to keep Maia down by the boats. But the Xanti had been so surprised and hurt by this that she gave in, and now she and Maia sat on the edge of the circle of firelight and watched.

Maia's "sisters" had implored her to smarten herself up a little; they brought bowls of red uruca dye and black genista and she let them paint her face, and even Miss Minton agreed to a dab or two of red on her forehead and a coronet of toucan feathers. Not that Miss Minton needed dressing up. As soon as there was any sign of a party, the women fetched Miss Minton's milk-tooth necklace and hung it round her neck. She had tried very hard to give it as a present to the tribe, but they refused to take it. It was too valuable, they said.

Finn was sitting with the old chief and his brothers. It was strange, thought Maia—in Manaus, Finn had looked Indian and exotic; here, as he looked thoughtfully into the fire, he looked European.

Maia loved the beginning of the feasts, before everyone got

too drunk. The smell of roast pork mingled with the smell of the wild lilies that grew round the huts, the soft breeze fanning her hot cheeks, the firelight, and above it, the brilliant stars.

Soon the men began to dance, and presently the women joined in.

But then came the words Maia dreaded.

"SING, Maia," called the Xanti, and her "sisters" came and pulled her to her feet.

So she sang, and because feasting was a serious business, she sang a song that her mother had loved particularly: "The Ash Grove."

Her pure, clear voice, the English words, carried across the compound and down to the river. . . .

And:

"My God!" said Captain Pereia, aboard a gunboat of the Brazilian River Police. "Listen! We've found them! The girl must be a prisoner to sing for the little swine. Shut down the engines; we'll take them by surprise. But don't shoot till I give the word."

Maia had stopped singing. She was making her way back to Miss Minton when she saw them.

A dozen men or more with blackened faces, carrying rifles, creeping up from the river.

"Don't try anything," the captain shouted. "We're armed."

A single shot was fired over their heads.

"Run!" hissed Finn to his mother's people.

With a cry that seemed to be one cry, the Xanti vanished into the forest, leaving the four Europeans staring in horror at the invaders.

*Her pure clear voice, the English words, carried across
the compound and down to the river....*

But it was not the Xanti who were being rounded up.

"Who are you!" said Miss Minton furiously, to the leader with his blackened face.

"What do you want?" said Finn.

Captain Pereia stared. A tall lady, a boy who spoke perfect English, an elderly gentleman, and the girl who sang.

These must be the people he had been told to rescue . . . but the lady in feathers and human teeth . . . a boy with a painted face! He was shocked. Had they gone native?

"You're safe now," he said. "We've come to take you back. Don't worry, you're safe."

Finn looked at the deserted village, the flickering firelight, the feathers dropped by his friends as they fled . . . And then at the men with their blackened faces and their guns.

"We *were* safe," he said bitterly. "We were safe with the Xanti. But now . . ."

It was Miss Minton's corset that had set off the alarm. For longer than expected, it floated down the Agarapi River. Then, when it was about to sink, it landed on a log of balsa wood and was carried into the Negro itself, where it became entangled in a fishing net.

The man who found it took it to the local policeman, who sent a report to the police station in the next town, where the officer in charge confirmed that it was a British corset and sent it to Colonel da Silva in Manaus.

When a name tape saying *A. Minton* was discovered inside the whalebone bodice, the fat was on the fire. Seeing Miss Minton's waterlogged corset very much upset the colonel. He knew Miss Minton and did not think she would have removed her underclothes willingly. She must have been captured by a hostile tribe, and if she had been caught, so, probably, had the professor and the children they had been pursuing.

So Captain Pereia of the Brazilian River Police was called and told to pick his men and take the fastest and best armed of the boats in the patrol fleet and look for them.

The captain wasted no time. He had led several missions: it was he who had put down a riot of the Talapi Indians when they turned against their employers in the Matto Silver Mine; he had broken up a battle between rival drug traffickers on the Venezuelan border; and he'd rescued a kidnapped missionary from the Kalis shortly before they planned to kill him.

And less than six hours after he had been sent for, Captain Pereia and twelve of his best men were steaming out of Manaus at a speed which made the urchins on the waterside dig each other proudly in the ribs.

But now, though his mission had been so successful, Captain Pereia was disappointed. None of the people he had rescued had thanked him. They seemed stunned rather than pleased, and the boy's wretched dog would not stop barking.

"There's no gratitude left in the world," he grumbled to his second-in-command. "Anyone would think I was taking prisoners instead of freeing them."

But they came aboard with him. They even agreed to return on the fast patrol boat and let the spinach boat and the *Arabella* be brought back by Pereia's men. It seemed that there were urgent messages waiting for them in Manaus. Maia had thought that Finn might refuse, but he came, too.

The dream was over.

The messages, when they reached Manaus, pleased no one. Mr. Murray had sent no less than three cables ordering Miss Minton to bring Maia back to England at once. He had heard about the fire from the consul, and read about Maia's flight in the newspaper, and was both alarmed and annoyed. And in an envelope, addressed to the professor, was a frantic note for Finn from Clovis.

"Westwood?" asked Maia, watching him.

"Yes. Clovis is in trouble."

"Does he say what kind of trouble?"

"No. But he says he's desperate and I must come at once."

"And will you?"

Finn nodded. "One can't run forever," he said. "If Clovis is in trouble, it's my fault."

But Maia had to turn away from the misery in his face.

24

THE THREE OF them traveled back on the same boat as Maia and Minty had come out on: the *Cardinal,* with her blue funnels and snow-white hull.

Maia had thought that having Finn with them would make it easier—at least they could all be miserable together—but it didn't. Finn had disappeared into himself. He was very quiet and stood hunched up over the rail, looking out at the gray sea. The cold surprised him; he would shiver suddenly in the wind.

He had decided that Westwood was to be his fate.

"It's what you said in the museum," he told Miss Minton. "'*Come out, Finn Taverner, and be a man.*' I thought I could run away forever, but if Clovis is in trouble, I've got to help him."

It was his time with the Xanti which had changed him. They thought that everyone's life was like a river; you had to flow with the current and not struggle, which wasted breath and made you more likely to drown. And the river of life seemed to be carrying him back to Westwood.

He had left his dog behind with Furo because of the quarantine. Rob would never endure six months shut up in kennels. As soon as they knew Maia was safe, the Carters' servants, with old Lila, had returned, offering to work unpaid, and Miss Minton had set them to repaint the spinach boat, which she had christened *River Queen*.

As for Maia, she was to go back to school.

"She will be safe there for a few years till she is ready to go out into the world," Mr. Murray had written to Miss Minton.

So now Maia was collecting her memories.

"We mustn't only remember the good bits," she said. "We must remember the bad bits, too, so that we know it was real."

But there weren't really any bad bits once she had escaped from the twins. The fried termites which the Xanti had cooked for them hadn't tasted very nice, and there had been a tame bush turkey which woke them up at an unearthly hour with its screeching.

"But it was all part of it," said Maia. "It *belonged*."

Miss Minton knew she was going to be dismissed, and she thought this was perfectly fair. A governess who let her charge sail up the rivers of the Amazon and live with Indian tribes could hardly expect to keep her job.

She missed the professor.

"Would you like to marry me?" he had asked her politely before they sailed, and she had thanked him and said she did not think she would be very good at being married.

When the boat docked at Liverpool they went their different ways. Finn was determined to go to Westwood quite alone. He had never bought a train ticket or looked at a timetable, but he seemed to know what to do and he would let no one help him.

"I wish he didn't look as though he was going to have his head cut off," said Maia.

The moment when the children said good-bye passed quickly. Finn was taking the train to York; Maia and Minty were bound for London. The bustle of getting their luggage on and finding their seats muffled everything. Maia had sent her love to Clovis, and it was only when the train steamed out that she realized that she might not see Finn again—and heard the snap of Miss Minton's handbag as she had heard it on the day they left England, and was again handed Minty's large white handkerchief to wipe her eyes.

The school, as they drove up to it, was just the same—the brass plate saying THE MAYFAIR ACADEMY FOR YOUNG LADIES, the row of desks she could see through the window. In Classroom B, Miss Carlisle was probably still teaching the source of the River Thames.

"I'll see you tomorrow," said Miss Minton, and drove quickly away. Mr. Murray was coming to interview her at the school on the following afternoon.

Everyone was so welcoming and friendly, and somehow that made it worse. The girls clustered round Maia; Melanie had painted a picture of her with a boa constrictor round her neck, and they'd made a banner saying WELCOME BACK. Some of them had read about the police boat sent to find her and thought she was a heroine.

"What was it like being rescued?" they wanted to know.

"It was like being rescued from Paradise," said Maia, but no one believed her.

They listened while she tried to describe the journey in the *Arabella*, and life with the Xanti, but they couldn't take it in.

"Aren't you glad to be back?" they kept asking her. "It must have been so scary!" And they told her that she had been given her old bed back and that there was a new history teacher who dyed her hair.

So Maia gave up. She realized that adventures, once they were over, were things that had to stay inside one—that no one else could quite understand.

The headmistress, Miss Banks, and her sister Emily understood a little better. They were happy to take Maia back, but they thought it might not be easy for her to settle down again.

"You must give yourself time," they said kindly, and Maia patted the spaniel and remembered the howls of Finn's dog as he was left behind with Furo.

But in the evening, when at last she had a moment alone, she slipped into the library and leaned her head against the mahogany steps she had climbed the day she knew she was going to the Amazon. The dream she had dreamed there had been a true one. She had found a land whose riches she had never before imagined, and she had found Finn.

Well, now it was over. In ten minutes the bell would ring for them to go to their dormitories, then another bell for them to kneel and pray. And why not? How else was one supposed to run a school?

"Oh Finn," said Maia. "How am I going to bear it, day after day after day?"

When he reached York, Finn changed onto a very small train which stopped, after a while, at Westwood Hall.

Clovis had said he would meet him there, but there was no sign of him. Finn left his bag in the ticket office and began to walk.

It was a cold, dank afternoon, and however fast he walked, he could not get warm. The light was already going—or perhaps on this bleak day it had never really come.

He saw the high pile of his ancestral home from a long way off. It looked unspeakably dismal, with its useless turrets and jagged battlements. He tried to imagine living there year in and year out, and had to clench his teeth so as not to panic.

The gate, when he reached it, was closed and surmounted by jagged spikes.

As he stood there the lodge keeper came out. "This is private property," he said. "No loitering. You'd best be getting along."

Finn glared at him. The rudeness and snobbishness was just what he had expected from this awful place. But before he could tell the man what he thought of him, he saw Clovis hurrying down the drive. He wore a tweed suit and a cap—but round his neck was a large white bandage.

Oh God, thought Finn. Have they tried to cut his throat?

Clovis came up to the gates and the lodge keeper touched his cap in a humble manner and said, "Are you going out, sir?"

"Yes, Jarvis," said Clovis. "I'm going into the village."

As he came through the gate, Finn saw that the white thing round his neck was not a bandage but a scarf—rather a bumpy one knitted in white wool.

"I thought they'd cut your throat."

Clovis shook his head. The scarf was a present from the middle banshee, who had taken up knitting. "There's a tea place just down the road. No one goes there much on a weekday. We can be alone."

The tea shop was a tiny room in the front parlor of a brick

cottage. The lady who ran it greeted Clovis as respectfully as the lodge keeper had done, and asked after Sir Aubrey.

"You'd better tell me exactly what's happened," said Finn, after they had given their order. "You said you were in a mess. Well, I'll help you out, but I must know. Obviously you haven't told him who you really are. You haven't confessed."

"But I have," said Clovis. "I have—and it was absolutely awful."

So then he told Finn what had happened when at last he found Sir Aubrey alone and willing to listen to him.

"I told him I wasn't Finn Taverner, and it was all a mistake. I was going to explain everything properly, but as soon as I said I wasn't really his grandson, he went a ghastly sort of blue color and started clutching his chest, and then he crumpled up and fell on the floor. I knew his heart wasn't good, but I didn't imagine . . ." Clovis shook his head, remembering the horror of that moment. "I was sure he was going to die and that I'd killed him. The servants came and carried him off to bed, and the doctor said he'd had some sort of a shock and I wasn't allowed to see him."

Clovis picked up a cut-glass ashtray and started fiddling with it.

"When they did let me in," he went on, "he tried to sit up in bed, and then he said, 'You were only joking, boy, weren't you? Tell me it was a joke and you're really my grandson. Boys like to play jokes, I know.'"

"And?" Finn's voice was sharp. "What did you say?"

"I said, yes of course it was a joke. Of course I was Bernard's son and his grandson. I know I shouldn't have done, but if you'd seen his face . . . And then he began to get better quite quickly. But he wants to make everything legal because I don't have a birth certificate or anything. He wants to name me officially as heir to Westwood and give me an allowance—quite a big one. And I don't know what to do. He's absolutely certain I'm his grandson. There's a painting of some admiral who's supposed to have my nose. . . ."

Finn was leaning across the table, staring at him intently. "And you don't want it? You don't want Westwood or the money or anything? That's why you asked me to come?"

The lady brought their muffins and the teapot in a knitted cozy. When they were alone again, Clovis said, "It isn't that I don't want it—the old man's been very good to me, and well . . . there are things I could do. I'd like to bring my foster mother here to cook. She's always wanted to work in a house like this, and the cook we've got is leaving. And my—your—cousins are nice. The Basher's girls. You wouldn't think she'd have nice children, but she has. But I couldn't take it from you for the rest of your life. For always. How could I live in a great house and take the money that's really yours when you live in a wooden hut . . . I mean, now that you've seen it, surely—"

He broke off. Finn was looking very odd. Different. He reached for Clovis's hand.

"Clovis, do you *swear* that you don't mind staying here as Master of Westwood? Do you absolutely swear it?"

"I swear it."

Finn, as he walked back with his friend to the station, seemed to be made of something quite different. Not muscle and bone—feathers and air . . . and lightness. He did not actually intend to fly, because that would have been showing off, but he could have done so if he'd wanted to.

"You'll never know what you've done for me," he said as they reached the gates of the level crossing. "If there's anything you want—"

Clovis grinned. "Can I have Maia when she's grown up?"

Finn's smile vanished in an instant.

"No," he said.

"Oh well . . ."

Maia would probably want to go off adventuring again one day, thought Clovis, and that wouldn't suit him. He'd settle for one of the Basher's banshees. There was plenty of time to decide which one.

At two o'clock, Maia saw Mr. Murray's motor stop outside the school. Five minutes later Miss Minton arrived, walking across the square.

The interview took place in Miss Banks' private sitting room while Maia waited in the hall, and as soon as she saw Mr. Murray's face, Miss Minton knew there was no hope. She would not even be allowed to look after Maia during the holidays. She was in complete disgrace.

Miss Minton had spent the night with her sister and bought another corset, because the good times were gone. She sat up very straight, and before Mr. Murray could begin she opened her purse and took out ten sovereigns.

"This is Maia's money," she said. "We sold the things we had collected on the journey, and since there were four of us, it seemed proper to divide everything we earned by four."

Mr. Murray looked at the heap of coins in surprise.

"And I have, of course, kept a list of expenses. Anything I bought for Maia out of her allowance, I have written down here."

"Yes, yes . . ." Mr. Murray had no doubt about Miss Minton's honesty. It was her sanity he was not sure about. He cleared his throat. "I have to tell you that before this . . . escapade . . . I was considering making you joint guardian with me of Maia. I'm getting old, and a woman would be able to help her with the problems she might soon meet. But now I'm afraid I shall have to dismiss you and arrange for Maia to spend her holidays at school."

Miss Minton bowed her head. "Yes," she said. "I was expecting that."

Mr. Murray pushed back his chair.

"Miss Minton, what on earth made you let a young girl travel up the Amazon and spend weeks living with savages? What made you do it? The British consul thinks that you must all have been drugged."

"Perhaps. Yes, perhaps we were drugged. Not by the things the Xanti smoked—none of us touched them—but by . . . peace . . . by happiness. By a different sense of time."

"I don't think you have explained why you let Maia—"

Miss Minton interrupted him. "I will explain. At least I will try to. You see, I have looked after some truly dreadful children in my time, and it was easy not to get fond of them. After all, a governess is not a mother. But Maia . . . well, I'm afraid I grew to love her. And that meant I began to think what I would do if she were my child."

"And you would let her—" began Mr. Murray.

But Miss Minton stopped him. "I would let her . . . have adventures. I would let her . . . choose her path. It would be hard . . . it *was* hard . . . but I would do it. Oh, not completely, of course. Some things have to go on. Cleaning one's teeth, arithmetic. But Maia fell in love with the Amazon. It happens. The place was for her—and the people. Of course there was some danger, but there is danger everywhere. Two years ago, in this school, there was an outbreak of typhus, and three girls died. Children are knocked down and killed by horses every week, here in these streets—" She broke off, gathering her thoughts. "When she was traveling and exploring . . . and finding her songs, Maia wasn't just happy, she was . . . herself. I think something broke in Maia when her parents died, and out there it was healed. Perhaps I'm mad—and the professor, too—but I think children must lead big lives . . . if it is in them to do so. And it is in Maia."

The old lawyer was silent, rolling his silver pencil over and over between his fingers.

"You would take her back to Brazil?"

"Yes.

"To live among savages?"

"No. To explore and discover and look for giant sloths and new melodies and flowers that only blossom once every twenty years. Not to find them necessarily, but to look—"

She broke off, remembering what they had planned, the four of them, as they sailed up the Agarapi. To build a proper House of Rest near the Carters' old bungalow and live there in the rainy season, studying hard so that if Maia wanted to go to music college later, or Finn to train as a doctor, they would be prepared. And in the dry weather, to set off and explore.

Mr. Murray had risen to his feet. He walked over to the window and stood with his back to her, looking out at the square.

"It's impossible. It's madness."

There was a long pause.

"Or is it?" the old man said.

Maia had been sitting absolutely still on a chair in the hall, waiting.

Now she heard a loud peal on the street bell and turned to see a dark, wild-haired boy running up the steps. Taking no notice of the flustered maid, he came up to Maia.

"I'm going home, Maia," shouted Finn. "I'm going home!"

Upstairs a door had opened, and Miss Minton came slowly down the stairs, dabbing her eyes.

Then she drew herself up to her full height.

"We are *all* going home," she said.